Written To Death

Written To Death

Alex Warren Murder Mysteries Book III

Zach Abrams

*My thanks and undying love go to my family
Special thanks go to authors Elly Grant, Brenda Perlin
and Carol White for their help and support.*

Chapter 1

When Sandra and Alex disembarked from the Boeing 737, they had to brave the damp, cold April wind. They hurried across the tarmac before escaping through the doorway then climbed the staircase into the terminal. The welcoming five-tone Nokia jingle from Alex's phone heralded their arrival.

Sandra playfully punched Alex's shoulder, chiding him, "I thought you enjoyed the holiday. We've been back in Glasgow for twenty seconds and already you've switched your phone on. Can you never relax?"

"Although it was only a short break, I can honestly say that was the best holiday I've ever had. Sorry, switching the phone on was a reflex reaction. In any event, I need it to contact the mini-cab we booked to say we've landed. Don't you remember? It was much better value than the airport taxis. So, I'm totally innocent. You're off work until Wednesday. Although,

I'm back tomorrow, we still have the rest of the day to do what we like."

Alex sent the text, but as they took their place in line for passport control, his phone rang. He pressed receive, expecting it to be a call confirming his booking before noticing the caller was Sanjay.

"Hello, Boss. How was the holiday?"

"I'm still on it. I've only just landed in Glasgow. Why are you calling?"

"Sorry, Boss. I didn't realise. Do you want me to call back later?"

"You've started. I'm guessing it's something important, out with it."

"It's a mysterious death. I wouldn't have bothered you normally, but this one's happened in your backyard."

The queue shuffled forward and Alex and Sandra were now at the front.

"You have to switch that off before you step forward. Can't you read?" the immigration officer announced to Alex. He pointed to a large sign stating the use of mobiles was prohibited while passing through the check point.

In response, Alex opened his wallet, showing his warrant card displaying *DCI Alex Warren,* and replied, "Police business."

"I don't give a stuff," the border said. "You have no jurisdiction here."

"I'll get back to you in a minute, Sanjay. I have a man with a small problem here, or maybe it should be a small man with a problem." Alex ended the call and placed his phone in his pocket. His towering frame dwarfed the man as he handed his passport to the official. The border guard took his time scanning, then carefully examining it before returning it to Alex with a curt nod and a whispered, "Thank you, Sir. Have a nice day."

Stepping past the desk, Alex was approached by one of the airport police who'd recognised him. "I'm sorry about that, Sir. He was within his rights so I couldn't do anything. He's not really a bad lad, but he had his balls chewed the other day by one of his supervisors for being too lax, so perhaps he's over-reacting a bit."

"No sweat, it'll take more than the likes of him to put me off my stride. Besides, I'm chilled out. I've had nearly a week away from the job."

Sandra raised her eyebrows, clearly amused. Although she realised Alex's statement had been meant in earnest, she observed the falseness of his words. As she steered him forward, he fumbled in his pocket to recover his mobile and reconnect to Sanjay.

"I'm back, now. You were saying something about it being in my backyard and precisely what did you mean by 'mysterious'?"

"Well, we can't completely rule out an accident but personally I think it most unlikely. The victim was stabbed through the heart," Sanjay stated. "As for the location, it took place on the stage of the main hall at Eastfarm School."

"Oh my God, that's my kids' school. Was it one of the pupils? What age was the victim? How did it happen?" There was a distinct note of panic in Alex's voice, any residual trace of being chilled out after his holiday totally disappeared.

Sandra stopped walking and instead directed Alex towards a quiet corner of the baggage reclaim area, a deep frown now furrowing her brow.

"Relax, Boss, it had nothing to do with the kids or the school for that matter, other than the venue," Sanjay reassured. "The stage had been loaned out to a local community group to rehearse a play."

Alex raised his hand to indicate to Sandra not to worry. "Okay, who was the victim? Was he from a local am-dram group?"

"Not quite, Sir. To start with, he's a she and it wasn't an acting group, it was the local writing group. It's quite bizarre really."

"I'm a bit confused here, Sanjay. I want you to go back to the beginning and tell me what's happened."

"Yes, sorry, Boss. It is a bit mixed up and it's getting more so the deeper we dig. We were called to the school earlier this afternoon. A woman is dead as a result of being stabbed through the heart. Her name is Sheila Armstrong and she's a member of the East-farm Writers' Association. They meet on a regular basis at the Community Centre. Their members are apparently working towards a national competition to produce a one act play. They need to perform it for the competition, so they've been allowed to use the school's stage facilities to rehearse."

"Okay, now it's starting to make a bit more sense," Alex said.

"Here's the really bizarre bit," Sanjay added. "The play they were rehearsing was written by Sheila herself. It was a spoof about a stage production where the female lead is a writer and she's stabbed to death, on stage."

"You're telling me she designed her own murder?" Alex asked.

"Well, yes, in a manner of speaking," Sanjay replied.

"Listen, you can give me the details later. I take it you'll be there for a while. I'll be out of the airport in a few minutes. Sandra's at the baggage belt looking for our cases as we speak, so I need to go and give her a hand. I should be home within the hour which means I can be with you within two. Who else is there helping you?"

"Phil, Steve and Mary are already here and Donny's on his way. We have a few uniforms as well, keeping order. Scene of crime are already on the job and Duffie's due at any minute. Mind you, I can't see them telling us too much more. We already know how and when she died and we've got the knife. We also have about a dozen eye witnesses, but I suppose we still have to go through the motions."

"Don't be so complacent, there's an awful lot more the technicians can tell us than we can hope to learn from witnesses. What's more, the scientific evidence doesn't have a vested interest. It isn't biased the way people are."

"Sorry, Boss, you're right of course."

"Get everything set up and I'll be with you as soon as I can."

As Alex disconnected the call, he spotted an incoming text confirming his taxi booking. It identified the registration number of a grey Skoda Octavia which would be waiting for him at the pick-up point. He rushed over to help Sandra manoeuvre their cases onto a trolley.

"I guess the holiday's over earlier than planned. What's it all about?" Sandra asked.

Alex repeated what he'd learned from Sanjay.

"Do you want me to take the luggage home, then you can take a separate taxi and head straight over to the school?" Sandra offered.

"No, it's okay. Our plan had been to go back to my flat in Shawlands and it's practically on the way. We can drop you there with the bags and I'll go on to Eastfarm. As soon as I've made sure everything is set up properly, I'll be straight home. It shouldn't take me too long."

"Yeah right! With a bit of luck, you might be back before midnight," Sandra noted.

"No, but ..." Alex paused. He grinned before continuing, "I guess you know me better than I know myself."

"Remember, I'm used to working on investigations with you. I've only been out of your team for three months. Even that was just because it made sense for us not to work together when it become public knowledge we were a couple. I've seen what you're

6

like once you've started. You don't know how to stop."

Alex gave a leering expression and pulled Sandra into an embrace. "Better get started then. I need to go to work soon," he whispered.

Laughing as she spoke, Sandra pushed him away. "Idiot, you know what I was talking about. But come to think about it, couldn't Sanjay look after things for a bit longer?"

He pecked her on the cheek and clasped Sandra's hand in his. "Okay, you've called my bluff. I did say you knew me too well." Using his other hand, Alex pushed the trolley through the Customs post and out of the terminal.

The mini-cab was one of seven waiting at the designated pick-up point in Car Park 2. After identifying themselves by calling, "Taxi for Warren," they quickly loaded their luggage and jumped in.

"The booking's for Shawlands isn't it? Been somewhere nice?" the driver enquired, striking up a conversation. "You certainly didn't turn that colour in the U.K. It's been pissing down for the last week."

"Good detective work," Alex joked. "We've just spent a few days in the South of France, although we flew back from Barcelona. The weather was terrific, bright and sunny every day with temperatures in the high twenties and low thirties."

"The temperature's not been too different here, although that would be Fahrenheit not Centigrade. So you don't need to rub it in," the driver continued. "I've another month to go before I have a chance to get away. Even that's only for a lads' weekend in Black-pool. There's not much chance of seeing any day-light, never mind sunshine."

"Well, don't ask me for sympathy. Your hardship will be self-imposed. Listen, there's a change of plan. I still want you to take us to my address in Shawlands, but just to drop off my partner and the cases. Then I'd like you to take me to Eastfarm School. Will that be okay?"

Although they'd been a couple for several months, Sandra still felt a thrill hearing Alex describe them as partners and realising it was no longer in the busi-ness sense. Alex and Sandra had worked together for several years. She'd been a Detective Sergeant in his team, sharing a close friendship and risqué banter be-fore their relationship was consummated. Since then they'd been practically inseparable, other than dur-ing work hours, with Sandra moving to a different department and collecting her inspector's badge in the process.

"Yeah, no sweat. But why the change? You're just back from holiday, you said. You must be awfully anxious to get back to work. What's it all about?"

Alex didn't have an answer. So far, he had only a scant idea about the incident he'd been called to attend. Irrespective, he had no intention of impart-ing any information about an ongoing investigation. Nevertheless, he felt compelled to give a justification for the late alteration to his booking.

"No rest for the wicked." He winked at Sandra and added, "And I've been very wicked."

"What is it you do?" the driver persisted, not taking the hint.

"Whatever I'm called to, I'm a public servant," Alex answered, with sufficient vagueness.

"Oh, right," the driver answered, implying an understanding which he clearly didn't have. "I know the feeling, Mate. In this job, you have to be at everybody's beck and call."

Arriving outside Alex's building, he quickly jumped out and lugged their main bag up to the flat. Sandra followed carrying a smaller one plus their hand luggage while the cab waited, its taximeter running.

Alex lifted his leather jacket from a peg, pecked Sandra on the cheek and added, "I'll try not to be too long. You will stay? That's what we'd planned."

"It's not really what we planned," Sandra replied. "But if I'm going to be sitting alone, I'm as well here as in my own flat. I've had enough travelling for one day. So yes, I'll be here. I think I'll pop across to Morrisons to pick up cold meats and salads then we can snack. I can chill a bottle of Rose so it's ready for when you get back." She pulled him into a longer and more lingering embrace.

"Was that to dissuade me from going or to encourage me to come back quickly?" he enquired. Then without waiting for a reply, Alex gave a final squeeze to her shapely rump, before racing down to the waiting vehicle.

Less than ten minutes later, the cab slowed in front of the school's main entrance. Seeing several police

vehicles parked in the vicinity and a throng of people crowding outside the entrance, the driver asked,
"Hey, looks like something big has happened here.
I don't think you'll be allowed in. Do you want me
to take you back, or else I can wait to see how you
get on?"

"No, I'll be absolutely fine," Alex peeled off a couple
of banknotes, settled the bill and exited the vehicle,
almost before it had drawn to a halt.

Chapter 2

Spotting Alex's approach, a uniformed constable rushed to hold the door open. Out the corner of his eye, Alex saw the cab driver's open-mouthed expression as he pulled away.

"Where's the action?" Alex enquired loudly, struggling to be heard over the barrage of questions from the mob gathered outside.

"The body was found on the stage in the assembly hall. Sergeant Guptar was there coordinating everything, the last I heard. I've been left here to try to keep order and stop anyone unauthorised from getting in."

"Alex, I'm glad you're here. Can you tell me what's going on? Since your people arrived, we've been kept back and not told anything." Alex glanced around to see his friend, Brian Phelps, deputy headmaster of the school. Colleagues at university, they'd practically lost touch afterwards, but had re-established contact in recent months. This followed a series of incidents with a delinquent pupil who'd made spurious accusations against one of his teachers. Alex didn't have any formal involvement with that investigation, but he'd been drawn into making unofficial enquiries as his son had been in the same class. Alex and Brian now met infrequently for a drink, taking the opportunity to catch up on old times.

They shook hands in greeting.

"There's nothing much I can tell you. I've only just arrived back from holiday. I was in France this morning and Barcelona this afternoon. In fact, my plane landed little more than an hour ago. What have you learned so far?"

"I suppose that explains the tan. I've been told very little. I was taking a class when everything kicked off. I heard someone was stabbed in the main hall and none of the pupils or teachers or any of the school staff was involved. The police and the ambulance service were called. All the kids were sent home early to keep them away from the incident and we've been trying to put the word out to cancel the evening classes too. Some parents and the press are camped outside the door, but what can we tell them?"

"Don't worry, that's not your problem. No doubt, we'll be making a public statement soon. Can you tell me anything about the victim?"

"Haven't a clue. I know the local writers' club was using the hall, but that's about all."

"I've not had an update yet, but I can confirm what you've told me is correct. There's been a stabbing, the incident involves the writers and the victim is dead.

But keep it to yourself for the time being; our people will make the announcements."

"Which one was it? I've met a number of their group. They get quite involved with the school, judging our essay competitions and providing prizes. It's quite prestigious for them to be involved with the school as a couple of them are published authors. In return, they get the free use of our facilities. It's a 'win - win' scenario, or it was until now."

"I'm sorry, Brian, but there's nothing more I can tell you at the moment. We'll get a chance to talk later. I'd better get on."

Alex had been at the school many times, so didn't need to be shown the way. He raced along the corridor throwing open fire doors as he went and leaving them to ease shut. Arriving at the main hall, he was far more cautious entering, to ensure nothing would be disrupted. He needn't have worried as the large room itself was almost empty, save for an ambulance crew standing in the corner. All the action was taking place onstage and the unfolding scene was macabre. Alex stepped forward and could make out the heavily bloodstained body of a smartly dressed middle-aged woman lying prostrate on the floor. As far as he could judge, she appeared to be of average height and build, with pale skin and neatly coiffed hair framing a round attractive face. He recognised Doctor Duffie in attendance, examining the corpse. Sergeant Sanjay Guptar was standing behind, notebook in hand, fastidiously recording every detail which came to mind. Sharing the stage were four, white-suited, 'scene of crime' specialists each carefully examining, measuring, sampling and photographing anything which sat still long enough for them to record.

"What have you got for me?" Alex's voice resounded through the large empty hall and all but one head turned.

Sanjay bounded from the stage while the others returned to their duties.

"Nothing new, Boss. Just going through the formalities."

"Where's everyone else?" Alex asked.

"I sent the kids and most of the teachers home. Anyone who'd been on or around the stage at the time and anyone else thought to be even remotely connected are still here. We've taken over some of the classrooms to get them out from under our feet. Also, many of them were rather upset. It's hardly surprising, really. I thought it best to keep them out of sight of the body."

"Good, where are they?"

"First, we moved them to the music room next door. We have a couple of uniforms sitting in with them and we're taking them out one at a time for interview. Donny and Mary are in one room and Phil and Steve in another."

"Any feedback?"

"Nothing much yet, but it's early days. The man holding the knife when she was stabbed is suffering from shock and had to be sedated, so I doubt we'll make much progress there. His name's Bert Singer. He's aged about seventy and looks pretty frail. We're lucky he's not had a coronary. One body's enough to cope with."

"He can't be too frail," Alex mused, "if he's been able to carry out a lethal stabbing. What can you tell me about the knife?"

"It's been thoroughly examined, bagged and tagged. There's nothing particularly unusual about its appearance. It has a solid steel, double-edged blade, about five inches in length. The hilt's made of heavy plastic and is another six inches long. However, there is something special about it. It's been designed especially for theatre and is one of a pair. The second one looks identical, but the blade retracts on contact. If you stab it against anything, it does no harm. They're used in performances like magic acts or stage murders as substitutes for each other. The real knife is shown first to prove how dangerous it is. Then the knives are switched and the dummy one is used for the act. It appears to cut into someone, but no harm is done."

"Except it didn't work this time. What went wrong? Did the blade stick or did something go wrong when they did the swap?"

"Neither. The switch happened as planned, but there was a third knife, identical to the first and someone swapped it for the dummy one."

"Give me that again."

"Okay," Sanjay replied. "There's meant to be two knives, a real one and a dummy. The actors watch the real one being demonstrated and see it's solid so, by default, the other must be the dummy. Then they can feel confident using it when they're exchanged. As a further security, the dummy has a little notch in the handle so the actor can tell the difference. It should be idiot proof, except in this case the dummy was replaced by a second real knife which also had the notch in the handle."

Alex exhaled slowly in a quiet whistle. "Could it still be an accident? Could the supplier have sent the wrong thing?"

"Not a chance. The two knives were tested before they went onstage. They were even larking about with it, from what I've been told. Besides, we've found the dummy. It had been dropped in a litter bin in the side room offstage, the one they used for storing their costumes and props."

"It's definitely premeditated then," Alex surmised.

"It sure looks that way, Boss."

"Okay, give me a full rundown. How many of the group have we got here? And what can you tell me about them?"

"Right, I've already told you about Bert. We have another twelve of the actors, or writers actually. First, there's the victim's husband, Graeme Armstrong. He's not one of the writers, but he helps with the sound and lighting. Apparently, he's in a drama group and knows about all things technical. He's an engineer in his real life."

"Now that is interesting," Alex's attention fully focused. "Family are always the first suspects needing to be eliminated, and if he was at the scene and he has technical skills, then we need to closely examine his story."

"Yes, Boss, we have it covered. Phil and Steve are talking to him as we speak."

"Good, we can follow up later if necessary. What are Donny and Mary doing?"

"You mean 'The Osmonds' or our very own pairing?" Sanjay jested.

"That was Donny and Marie, not Donny and Mary. Anyway, I thought you're the one who slags off Phil for his schoolboy humour and bad jokes. Now here you are trying to compete. I'm tired, I can't take much more. Just fill me in," Alex continued, labouring over his words to add emphasis.

"Sorry, Boss. I sent them to interview Patricia Bannister. She's the group's secretary. She was standing next to Sheila when the stabbing took place."

"Who does that leave?"

"The next in line are Scott Burton, Lionel and Aaron Goldstein, Fiona Wark and Debbie Quinn. Here's a list of all the Club's members noting which ones were here at the time."

As they were talking, they continued walking in the direction of the music room. Their progress was halted by the sound of a door slamming followed by a peal of laughter. Then they caught sight of Phil and Steve moving in their direction.

"You would hardly credit it," Phil's voice boomed out then stopped after spotting Alex and Sanjay.

"Keep your voice down," Alex barked. "It's hardly appropriate under the circumstances. Now what do you find so funny?"

Phil looked down at his feet, embarrassed, realising his insensitivity.

"Well, out with it," Alex pursued.

"We interviewed Graeme Armstrong, the husband of the victim. He told us about the play they were performing. Apparently, it was written by his wife and the story's about a group of actors performing a play when an accident takes place and one of them gets stabbed."

"Yes, Phil, I was aware of that already and the parallels are clear to what's actually happened. But I still don't know what you were laughing at," Alex confronted.

"No, it's something else I found funny. Armstrong said to us that although it was his wife's play, he'd come up with the idea for the title and his wife agreed. He called it, *Abridged Too Far*," Phil replied.

"Clever, yes, but not funny," Alex stated. "Hardly a justification to laugh out loud."

"Okay, Sir, I suppose not. It appealed to me, though," Phil answered.

"I was quite taken with it too, Boss," Steve added, supportively.

"Maybe it wasn't such a good idea to put you two together," Sanjay sighed. "More importantly, what have you found out that's relevant to the enquiry?"

"Yes, of course, sorry. To start with, he was unusually calm. It was quite bizarre. His wife has been murdered, stabbed through the heart. Now here he is, all matter of fact, talking to us as if he was describing a television programme," Phil replied.

"It really was quite surreal," Steve added. "He gave us a graphic description of what happened and showed no emotion whatsoever."

"He could be in shock," Alex suggested. "Perhaps it hasn't sunk in yet, what's really happened, and he's working on autopilot. Has he been seen by a doctor?"

"The medical crew offered to examine him, but he'd have none of it," Steve said.

"Well, what did you get from him?" Alex asked.

"He seemed to be completely open. He answered everything we asked. His wife wrote the play as entries for a national competition. A number of the Association's members submitted an entry, but Sheila's was the one picked by the writing group to represent them."

"Interesting," Alex replied. "Might any of the others have been aggrieved not to have been picked?"

"I asked the same question," Phil said. "He thought it was unlikely. He said all the submissions were examined by a sub-committee then read out at one of their meetings and Sheila's won overwhelmingly. There was no serious competition."

"It doesn't mean someone wasn't upset by the decision," Sanjay posed.

"True," Phil replied, "but there wasn't any suggestion of anyone taking umbrage."

"Early days, wait 'til we've noted everyone's version before drawing any conclusions," Alex admonished.

"Yes, Sir," Phil said. "How was your holiday? I thought you weren't going to be back until tomorrow."

"I'm not," Alex stated. "Or rather I shouldn't be. This is my boys' school and Sanjay rightly thought I should be told what was going on. While I had a good break, the holiday's most definitely over."

"And how's the lovely Sandra?" Phil persisted.

"She's fine, at home doing the unpacking, I hope. But you should be aware that it's Inspector McKinnon to you, now she's had her promotion," Alex chided.

"Yes, Sir, of course, Sir, right away, Sir, three bags full, Sir," Phil responded, while mocking a boy-scout style salute.

Alex could only smile and shake his head as he walked away with Sanjay.

Steve turned to Phil, "How do you get away with talking to the Chief like that?"

"Like what? That's how I talk to everyone. But seriously, the boss is a really good guy. I've worked with him for years. Most of the time he's one of the lads, but he knows how to crack the whip when he has to. Sandra, his partner, worked in this unit too, until she got her promotion. The Boss is a lucky man. She's really smart and quite a doll, not at all bad to look at. But I'd better not let her or the Boss hear me saying it. You're new here. You just need to learn the ropes. You'll soon settle in. I'll help you."

"I'd appreciate it," Steve replied. "I worked CID in Edinburgh for two years before transferring here. There was no eye candy there and my chief was a real tyrant. You were frightened to open your mouth in his presence if he didn't ask you to first. It may take me a while to adjust."

Chapter 3

"Good afternoon, Ms Bannister, please take a seat," Mary ushered while depositing a portable recorder on the table and then switching it on. "I am DC Mary McKenzie and this is DC Donald McAvoy. We're here to take your statement, to find out everything you know about what's happened, and we'll be recording all that's said. Afterwards, we'll prepare a transcript of what you've stated and we'll ask you to check to make sure it's correct and then sign it. Do you understand?" The lady had been standing staring out of the classroom window as the two police officers entered the room.

"Of course I understand, I'm not stupid. But aren't you meant to read me my rights or something like that?"

Patricia Bannister's voice was sharp and nippy matching her small-featured, narrow, angular face. She was tall and her slender frame slouched forward with her shoulders turned in protectively. Her movements were hesitant and belied her aggressive words.

With thirty years of experience as an investigator, Donny immediately recognised this as her defence mechanism when facing unfamiliar circumstances.

"A caution isn't required unless we're charging you with something," Mary explained.

"Should we be charging you with something?" Donny added, capitalising on her discomfort and seeking to test her.

"Of course not," she spat back. "I want you to tell me exactly what's going on. I'm not used to being treated like this. I was told to come into this room and wait to give my statement. That was more than an hour ago. I want you to tell me what's happened to Mr Singer. He was looking most unwell when I last saw him. I'm used to being taken seriously and treated with respect. I worked as an English teacher up until I took my retirement. So don't play me for a fool."

"No-one would dream of it. We're sorry you've been kept waiting, but as I'm sure you can imagine, there are a lot of very important matters to deal with besides yourself. Now, so we can get started, will you please state your name, address and occupation for our records?" Mary requested and Patricia duly obliged.

"You've not told me yet about Bert Singer," Patricia persisted.

"Mr Singer had a nasty shock. He was sedated and I understand he was taken to hospital to be checked over. We won't find out any more until later. If you'll forgive me mentioning it, shouldn't you be more concerned about Sheila Armstrong?" Donny challenged.

Patricia's face paled. "Oh, yes, of course." She paused. "I was assuming there was nothing could be done to save her."

"No, I'm afraid not," Donny confirmed. "Now, can you please tell us what you saw?" Ordinarily, Donny would take more time to settle a witness before trying to draw out their recollection of an incident. In this instance, he could tell there was nothing to be gained by delaying the inevitable.

"Well, we were working through the script. Have you read it?"

"No, not yet," Mary replied. "Please explain?"

"It's a scene round about the middle of the play. Mrs Rathbone, that's the character played by Sheila, well, she gets stabbed by her husband, and he was played by Bert. It all seemed to go as expected. Bert lifted the knife and drove it into Sheila's chest then Sheila collapsed onto the floor. I thought she was acting and doing it quite realistically. But Debbie called out saying she should have acted the fall much better and played it to the audience with more flourish. More fool her, I suppose. Then Lionel started complaining that she was wasting all the stage props and shouldn't be using the fake blood for the rehearsal. It was only then Bert realised his hands were covered and so was Sheila's chest.

"Bert sank to his knees and let out a whine. Then everyone rushed forward. We didn't know who to look after first.

"Someone, I'm not sure who, yelled, 'phone for an ambulance,' and then everything became chaotic. It was all a blur after that and I can't remember who said, or did, anything. Some of the school staff rushed in. I came away from the stage and sat down and can't be certain what happened. Someone said, 'I think she's dead,' and then I heard someone else say, 'It's not the first time she's died on stage but probably the most effective.' I remember laughing at the thought, because it was true, she wasn't a good actress. Then I realised how awful it was and thought that we shouldn't be making jokes about such a terrible accident. I assumed she was dead, but I wasn't certain at the time."

Although the classroom was warm, Patricia pulled her cardigan tightly around her shoulders as if to ward off a chill. "I suppose it was an insensitive remark under the circumstances, but people say strange things when they're nervous or shocked." These words were spoken in little more than a whisper, expressed more as a comfort and a justification for herself than a statement to the officers.

"Can we get you a cup of tea or coffee?" Mary offered.

"No, I never touch caffeine. A good stiff brandy is called for, but I'd better not, I need to drive home to get back for Sammy, to make his supper."

"Is Sammy your partner?" Mary asked innocently.

"In a manner of speaking, he is. He's my cat and the closest living creature to me."

"Do you have any family?" Mary enquired.

"I'm a widow, my husband died eight years ago. My son lives near Motherwell, but I haven't seen him or his family for years. He's married with two children, but I've never met them. His wife's a strange one and won't let him or the children visit. The last contact I had was two years ago when he sent me a letter advising of his new address. I thought he was trying to resume contact and sent a 'welcome to your new home' card and flowers. Then *she* phoned me to ask why I'd sent it and told me she didn't want any contact. I asked her, if that was the case, then why had my son sent me the letter? Do you know what she said? She told me, it was for me to update my papers in case anything happened. The callous bitch only wanted me to correct the contact details in my will." Tears were welling up in Patricia's eyes.

Donny was unmoved, but Mary looked on sympathetically. "You've had a bad shock. Is there a friend or neighbour who you can go back to? It would be best if you weren't alone."

"It's all right, I'll be fine."

"There are a few more questions we'd like to ask you if you're up to it?" Donny continued.

"Okay, yes," she conceded. "Go on."

"Were you aware of the trick knives and how they worked?"

"Yes, we all were. It was Graeme who purchased them. I'm sure he said he'd bought them over the internet. He brought them to the meeting we had last week and showed us all how they worked. In one of the early scenes a knife is used and the audience sees Bert with it. He then places it in a box on the sideboard. Hidden inside is the fake knife and when it comes to the murder scene he lifts the fake one out of the box. What went wrong? Did Bert lift the wrong knife? Was it his fault?"

"We're still investigating so we can't tell you anything at the moment, but, as far as you were aware, were there only two knives?" Donny asked.

"Yes, that's how they came. They were kept in the container they were delivered in. It has inserts for the two knives. Why? Do you think there were more?"

"We're still checking, but we need to look at every option," Donny replied. "To move on, can you tell me if Sheila had been fighting with anyone? Had she upset anyone who may have had a reason to want to hurt her?"

"I really couldn't say," Patricia turned her head away, to avoid meeting their gaze.

"Couldn't or would prefer not to?" Donny challenged.

"I don't know anything."

"You must tell us anything you have knowledge of," Mary probed. "We're treating this as a murder enquiry and we need to identify anyone with a motive, however tenuous."

"Murder? Surely not?"

"We need to consider every possibility," Mary explained.

"Yes, I understand," Patricia's tone was unconvincing.

"Well, please go on," Mary urged.

"It's probably nothing, but if you insist, Sheila was not the most popular of people. She had a sharp tongue and a way of upsetting almost everyone she met."

Donny blinked a couple of times, unsure he was hearing correctly. From what he'd seen so far, he regarded Patricia Bannister as a nasty piece of work. She'd been nippy and unpleasant since they'd entered the room, only showing signs of humanity when talking about her own problems. He first thought, unsympathetically, that perhaps her unpleasant character was what chased away her family. Then considering again, it might be the trauma of losing them which made her bitter. In any event, based on what he'd seen, he wouldn't want her to teach him or anyone he knew. Here she was bad-mouthing Sheila Armstrong, talking about her being disliked, with the body not yet cold.

"Could you please give us more details?" Mary prodded.

"I'm not sure where to start."

Donny spotted a glint in her eye and reckoned she couldn't wait to dish the dirt. He also forecast they'd be in for a long session and was sorry Patricia had turned down the offer of a beverage as he was keen for one himself.

"Let's start with yourself," Donny said. "How long had you known Sheila and how did you meet?"

Patricia paused to think. "We live not far from each other. We both stay in the Giffnock area. I must have seen her about over a lengthy period of time. However, I didn't meet her properly until she joined the Association. That must be about six or seven years ago. I was already a member and on the Committee at the time. She was a very competent writer, but she specialised in slushy historical romances, not my type of thing. She was elected onto the Committee after a couple of years and became Vice President not much more than a year ago."

"Just a second, please," Donny interrupted. "You told us she was disliked by everyone. That being the case, how did she get elected to Vice President? Or even onto the committee for that matter?"

Patricia hesitated for a moment. "Well, you know what it's like with voluntary groups. It's often very hard to find volunteers to do anything, and one thing I'll say for Sheila, she was a worker. She was a great organiser and coaxed and cajoled and bullied other people into doing things. She was very effective in her role."

"Another thing," Donny pursued. "You said Sheila wrote historical romances but we were also told she was the author of the play you were performing. Now, from what we can gather, it's a crime drama, not a romance."

"You clearly weren't listening well enough," Patricia said, transforming to school teacher mode. "What I said was 'she specialised in historical romances.' It wasn't the only thing she wrote. In fact, the whole point of this writers' group is for us to set ourselves tasks to stretch our boundaries and take us out of our comfort zone. We try different genres and it makes us better writers. When I said Sheila specialised, it was because she has a number of books published. They're all part of a series and the theme is historical romance. She's written all sorts of other things, but none of it's been published."

"It sounds as if she's been very successful then," Mary commented.

"Well, I suppose it's down to how you measure success." Patricia sulked.

"Have many of the group members had books published?" Mary enquired.

"Not many."

"How about you?" Mary continued.

"Well, no, not yet," Patricia defended.

"And how do *you* measure success as a writer?" Donny questioned.

"It's hard to say, but in my opinion, it's more down to quality. I believe it's more important to be critically acclaimed than to make money. What's the point of having lots of people reading your work if it's wrong, or not good? I'm fastidious about anything I write to make sure the language and grammar are correct."

"And who would be the judge of something like that?" Donny enquired.

"Well, as I said, in my opinion critical success is what's important, the national writing competitions, for instance. I've had several prizes and commendations over the years, but I'm certain Sheila has never won any."

"Ah, you prefer to be judged by your peers than by the general masses?" Donny goaded.

"Exactly," Patricia replied, either ignoring or not realising the implied barb.

"Did she often enter competitions, or was she more interested in the commercial side?" Donny continued.

On this occasion, Patricia did rise to the bait. "I honestly wouldn't know, or care for that matter. From anything I read, the quality of her writing wouldn't have taken her very far anyway."

"This doesn't quite stack up," Donny pursued. "From what we've already been told, Sheila wrote the play you were performing here and it was chosen by the Club as its entry in a national competition. Now, here you are telling me her writing wasn't respected."

Patricia became quite flustered. "It was picked. But there weren't many other entries, and to be honest, it was only picked because of her status as V.P. It really isn't very good and will no doubt get thrown out at the first round."

"You didn't submit an entry yourself?" Donny asked.

"Yes, well not really, not this year. Last year I did and it took second place overall. It wouldn't have been right to put in a proper entry this year," Patricia defended.

"But you did have an entry?"

"Well, yes, I suppose."

"And you told me Sheila's work wasn't worthy of respect by other writers, but it would appear her publisher thought otherwise," Donny concluded. "In any event, this isn't taking us very far forward. More interestingly, you were talking earlier about Sheila being disliked."

"She was respected for what she achieved, but she wasn't liked," Patricia answered.

"Can you please be more explicit?"

"Well, she didn't take prisoners, she was quite brutal when giving critiques," Patricia continued.

"And this would be more aggressively critical than you think appropriate," Donny probed.

"Oh yes, I try to be constructive in my comments, particularly for newer members. I'm an educator, my aim is to help and encourage, not frighten people away."

Donny raised his eyebrows although he managed to stop himself gaping in amazement.

"I'm not always such a battle-axe," Patricia explained, correctly reading his reaction. "I do set high standards for myself and everybody else, but I try to be fair and not be unkind. I'm sorry, but Sheila was always able to bring out the worst in me."

"I gather you disliked her," Donny probed.

"I wouldn't put it like that. I can't say I was close to her, but I tolerated her. Dislike is too strong a word."

"Did anyone give the indication of being angry with her and wanting to get their own back?" Mary asked.

32

"Not that I'm aware of. Sometimes there were heated words exchanged, but it went no further. As writers, we're able to get our anger out on paper. The pen is mightier than the sword and all that."

"Well, in this case, it seems the knife was mightier than the pen. We have a corpse on its way to the mortuary to prove the point," Donny exclaimed.

Patricia's head slouched forward, unable to find an appropriate answer and unwilling to meet Donny's gaze.

"Okay, we can't go much further right now and we've several other people to interview. I would, however, like you to provide me with a list of all the members and anyone else you're aware of who knew her. I want you to attach comments against each, of any arguments or gripes they had," Donny requested.

"But that will take ages," Patricia complained.

"As may be, but it's very important," Donny concluded.

Chapter 4

"Do you have anything else to do at the murder scene?" Alex asked as he and Sanjay arrived in front of the classroom housing the other witnesses.

"No, I finished what I was doing and the 'scene of crime' team have everything under control. I'll check back in with them later. Shall we take on the next interview?"

"Yes, sure, but before we do, you didn't explain the line of command," Alex stated.

"It's your case, Boss. Sorry, I thought I'd said," Sanjay replied. "That's why I called you. It wasn't only because of your connection with the school. Realising you'd be back tomorrow, I was asked to kick things off on the understanding it was being allocated to you."

Alex looked quizzical.

"Yes, of course, it would be more normal for a higher ranking officer to be sent out in the first instance, but the department is short staffed. Inspector

Williams is away on a training course and Cairns is off sick with a recurrence of his back problem."

Alex rolled his eyes but said nothing.

"I was told to report directly to the Super if I didn't get you," Sanjay continued.

"Hmm, although I didn't realise it, I suppose I didn't have much of a choice," Alex said.

"I don't know, Boss. If you hadn't come in, they might have pulled Bill-Bill back or else seconded someone across."

"I guess you're right, but I wouldn't let Billy Williams find out you call him by his nickname if I were you," Alex warned.

"Thanks, I'll keep that in mind."

"Okay, who's up next?" Alex asked.

"We've got Scott Burton," Sanjay suggested. "If we take them alphabetically, then he's front of the queue."

Alex blinked a couple of times. "Are you being serious?"

Sanjay smiled. "He is next in line as he's the only one we've not already seen who was front of stage at the time of the stabbing. It's true that, alphabetically on surname, he's first as well and you've always lectured us on being methodical."

"Okay, okay, let's get on with it. It's getting late and I'm tired. I had a very early start travelling down from French Catalonia to Barcelona, El Prat, in time for our flight. And you need to remember, that for me, it's an hour later too, because of the time difference."

"Righto, Sir. I'll go and get him and we can use the second classroom over there on the left." Without waiting for an answer, Sanjay strode through the door to find Burton.

A few moments later they were all sitting around a table, with the interview already commenced.

Scott Burton lacked presence. Physically, he was the archetypal eight-stone weakling. Aged in his late thirties, he was puny in stature and softly spoken. He had a round, pudgy face and was clean shaven with almost no hair on top to compensate. The visual impression was like a child's drawing where you can turn a head through one hundred and eighty degrees and it looks the same. His speech was slow and reticent. He started by talking in a monotone, drawing out each word, even though he was using monosyllabic answers most of the time.

"Right, Scott," Alex proceeded. "Based on other statements, you were perfectly positioned to witness what happened."

"Ye, ye, yeeees."

"Please tell us in your own words what you saw. Don't leave anything out. I don't want opinions or theories, only a detailed account of what you saw. Can you manage that?" Alex asked.

"Ye, yes, I understand. I'm sorry. There isn't much I can tell you. You see I hadn't been paying too much attention," Scott said.

"You must have seen what happened, you were standing only a few feet away," Sanjay prodded.

"Well, yes, but as I said, I wasn't really paying attention to what was going on. To be honest, I was a bit bored. We'd rehearsed the previous scene four times and I was expecting this one to be the same. I'd been thinking about a letter I had to write, for work, when I got home and I wasn't exactly following what was going on. My speaking part wasn't due to come until further into the scene anyway. The plot was for Sheila's character to be stabbed by Bert's and a whole commotion to start. That's exactly what happened except it wasn't acted, it was for real."

"What did you actually see?" Alex persisted.

"From what I remember, Sheila gasped then fell to the floor and Patricia screamed, then everyone else gathered round. But that's exactly what was scripted to happen. Then someone, it might have been Aaron or Lionel, made a comment about wasting blood and Patricia told Sheila to stop hamming and get up. It was then we all realised Sheila hadn't moved and then Debbie screamed. A lot more realistically than Patricia's it was too. Someone shouted, 'get an ambulance,' and that was it."

"Up until that point, was there anyone there who wasn't part of your group?" Sanjay asked.

"I don't think so. There were two or three of the school's staff about earlier, but none were close-by. All the pupils had been kept well away to give us privacy."

"How about before the rehearsals started? Was anyone close-by or talking to the group or in or around the dressing room?"

"Nothing comes to mind. I was one of the last to arrive. I can't comment on what happened before," Scott replied.

"I want you to tell me about Sheila. How well did you know her? What was she like?"

"I only knew her from the writing group," Scott's answer was abrupt and seemed defensive.

Alex and Sanjay looked at each other for confirmation, both having picked up on the change in attitude. They continued cautiously with their questioning, seeking more background information and putting Scott at his ease before returning to the point.

"Besides your connection within the group, how did you get on with Sheila?" Alex resumed.

Scott paused for a second before answering. "She could be quite flirty. With all the men, not only me," he quickly added.

"And what about the women, did they get on with her?" Alex questioned.

"Not really, from what I saw, they mostly tried to keep a distance. I'm sure she wasn't liked by the other women. They might have been wary of her trying to flirt with their partners and didn't want to give her a chance."

"You've used the expression 'flirt' a couple of times. Will you please tell us more about what you mean?" Sanjay prompted.

"I'm not sure how to best explain. It was mainly when there weren't other people about. Let's see, staring into your eyes when she was talking to you, leaning in close and being tactile, a bit touchy-feely.

Sometimes she was a bit, how can I say, 'suggestive' in conversation."

"Okay," Alex continued. "And what particular interaction did you have with her?"

Scott's face reddened and he gulped in a large breath. "There was only one occasion. It happened a few months ago. It was as we were leaving the group and we were talking in the car park. Sheila leaned in close to me and whispered that she and her husband were going to be having a few friends over the following evening and asked me to join them. I thought she was being friendly and said I'd happily accept. I was new to the group and was pleased, taking it as an indicator of being fully accepted.

"I turned up the following evening at eight o'clock. I took a bottle of wine. It was a good Bordeaux label, a Saint Emilion, because I didn't want to appear cheap.

"She showed me into the lounge, poured us each a large glass and told me to sit on the couch. I asked where everyone else was and she said her husband had to attend a business meeting in Stirling so they'd postponed the party. She claimed she didn't have my number and wasn't able to tell me it had been cancelled. I thought it odd, because she could have contacted me if she'd really wanted to. She went on to say that since I was there anyway then I would be able to help her with a bit of her writing she'd been finding sticky.

"I felt quite flattered because, as I said before, I was new to the Writers' Association and I'm not that good. I'd only joined so I'd be able to learn. By contrast, Sheila was a published author and here she was asking my opinion."

Alex nodded indicating for Scott to continue.

"She left the room then returned holding a few pages she said she'd started. Then she went on to explain it was a seduction scene. She asked me if I would read it first then perhaps we could play it out, to give her ideas on how to take it forward.

"I felt a bit unsure, but really couldn't say no. She handed me the papers and then sat beside me and placed her hand on my thigh.

"I leapt out of the chair as if I'd had an electric shock. She wasn't unattractive, but I wasn't interested in having a fling. I told her I thought it best if I left.

"I was concerned she might be angry or upset, but none of it. She squealed with laughter and said that was exactly the reaction she wanted. She said she was truly writing a seduction scene and that I'd been a great help. I wasn't certain what to think, but knew her explanation was unlikely. Perhaps it's only my vanity, but I'm pretty certain it was for real. Anyway, I left and no more was said."

"What can you tell me about Mr Armstrong? How well do you know him?" Alex asked.

"Not at all. I met him a few times when he's attended our meetings as he helps out on the technical side. He seems to understand these things."

"What, in particular, is his expertise?" Sanjay asked.

"I can't say for sure. I've heard it said that he was an engineer by training and he understands all about producing plays. He can set up the lights and sound. I've been told he also makes a lot of our props."

"Oh really. He must be good with his hands?" Alex enquired. "What sort of thing? Is it woodwork or metal?"

"He can turn his hand to most things; wood, metal, plastic, material, even printing."

"Were you aware of Sheila having any fall-outs with anyone?" Alex asked, quickly switching subject.

"There's nothing I can tell you from my own experience. As I said before, she was a bit of a flirt, but it all seemed pretty harmless. Mind you, a few of the women may have had a different opinion. Also, I've heard talk that she had a major fallout with someone in the States, someone she met on the internet through a writers' support group. From what I was told, this woman took complete exception to a review Sheila wrote about one of her books. She was really angry and made threats about what she'd do if Sheila didn't change it or remove it."

"And did Sheila do anything about it?" Sanjay asked.

"Well, not that I'm aware of, but I only got it second or even third hand."

"Where did you hear this?" Alex asked.

"I'm not sure. It could have been Aaron."

With little more added, Scott had served his purpose. It was apparent he had nothing further to contribute for the time being. He was allowed to go home, with instructions not to discuss the happenings of the day.

The two officers were sitting collating the information received to date when Alex felt the vibration from his phone against his leg. He'd set it to silent before the interview and hadn't corrected it yet. Looking at the screen, he saw his own landline displayed.

"Hi, Sandra, is everything okay?"

"Yes, I'm just checking on you to make sure you're alright. It's getting late and you haven't eaten since Barcelona, not unless you've sent out. I've bought in a nice supper for us and a good bottle of plonk. When do you think you'll be back, or should I start without you?"

"You'd better go ahead. I'll be back in another hour or so. I'll be as quick as I can. Hopefully, you'll still be awake as I'm not into necrophilia, or even somnophilia, for that matter" Alex whispered.

"I'll see what I can do, but you'd better not leave it too long. There's something I need to discuss with you if we're both not too tired. Oh, and to cap everything off, my holiday's over too. I received a call asking me to come in tomorrow as I've been seconded back to CID because your lot are short staffed. I've to fill in on the Court Investigation because McTaggart's been hospitalised with suspected appendicitis."

"McTaggart's a lazy bastard. He's never done calling in sick over some invented disorder or other. As for appendicitis, that sounds a bit too high, he's more of a pain in the arse. Anyhow, what's this Court Investigation?" Alex enquired.

"Didn't you hear? It's all over the news, an armed holdup at the Sheriff Court. It happened this afternoon," Sandra explained.

"I've been too tied up. I've not heard the news. What happened?"

"The details are fairly scant. But from what I've been able to find out, two men forced their way into the fines office at the Court and made off with all the cash. At least one of them was armed."

"Aw, come on, you must be joking. Why would anyone do that? It's not as if they collect very much money and most of what they do take in will be cheques or electronic payments. There can't be too much in readies," Alex conjectured.

"I had the same thought," Sandra answered. "I don't reckon the motive was money. More likely, their aim was to cause embarrassment to the fiscals' office and to us. It was either that or to cause a distraction to take our attention away from something else."

"Mmm, an interesting theory. Well, it looks as if we're both going to have our work cut out for us over the coming days, or more."

Sandra sighed. "A bit different from sunning it up on the Med or sampling the local vineyards of rural France."

"All good things come to an end, but we can look forward to the next time." Realising he was becoming pensive, Alex decided to get back to work. "I'll go now and I'll try to come home soon."

Alex clicked off and noticed Sanjay looking questioningly at him. He explained about the heist at the Court and Sandra being drafted across to work the case.

"We're pretty much finished here for tonight and I can handle anything else. You've still a few hours of what was meant to be holiday left. Why don't you call it a night? We can pick up where we've left off in the morning," Sanjay offered.

Alex didn't need too much persuading and called to arrange for a driver to take him back to Shawlands.

For the last couple of hours, he had functioned on adrenaline. Now standing waiting in the school's entranceway, exhaustion caught up. But it was a good tiredness. Alex had been doing what he enjoyed most of all.

The few days break he'd had with Sandra, living in her parent's French holiday home, had been wonderful. Days spent under a clear blue sky; sometimes walking in the fresh mountain air or basking on a Mediterranean beach with sand stretching as far as the eye could see and hardly a soul in sight. Other times pottering at galleries, 'brocantes' or 'vide greniers' seeking out novelties and bargains. There was delicious local produce to sustain them, often hand-picked from their own garden. Their nights were spent snuggled cosily in bed interspersed by episodes of exercising sexual prowess.

Despite this, Alex was happy to be back doing the job he loved. He was good at it. He knew he was and so did everyone else. He was well respected and liked too, by his subordinates as well as his bosses.

He was enjoying his life and couldn't remember a better time. They each continued to rent their own flats, but in the months since he and Sandra had come together, they'd lived in one or other property. They shared a bond he'd never experienced with Helen, his ex-wife. Sandra loved police work and was driven in the same way he was, in a way Helen could never understand. Time had moved on and Alex and Helen now had a tolerable working relationship which allowed him to have full access to his two boys.

After his divorce, money had been tight for a while. There was little left after paying his living costs, making his monthly contribution for child support and keeping up the mortgage payments on the family home. However, his imposed frugality had already started to ease before being helped by sharing his living expenses with Sandra. Her recent promotion to Inspector rank meant they would now be able to afford more luxuries. Were they to take the next step of formally living together, renting only one house, they would be even better off. But somehow, they never got round to making the decision or even discussing the option.

Alex was very content, his musings considered his long and successful police career. He wasn't too far off having twenty years of service and not many more would give him entitlement to a full pension. If he chose, he could retire and take on a security advisor or consultancy role and then he would be rolling in money. However, to do that would mean giving up the work he loved and any such thought couldn't be contemplated, not at this stage.

"DCI Warren? The car's over here." Alex was startled from his deliberations by a fresh-faced, young constable, a tall lanky boy who looked hardly any older than Alex's son.

He climbed into the passenger seat of the Astra and clipped his belt.

"Okay, Sir, I'll get you down the road in no time. You've got quite a tan there, are you recently back from holiday? Lots of sun, sea and sex, I trust."

Alex prized the good and friendly rapport he had with his staff and other police officers, but he was taken aback by the constable's brashness. When Alex started in the force, superior ranks were always treated with the utmost reverence. Where there was more than one level of difference, a subordinate would never speak unless by invitation and most likely then only to provide information or evidence pertinent to an enquiry. Alex considered how times had changed. The youngsters nowadays were so much more confident and forward.

He wasn't unhappy to encourage enthusiasm, but neither was he prepared to tolerate any lack of respect. "You're not in the pub now, young man, and you'd do well to remember it." Alex then barked his address and the rest of the journey passed in silence.

Chapter 5

Hearing a key turn in the lock, Sandra jumped to her feet. "You're earlier than I expected, come on in and relax."

Sandra helped Alex out of his jacket and ushered him towards the lounge as she diverted to the kitchen. She reappeared a few moments later proffering a large glass of red wine.

Alex was already stretched across the couch and hauled himself to a more upright sitting position to accept the offering and take a first sip.

Although as a couple, they'd both been caring and attentive to each other's needs and comforts, Alex detected something unusual about the welcome he'd received.

"Where's your glass?" he enquired.

"I'm not quite ready yet. I mentioned on the phone that I'd something to discuss if you're not too tired."

"I am pretty exhausted, but I'm sure I can cope. Is it about your reassignment to the Court enquiry?"

"I'm late," she whispered.

"It is late, but that's okay. I'm still awake enough."

"No, I'm late," she continued, enunciating the 'I.'

Alex looked expectantly for a further explanation and then it dawned on him and his face froze.

"I wasn't certain I'd got my dates right these last few days, so I picked up a pregnancy test at the chemist. I tried it this evening. It showed positive," she blurted.

"But how?" he asked.

"I'm sure you don't need me to explain how," Sandra replied without any hint of a smile. "As for why the pill didn't work, I can only guess. It could have been when I had a tummy bug. You remember, I was throwing up, on and off, for a couple of days. It's the only thing I can imagine, and the timing would be right."

Alex placed his glass on the table, jumped to his feet and enveloped Sandra in a comforting embrace. His heart was racing, delighted at the news, but reticent to show his feelings, fearful of Sandra's intentions.

"How do you feel about it? What do you want to do?" he asked hesitantly.

Sandra pulled back from the hug to see Alex's face. "What do *you* want to do? How do you feel about having another child?" She too was apprehensive, inwardly quaking, terrified he would be unwilling to take on more commitments.

Alex drew in a deep breath. "I don't know what you want me to say."

"The truth, the whole truth and nothing but the truth, you're more than familiar with the routine." Sandra's words were making light of the subject although her expression lacked any humour.

Again, Alex paused as if to summon up energy and compose his thoughts. "Whatever we decide, this will be a defining moment for us. Things will never be the same again."

Alex saw Sandra's eyes welling. She had a fearful look he'd never seen before. He instinctively reached out and held her hand.

"I love our life, exactly as it is now and I truly hadn't contemplated us having a child. It's not that I don't want one, but because I understand how driven you are with your career and I hadn't expected you to change. I've always wanted a big family, but Helen wanted to stop after the two boys. Nothing would make me happier than having more children, but it's not only about me. How about you? Do you want to be a mother? You've already shown how great you are with Craig and Andrew when we've looked after them. They both adore you, but they're teenagers, almost adults. How do you feel about looking after a baby? Would you want to do that? I know what you're like and I'd never pictured you as a 'stay at home' mum."

Sandra threw her arms around Alex's neck and pulled him into an embrace. She exhaled a flood of air, not having realised she'd literally been holding her breath.

"Alex, I'm so happy you feel this way. I didn't want to get pregnant and hadn't expected to, but now that I am, I really want to have your child, our child. But there's so much to consider." Sandra took Alex's hand and placed it on her abdomen. "It's in there, living and growing, a part of you and me, I couldn't countenance a termination." Her tears were now in full flow. They were tears of joy.

He leaned over to wipe her cheeks then gently kissed her on the lips. "We'll manage," he said.

"What about your boys, how will they take the news?" Sandra asked.

"Their reaction to the prospect of a new baby brother or sister with them already teenagers might be interesting. We won't know until we tell them," he replied.

"Let's take them for a day out this weekend. We can talk to them together and gauge their reaction," Sandra suggested.

"Sounds like a good idea. I suppose I'd better give Helen the news too. I'm not too bothered about her opinion, but I'd prefer to keep her sweet. Then there's less chance of her trying to poison the boy's reaction to it," Alex commented.

"Humph, I suppose you're right. Just provided I'm not expected to be nice to her. She's never even given me the time of day."

"I don't expect you to do anything where Helen's concerned, although I'd prefer to minimise hostilities if possible. But on a more relevant issue, what about work? What do you think you'll want?"

"As you rightly said, I love what I do and the position I've achieved. I don't want to give it up. I don't believe that I'll need to. I can keep working until the seven-month stage, I reckon. I'll possibly need to move to desk work in the later stages, but that's a long way off. After the baby's born, I'll want to take a period of maternity leave, but then we could employ a nanny or a child-minder and that way I could go back to work."

"Would you be okay doing that?" Alex enquired.

"We don't need to jump to any immediate decisions, but I don't see why not. It's not uncommon and we are in the twenty-first century. Of course I want to be an attentive mum, just as you'll want to be an attentive dad. But there's no more reason for me to give up my career than there is for you to give up yours. Is that a problem for you?"

"Of course not, I'm only trying to talk it through. I truly believe a large part of the problem with society today is children growing up without parental supervision, or interest, really. You know as well as I do what we deal with each day. But that's not down to whether or not both parents are working. Consider how many little toe-rags we deal with where neither parent has ever worked.

"In Helen's case, she couldn't wait to give up work when she became pregnant. She had no wish to go back after the boys were born, but that in itself was no recipe for success and we weren't without our problems either.

"If we're both going to be working, then we'll be able to afford whatever care and support is necessary and we'll still be active parents. If you choose to give up work, then money may be tight, but we'll find a way to manage. Don't think you need to do anything immediately as there's no rush to make any decisions. Let's take things as they come."

Sandra's tears were again running and Alex looked on, concerned. "Don't be upset, we'll make this work."

"I'm not upset. I didn't expect this to happen. If you'd asked me before how I'd react, I'd probably have been appalled at the thought. But I'm really happy. Maybe it's my hormones or something but that's how I am, for now at least."

"Do you want to get married?" he asked sombrely.

"Is that your idea of a romantic proposal?" she replied.

"I'm sorry. That was stupid of me. I was being crass. I was thinking the baby should take my name."

"The baby will have your name whether we're married or not. It won't make a difference. This is something we've never discussed, but what makes you believe I'd take your name if we did get married?"

"I didn't think. I just assumed..."

"There's an awful lot to consider and we can't do it all now. We're both tired and more than a little bit stunned. It would probably be better if we didn't try to dwell on it now. Let's go to bed."

"Isn't that how we got into this position?" he quipped.

* * *

Hours later, Sandra was rudely awoken by loud grunting noises and Alex was thrashing about in bed. He seemed to be sparring with an invisible demon. It took her a few moments to realise he was sound asleep and literally in the throes of a nightmare. Gently, she roused him, taking care not to be caught by a wayward blow from his flaying arms.

"Alex, are you okay?"

Gradually he came to. "Sorry, love, I didn't mean to disturb you. It was really strange. I was fighting with someone, but it was all very vague, I don't know who or what it was about."

"Was it a reaction to the news I gave you last night?" Sandra looked dismayed.

Alex gathered her into his arms. "Oh, don't say that, for God's sake. I'm delighted with the news. It has nothing to do with it. More likely it's with me starting a murder investigation yesterday. I've quite often had nightmares after the first day of a gruesome enquiry. You wouldn't have realised because last night must be the first one we've spent together immediately after a major case has started. If I'd only thought, I'd have warned you, but I didn't think. I remember Helen talked about it. In the past, I sometimes stayed up all night or slept on the couch to avoid it causing a problem."

"Would it help to talk it through?"

Alex looked at the bedside clock, showing 5.30 am. "No, you go back to sleep. I'll get up and make myself a cuppa."

"No, lie here and tell me about the case. It might help you and I might even be able to make suggestions," Sandra offered.

"I don't think it right to be lying in our bed talking about violent murders."

"In that case, I'll get up too and we can sit together and have tea in the kitchen," she replied.

"But it's too early for you. You need to get more sleep. It's likely to be a heavy day ahead."

"I'm wide awake now. Let's do it." Before Alex could protest, she leapt out of bed, threw on her dressing gown, walked through to the kitchen and filled the kettle. "It's cold. I'm going to put the heating on if you don't mind."

"You go ahead. I don't know if it's that cold or we've become soft after a few days waking up to the Mediterranean sunshine."

"Okay, I'll make the tea while you tell me all about your case."

Alex sat down at the kitchen table and systematically ran through all the information and evidence the enquiry had so far amassed.

"Well, what's your next step?" Sandra asked.

"There are several," he replied. "First, I need to catch up on any further information collected after I left. I doubt there'll be much of importance or Sanjay would have called, but I need to check. Obviously, there'll be the technical reports to gather in too, but again I'm not expecting much as we're already certain of how she died. We can always hope forensics will give us more leads though.

"We've not yet been able to speak to Bert Singer to see if he has any more to tell us. He was sedated after the shock of delivering the fatal wound. He's quite elderly and has a dickey ticker, so we may need to walk on eggshells a bit. I also want to speak to the husband, Graeme Armstrong. Phil's description of his interview sounded a bit odd and I'd like to talk to him myself so I can form my own opinion. A bit of time has passed to let the news sink in. We'll see what difference that makes. The other thing I want to check is this business about a fall out with an American author."

"Well, it's hardly surprising you've been having nightmares with so much on your mind."

Alex smiled, ruefully.

"If you'll excuse me trying to teach my granny how to suck eggs, I'd suggest you take a deeper look at Sheila and Graeme's relationship. The accumulated impact of Bannister's statement about her being disliked, with the implication of it being more by women, together with what Burton said about the attempted seduction, gives rise to all sorts of possibilities. Was Sheila having an affair? Was Graeme for that matter? Or did they have an open relationship."

"Fair point," Alex replied. "Murder almost always comes as a result of greed, jealousy or revenge and invariably the root cause is either money or sex."

"Okay, now we've put the world to right and we don't need to be out for another hour. Do you want to grab some more shut-eye?" Sandra asked.

"Thanks, no. I'm wide awake now and I'm rested. If I were to sleep again now I'd either not be able to get up or I'd be groggy all day. I'll refill the tea and you can give me your thoughts about telling anyone our news," Alex added.

"It's too soon, Alex. First things first. I want to make an appointment with my G.P. to confirm everything's alright. Up to now, the only thing I'm certain of is that the pregnancy test showed positive. In the meantime, I'm not going to drink alcohol and I'll try to be more careful with my diet. Once we know for sure and we've worked out our immediate plans, then I'd like us to tell my family and, of course, yours. After that, we'll need to advise our bosses and our teams."

"Have you thought any more about what I asked you?" Alex asked.

"What was that?"

Alex took Sandra's hand then theatrically knelt on one knee but almost immediately his face contorted in pain.

"What's wrong?" Sandra asked, helping him back to his feet.

"I hadn't noticed one of Jake's toys was lying on the floor. I must have forgotten to take it back with him last time I had him here. Bloody dog's spoiled my romantic moment. Now what I was trying to ask was, 'Will you marry me?' "

They both looked at each other – Alex dressed in pyjama shorts, Sandra wearing a midi nightie and both wrapped in towelling robes – then burst into fits of giggles.

"You sure know the way to make a woman happy," Sandra blurted between guffaws.

"Does that mean yes?" Alex questioned.

"No, I didn't mean me. I was talking about my mum. It would make her dreams come true to see me married. It was the last ambition she wanted to achieve before she reached retirement age, having all her children wed. Besides, she approves of you, probably quite fancies you herself, truth be told."

"I doubt it, but even so, I'm less sure about your dad," Alex replied.

"No, he definitely doesn't fancy you. You're not his type." Sandra countered.

"I meant…"

"I know what you meant. I'm sure Dad quite likes you, but to him I'll always be his little girl, and for that reason he wouldn't be completely happy with anyone. It concerns him that you're a few years older than me, but otherwise he approves, as much as he could ever do at least."

"And you?" Alex pursued.

"You need to ask? I love you, Alex. I'm carrying your baby. What more proof do you want?"

"You haven't answered. Will you be my wife?"

"Alex, I love you and I'm flattered you've asked, but I'm really not sure about marriage. Let's not rush into anything and do something just because

I'm pregnant. If we are going to get married, then I want it to be for the right reasons. Not as a result of the pregnancy and not only to please my parents. It needs to be because it's right for us and for our child and most of all because it's something we both want."

"Okay, I won't rush you. You're right, the subject only came up because of the baby. But that doesn't mean I don't love you, or that I want to be with you any the less. I ought to have asked you before, but I needed this catalyst to wake me up. Anyway, there's no pressure, we can take it a bit slower. We'll leave the matter open."

Chapter 6

Sanjay was already at his desk poring over reports when Alex entered the office. Despite his Asian complexion, his face appeared pale, making the dark rings around his eyes more pronounced. This was further accentuated by the white surrounding his deep brown irises appearing badly bloodshot. His jowls were heavy, giving the effect of his face lacking definition.

"You look like shit. Are you okay? And once you've explained your condition, can you fill me in on what's happening?" Alex enquired before allowing Sanjay to get a word in.

"Yeah, I'm fine, Boss. A bit tired though. We stayed late last night so we could take preliminary statements from everyone; the techies finished up too. It means the school can get back to normal today. Well, as normal as possible under the circumstances. I didn't get away until after one in the morning by the time I'd collected and collated all the reports. I've been in here since six, checking everything through."

"I've no doubt that you've been doing a first-rate job, but we'll need to train you to delegate more," Alex suggested.

"I guess you're right, but this is the first major enquiry where I've had as much responsibility. I wanted to make sure I had everything under control," Sanjay stated.

"I understand and approve of your sentiment, but it will all count for nothing if you burn yourself out."

"Thanks, Boss. I'll remember that, but for the record, can I repeat it back to you when you do the same thing?"

"Certainly not," Alex replied, smiling. "I go by the traditional leadership rule of 'do what I say, not what I do.' Anyhow, what do you have for all this effort?"

"You mean besides a headache and the first symptoms of an ulcer?"

"Of course, but keep your medical symptoms to yourself."

The banter out of the way, Sanjay became very business-like. He stood, straightened his tie then leafed through his papers and handed a sheet to Alex.

"This is the list showing all the Club's members. It also shows everyone else known to be in the vicinity of the stage, at any time, on the morning before the incident, through until after it had taken place.

"The ones highlighted in yellow were on or near the stage at the time of the murder. The pink ones were in the general area. The blues are members of the Club who weren't in attendance and the green ones are non-Club members who were or had been near the stage. Then the non-highlighted names are ones we've been told about during the interviews. They're people who, at first, don't appear to have a direct link to what happened, but nevertheless sounded of interest and worth talking to."

"Very methodical. Well, who's been spoken to?"

"All the Yellows were interviewed yesterday, with the exception of Bert Singer. He's been kept in hospital under observation and we've not been permitted access yet, but hopefully this morning."

"I'd like to sit in on that," Alex stated.

"I expected you would. I've placed a call to his ward. They said they'd call back in the next half hour. We've taken initial statements from all the Pinks, but I'd like to follow up with a few of them. I think we've seen all the Greens we're aware of, but I've still to check. We've yet to talk to any of the Blues or the last, unmarked, list."

"I see you've Brian Phelps listed as a Green; he won't like that."

"Sorry, Sir, I don't understand. Why not? He falls into that category."

"He's a Rangers fan. A real blue-nose if ever I saw one."

It took Sanjay a moment to follow Alex's quip but then his face became creased by a broad smile. "I take your point. It hadn't occurred to me before. I've never been much of a football fan. I don't understand how fanatical folk can become about a bunch of lads chasing a ball around a field."

"Careful what you say here. Although not as obsessive as some, I'm one of these fanatics and I support Rangers too, well what's left of them. That's why I can appreciate Brian's likely reaction."

"I'll bow to your superior knowledge in that case," Sanjay replied, simultaneously enacting the gesture. "What's planned next?"

"My first priority is to talk to Bert. I'll wait to hear from the hospital before scheduling anything else for myself, but I've planned interviews with the other Club members. Phil, Steve, Mary and Donny will handle those as well as the follow-ups. They'll also take statements from the family and neighbours."

"It seems you've got it all covered, except, what about a follow-up with the husband?"

"You're right. Yesterday's reaction was anything but typical. Now a bit of time has elapsed, he'll have been able to absorb the news and we can go and talk to him after Bert if you'd like."

As if on cue, Sanjay's phone rang.

"Sergeant Guptar. Yes, that's correct. Ah, good, I'm pleased he's more settled. Aha, it shouldn't take too long and yes, I'll be able to put his mind at ease. No, we won't be rushing to arrest him. We know he was the one who held the knife when Sheila Armstrong was stabbed. But we've every reason to suspect he was the instrument of death, not the cause. Thank you, we can be there in thirty minutes."

Sanjay replaced the receiver.

"You don't need to explain. I picked up enough from hearing your end. Let's get going. It's not too far to the Vicky and we'll be travelling against the flow of traffic. I presume it was the Victoria he was taken to?"

"Yes, Sir. He was taken to A&E, yesterday. At first, they were treating him for shock but he was showing irregular heart rhythms and he has a history. They've kept him under observation in the C.C.U. He had a restful night and this morning he's been moved to a regular ward."

* * *

When Alex opened the passenger door of Sanjay's Renault Megane, he had to clear the baby carrier and other assorted accoutrements into the back before being able to lower his large muscular frame onto the seat. There wasn't very much room in the back either with a cricket bat propped between the baby seat and two booster cushions.

He looked back pensively at the array of accessories, remembering his own experiences when his boys had been younger. It made him acutely aware of what lay ahead resulting from Sandra's news.

Misinterpreting his reaction as a mild rebuke, Sanjay started to explain, "Sorry, Sir. My wife had the car yesterday and I've not had the opportunity to clear it out. You'll have forgotten what it's like travelling with youngsters."

Alex smiled, battling an irresistible urge to share his news with Sanjay, yet knowing it was too soon.

"Not something you ever forget," he settled for.

The aggregation of traffic approaching the city neared gridlock. However, the road south was quiet and provided an unimpeded passage, other than the inevitable succession of red traffic lights. Shortly after crossing the Jamaica Street Bridge, Alex's eyes strayed left beyond the elegant red sandstone terraces of Carlton Place towards the modern block structure of the Sheriff Court. It occurred to him Sandra would no doubt be close-by, enmeshed in her enquiry.

Continuing along Bridge Street, they travelled beyond the subway station and Alex noted a queue had already formed outside the O2 venue waiting for the ticket office to open. On closer examination, he realised some were carrying sleeping bags and had obviously been waiting overnight. He glanced up but was too late to catch the details of who was going to be performing. He reminisced the many concerts he'd attended over the years at the venue in its previous incarnations as the Bedford, Greens and the Academy before reaching its current designation.

"Did you see who was playing?" he asked Sanjay.

"Sorry, Boss. I was watching the road."

"I've spent many a good night in there and in some of Glasgow's other famous gig venues: the Barrowlands, King Tut's and the Apollo. Over the years there can't be a band which hasn't played in at least one of them. A band that's worth listening too, that is."

64

"A lot of changes now though," Sanjay said. "Who's to say whether any will survive? I can't even remember the Apollo, it closed years ago. Isn't that the site where the Cineworld multiplex is now?"

"Yeah. That's right. It went from being the biggest concert venue in the country to the tallest cinema."

"Anyway," Sanjay continued, "now there's now all these new places with much better acoustics. The Hydro, the Armadillo and the Concert Hall are all state of the art and the Hydro's enormous."

"That may be the case, but none of them can ever match the atmosphere."

"And that's a bad thing?" Sanjay asked. "In the old days, you could cut the atmosphere with a knife and it wouldn't be so bad if that was the only thing that got cut."

"Maybe," Alex smiled. "Perhaps I'm just being nostalgic."

Sanjay thought it best not to comment and they continued driving in silence with Alex pensive, remembering times past.

Arriving at the Victoria, Sanjay drove around the complex for some time, unable to locate suitable parking. Eventually he gave up and crossed Battlefield Road to find a space in the underground car park of the new hospital. Having lost several minutes seeking a space, they left Sanjay's car abandoned rather than parked to avoid wasting further time.

They exited the car, crossed back over to the old sandstone fronted building and took the elevator to the fourth floor. Although exhaustive efforts had been made to maintain the property and keep it clean, any major investment had been reserved for the new Southern General, earmarked as the hospital for the whole of the south of the city. The new Victoria was planned predominantly as a facility for outpatients. Time had taken its toll on the old building and the deterioration was evident.

Their heavy footsteps echoed as they proceeded along the corridor.

"Much as the new Southern looks incredible, the South-Side will sorely miss this place," Alex said.

"You're right there, Sir. Can you imagine having an emergency and needing to travel all the way to Govan to get to an A&E?"

"Yeah, even when the roads are quiet, it will take fifteen minutes, but in the rush hour you could double or even triple that."

"Too true and worse still, if you have an emergency on match day and there's a game on at Ibrox. They'd be no point calling an ambulance, you'd be as well to save time and bring in a hearse instead," Sanjay joked.

"We're in here," Alex advised, turning off the main corridor.

Within moments they'd located the nurse's station. Alex displayed his credentials and was shown towards a small private room overlooking the side of the building. A feeble looking man dressed in striped winceyette pyjamas was sitting on the bed which was angled upwards, his posture supported by pillows.

"Good morning, Mr. Singer. I'm DCI Alex Warren and this is Sergeant Sanjay Guptar."

"I've been expecting you," Bert answered and held out his arms as if waiting for handcuffs to be applied.

"Please relax. We haven't come to arrest you. We're here to take your statement," Alex reassured.

"I still can't believe what happened. It's my fault. I should have been more careful," Bert offered, tears welling up in his eyes.

"Let's take this one step at a time, shall we?" Sanjay asked.

Alex took several minutes checking Bert's details and asking mundane background questions, allowing him to settle before addressing the key issues.

"Had you handled the knife prior to the incident?" he enquired.

"Incident is a very mild way of describing it," Bert started. "Yes, the two knives were brought to the last Club meeting. I was particularly interested as it was my character in the play who'd be using them. I closely inspected them and played about with the trigger mechanism so I'd feel comfortable handling it. Sheila and I also had a bit of a rehearsal for the murder scene. She thought I was being too gentle and told me to be more forceful when I lunged with the knife. If only I hadn't listened..."

"Let's go back a bit. How well did you know Sheila?"

"She was a wonderful person. We go back a long way, it must be more than ten years. She and Graeme are very good friends of mine. They were very supportive when my Rachel passed away. I don't think I could have coped without them. She's a lovely lady, very pretty and very talented. She's a published author, you know, and she took time to help and encourage the rest of us in the group."

"Yes, we've heard," Sanjay interrupted. "Please run us through what actually happened from the time you lifted the knife."

"I walked over to the sideboard, as directed in the script. I lifted the knife from the box and I did check it was the right one. The one with a notch on the hilt. I turned to face her and waited for her to walk towards me. Right on cue, when she said, 'get out,' I lunged forward to stab her in the stomach, just below the sternum. I did it quickly and with power, the way Sheila said I should. Her knees buckled and she collapsed onto the stage. It looked very realistic and blood started to flow. I was marvelling at how well she'd acted and wondered how she'd produced the blood. I thought it looked very real and then I realised it was." Bert raised his hands to cover his face. "It was awful."

Following a lengthy pause, he added, "I don't remember anything after that."

"How about before?" Sanjay enquired. "Did you see anybody milling around who didn't belong to your group?"

"Not that I can think of."

"What about teachers and school staff, pupils even," Alex prompted.

"There were definitely no pupils. I remember one of the staff brought us a trolley with tea and biscuits.

I remember because we all considered it unusually kind."

"Can you remember who? Can you give us a name or description?" Sanjay's attention perked up.

"I'm sorry, but I have no idea of the name. Sheila seemed to know her quite well though. Let me think, she was quite tall and slim. Blonde hair, it was shoulder length, and she had freckles, lots of freckles."

"You said you were friends with both Sheila and Graeme. How did they get along?" Alex asked.

"How do you mean?"

"Obviously, they were a married couple, but were they close? Did they seem to get along well or were they prone to argue? You know the sort of thing," Alex pursued.

"They got along fine. They helped each other a lot and I never heard a cross word between them. Mind you, there were times when there was an atmosphere. I'm not sure how best to describe it, but there were uncomfortable silences."

"You mean like they'd been arguing, but didn't talk about it?" Sanjay asked.

"I really shouldn't have said anything," Bert replied.

"No, you really should. We need you to tell us everything you know or even think you know, no matter how trivial. We can be the judge of what's important," Alex continued. "Now is there anything else you can think of? Anyone you may be aware of, who had a grudge against Sheila?"

"Nobody comes to mind."

"Well, that's all for now." Sanjay advised. "We may wish to talk to you again though."

"That's it?" Bert asked, his face showing clear surprise.

"For now, it is," Alex confirmed.

Chapter 7

As the automatic door slid silently open, a cold, damp gust of wind greeted Alex and Sanjay. Almost as a reflex reaction, they both pulled up their collars to offer some protection from the elements while they made their way out of the hospital, darting between the fast moving vehicles on Battlefield Road and towards their car.

"I'm not used to this. It was in the mid-twenties where I was last week, not to mention bright and sunny," Alex muttered.

"You're back in Glasgow now, though. There's not a lot of point dwelling on it or you'll just get depressed."

"Too bloody true. I'll keep my mind on the job then maybe it won't seem as bad."

"Shall we see if Graeme Armstrong's about?" Sanjay suggested as he lifted his mobile to call ahead. At that same moment, Alex's ringtone sounded, indicating a call from Sandra.

"Hello, luv. Are you still at the court?" Alex said, letting Sanjay walk ahead to the car to allow himself some privacy for his call.

"Yeah, that's why I'm calling. I'll be here for some time; there's been another incident."

"What, while you were there?"

"Yes, I'm afraid so. We were in the cash office at the time and didn't see anything. It happened only a few yards away, in front of the main entrance. It's a bad one. GBH at least, more probably attempted murder," Sandra advised.

"Christ! Whatever next? What happened, was it a gang fall out?"

"A hit, more like. The victim was a lawyer, Fergus Hardy. I've come up against him before."

"Really, now that is interesting. As you're probably already aware, he handles a lot of dodgy characters; there's suspected mob connections. He's frequently in the high court so he must have been slumming it a bit. Have you any clues on the motive yet?"

"Early days, but we've a few theories already. It happened outside the front entrance. He was standing talking to one of his colleagues, near the door, but where they were under-cover so they could have a smoke. You know where I mean, the place that all the smokers use, next to the no smoking signs. Apparently, someone asked him for a private word and, as he walked away, four youngsters grabbed him and chucked him over the wall into the car park."

"You mean the bit to the right of the entrance where there's a warning not to climb? It's about four or five feet high but has a drop of twenty feet on the other side."

"The very same and the warning says twenty-six feet to be more precise. Fergus found out for himself, the hard way, literally."

"How bad is he?"

"I don't know for sure. His fall was broken as he landed on one of the police vehicles used for ferrying prisoners. It didn't do the van any good but probably saved his life. Even at that, there are certainly broken bones, compound fractures in fact. There might be internal injuries too. He was conscious and screaming the place down. An ambulance has taken him to the Southern. We should hear soon."

"Witnesses?"

"Yeah, no shortage, but even so, not a lot to go on. Four young slim tykes wearing hoodies. Two were tall, one medium and a small one. They made off before anyone realised what had actually happened," Sandra advised.

"What about the guy who called him over. Can he be identified?" Alex enquired.

"We may have more luck there. He made off too, but we have a description and it sounds like our old pal, Pat Carson. We're trying to track him down."

"What else have you got?" Alex persisted.

"Hey, this is my case. I only phoned to tell you that I'm going to be tied up on it and not likely to be home until late," Sandra replied before adding, "We won't starve, there's some food in the fridge as we hardly touched what I bought yesterday. It's not very exciting though."

"I'm sorry about the interrogation; force of habit," Alex continued. "You should be used to me by now; tell me about an investigation and I want to run it."

"And how is yours getting along?" Sandra enquired.

"Slow but steady. I'm with Sanjay and we've just stepped out from the Vicky. We were seeing Bert Singer."

"Did he have anything interesting to tell you?"

"Only what we expected. He seems pretty cut up about it all, although maybe not as much as Fergus Hardy from what you've told me," he added with a chuckle. "I reckon Bert was besotted with the victim and he's having trouble handling the guilt. I'm hoping to go and speak to the husband now."

"What, to see how besotted he was?" Sandra asked.

"That might be an interesting approach, we'll see. Listen, I'd better get going. It's blowing a gale here and this place is really exposed. Wait a minute. While I think about it – you said Hardy was standing, talking outside the Court building. Does that not strike you as strange in this weather?"

"Not really, as I said, they'd gone out for a smoke. It's not permitted inside the building and the roof has an overhang at the front which affords some protection from the rain. It's a favourite spot for smokers. There are bins there, but the ground's covered in stubs. We could collect a fortune if we positioned an officer there to hand out littering fines. Anyway, this all took place more than an hour ago, and from recollection, it was brighter at the time. But you're right, the wind fairly howls up from the river."

"I guess it's another justification of why smoking's bad for your health," Alex offered. "Anyhow, I'd better go now. Sanjay's waiting and I'm sure you've lots to do as well. See you later."

The engine was already running when Alex pulled his door open. "Sandra's got her work cut out at the Court which means I'm free to work late. What's the word on Graeme Armstrong?"

"He's home; we can head straight there. It's not far from here. But what's all this with Sandra? Don't tell me she's got you under the thumb already if you need to check with her before working late."

Alex's face flushed with embarrassment, realising the inference of what he'd said. Although Sanjay's comment had been made as a quip and was well intentioned humour, Alex laboured over an answer, not wanting to give credibility to the comment, but neither did he want to downplay Sandra's significance in his life. Particularly so, after the news of her pregnancy. In the end, he opted to say nothing, but there followed an uncomfortable silence in the car.

"Do you know where you're going?" Alex asked unnecessarily, for lack of anything better to say.

"Sure thing, Boss. I've logged the address in the satnav but I'm fairly certain of how to get there. It's not far beyond Orchard Park."

"Did it occur to you to check if he's alone?" No sooner had he said it than Alex regretted his words.

Sanjay was a good detective and would have made appropriate preparations. To ask basic questions the way he had was insulting. He was angry with himself; he knew he shouldn't be releasing his frustration by being nippy with his staff.

"Sorry," he quickly added, before Sanjay replied. "Is anyone there with him?"

"Yes, Sir," Sanjay answered, showing no indication of annoyance. "His brother, Calum, insisted on staying with him last night to give him support and company. He's still there."

"Do we have any info on the brother?"

"Not much. We ran routine checks to find out about family. Graeme has one older sister who lives in Australia and Calum is his only brother. He's a couple of years younger. Sheila had no siblings. Her parents were divorced and both remarried. The father died a number of years back but the mother and step-father are still around. They live down the coast, somewhere in Ayrshire. Graeme's brother lives in Edinburgh, works in Holyrood. The first we knew he was on the scene was when I called a few minutes ago," Sanjay advised.

"Holyrood, what does he do there? I hope we're not going to suffer any political interference?" Alex sounded concerned.

"Relax, Boss. I doubt that there's much risk. He'd not an MSP or even an aide. His work is something to do with building maintenance," Sanjay reassured.

"Even so, be careful. You don't know who his friends might be."

No more than fifteen minutes later, Sanjay drove down a broad avenue of detached bungalows and drew up outside the Armstrong house. They crunched their way along a red whinstone pathway bordered by brightly coloured, flowering shrubs.

Before they had time to ring the bell, the front door was pulled open and they were greeted by a grim-faced, rotund man.

"You must be Sergeant Guptar, we spoke on the phone. I'm Calum Armstrong," he said, reluctantly offering his hand for the briefest of engagements.

"And this is DCI Warren," Sanjay replied, pointing to Alex.

Calum took slightly longer on this greeting, as if in appraisal, but declined any eye contact.

"Come in, have a seat in the lounge," Calum closed the door and led the way into a freshly decorated, bright room, illuminated by a watery sun flooding through a three-windowed bay.

Calum lowered himself into an armchair while gesturing for the officers to do likewise on the sofa.

They remained standing. "We've come to speak to your brother, Graeme," Sanjay said.

"I reckon I'll be able to tell you anything you need to know and save Graeme any unnecessary suffering," Calum claimed.

"If you have information to give us, then we'd be very pleased to hear it; however, we need to speak to your brother and we can only take his statement from him directly," Alex replied.

Calum looked at Sanjay, vainly seeking support. His imploring look was met by a blank stare.

Resignedly, he stood again, "I'll bring Graeme through, but I warn you, I won't tolerate you giving him a hard time. He's already had more than enough to cope with."

Believing discretion to be the better part of valour, Alex remained silent but nodded to Sanjay, indicating for them to sit.

A few moments later, the door opened and Calum returned, followed by his brother. There was a distinct family resemblance but Graeme looked a good twenty kilos lighter. He was a far taller and thinner version with handsome, well defined features, where Calum's were blubbery and blotchy. Despite his gaunt complexion and the dark rings around his eyes, on first impression, it was difficult to accept Graeme was the elder. Alex cruelly considered he must have used the opportunity to select the best genes from the family pool with Calum picking up the left-overs. Graeme shuffled slowly into the room.

Alex and Sanjay stood for the introductions before they all resumed their seats.

"To start off, can I say we are sorry for your loss and reassure you that we will do everything in our powers to catch whoever was responsible," Alex stated.

Graeme nodded, but didn't comment.

"I'm aware you already spoke to some of my colleagues yesterday and I have the notes on what was said, but I'd like to go over it all again, to make sure we have everything correct. There may be other things you've remembered or that didn't occur to you as being important yesterday, when it was so soon after the incident," Alex commenced.

"Now just wait a minute," Calum interrupted. "This isn't right. You shouldn't be harassing my brother and especially not now when he's upset. He already told you what he knows. Unless you've got something new to ask, then you need to stop now. Besides anything else, he's entitled to have a solicitor present. I'll have you know my partner's a clerk in the justice department at the Parliament, so we won't be messed about."

Alex looked fiercely at Calum. "Mr Armstrong, I don't give a monkey's fart where your partner works. For all I care she, or he, can be the Lord Chief Justice. I'm carrying out a murder investigation and I need to collect all relevant information as quickly as possible. For that, I need to interview your brother and I need to do it without your interference. You must either keep quiet or I'll be forced to make you leave the room. You are correct that your brother is entitled to have a solicitor present when he's being interviewed, but I hardly imagine that's necessary, particularly if he has nothing to hide. However, if that's what 'he' wants, we can adjourn this meeting and resume it at our offices. Of course, he'd be more comfortable here. It doesn't bother us if he does have his lawyer. A trained solicitor understands the process and knows how to conduct himself to allow us to get the information we need. Well, what's it to be?" Alex's words were spoken slowly and quietly in a controlled fashion, but the dispassionate delivery combined with his aggressive body language were all the more intimidating. It was a technique he'd mastered over the years and invariably it worked well.

Calum started to stand. His eyes bulged and his face flared bright scarlet. He tried to speak, but words seemed to catch in his throat. Graeme placed a restraining hand on his arm and drew him back into his chair.

"It's alright, Calum, I need to do this sometime. I'm as well to get it out of the way. I'm sorry, Officer, but Calum's only trying to look after my best interests. Now if this is going to take some time, would you like some tea?"

Calum looked between his brother and the detectives, unable to hide his resentment, then he slowly edged backwards into his chair.

"That's most kind of you to offer, but we're fine."

"What would you like me to tell you?"

"Let's start with the knives. We understood that you made the purchase on behalf of the Club," Alex said.

"Yes, I did. I bought them from a company called 'Top Hat,' over the internet. They're a magic and theatrical supply company in Las Vegas. I understand that they have an English associate, because they were delivered by Royal Mail and it had UK stamps on the package. I remember remarking on it to Sheila."

"You wouldn't still have the packaging?" Sanjay asked.

"I don't think so," Graeme replied. "It arrived about three weeks ago, and we recycle all paper and packaging. The Council pick it up every second week on a Monday. I reckon it must be gone by now. I may have the stamps though, as we collect them in a bag to give them to charity. It was a heavy box, so the postage would have been quite expensive. The stamps would be together on a section of the cover so shouldn't be too difficult to locate."

"We don't need it at this moment. Did you keep the order form?" Sanjay asked.

"I'll have it on the computer. As I said, I ordered on the net, which means I'll have email confirmation of the order and the payment, as it was electronic. I remember I printed the invoice too, so I could get reimbursed by the Club. I gave it to Lionel, he's the Treasurer. He's bound to have a copy, even if I can't find it."

"Thank you. That's most helpful. Can I ask you to try looking out the papers and the stamps after we finish speaking?" Alex asked.

"What do you want them for?" Calum interjected.

"Isn't it obvious?" Graeme snapped, irritated by his brother. "They want to know that I only bought two and not three knives and they want to find out where they came from so they can check who else bought the same thing. Am I not right?" he asked looking to Alex for confirmation."

"Absolutely. You should have been a detective, yourself," Alex quipped.

Calum scowled and looked away.

"Was it the first time you'd purchased anything from this company?" Sanjay asked.

Graeme paused for a few moments, contemplating. "Yes, I'm fairly certain. I've used many different suppliers over the years, not only for the writers, but also for my theatre group. But I can't remember using Top Hat before. I have bought from other companies in Las Vegas, but I can't be certain that they aren't connected."

"How did you find them?" Sanjay continued.

"I remember looking them up on Google, but I have a vague recollection that someone recommended them to me."

"Please try to remember," Alex asked. "It could be important. If you can try to remember who and how long ago it was."

Graeme closed his eyes for a few seconds, trying to recollect. "No, I'm sorry, nothing. I don't think it was recent. Maybe it'll come back later. I'll get back to you if it does."

"How long ago did Sheila write her story?" Alex asked.

"It was a short play, not a story," Graeme retorted. "She knew about the competition since the middle of last year and started writing for it straight away. She must have finished maybe two or three months ago."

"And had many people read it, or at least been told about the plot?" Alex continued.

"Everyone at the Group," Graeme replied. "They had to, so it could be cast and then acted out. Oh, I see what you're getting at. For someone to plan the murder in this way then they must have been aware of the theme of the play and they'd have had to know that before designing the plan with the knives."

"Keep going at this rate and you'll be doing my job soon," Alex joked.

"Okay, Sheila submitted the play for consideration about two months ago. At that time, there were only three people judging, plus Sheila – they weren't allowed to judge their own. Let me think; that would have been Lionel, Patricia and Bert, they're all on the executive committee. The decision took two or three weeks and then it was given out to the whole group. That must have been more than a month ago."

"How about anyone outside the writers' group –was anyone else given it to read?" Sanjay questioned.

"I really couldn't say," Graeme said. "She sometimes read her work to her cousin in Canada. They'd often talk for hours on Skype. She also quite enjoyed reading her work to friends and fans, so I'd only be guessing at who might have heard it."

"Well that doesn't narrow it down very much. What about your order for the knives? How long did they take to manufacture and deliver?" Sanjay continued.

"I don't think that will help you much either," Graeme stated. "They had them in stock and were able to deliver within a matter of days."

"How easy would they be to make? Could someone have made a copy?" Sanjay continued.

"I suppose. You'll have seen them yourself. There's nothing complicated about them, particularly not the one with the fixed blade." Graeme conjectured.

"We've heard that you're quite handy, yourself. Is it something you could have made?" Sanjay probed.

Calum was on his feet. "Now just a minute. You can't go making accusations…"

"Calm down, Calum," Graeme cut in, speaking dispassionately. "It's an obvious question for them to ask. Since they know I can work in wood and metal and that I've got my own workshop, they'd be negligent not to ask."

"That's very considerate of you to see it that way," Alex commented. "And the answer is…?"

"Yes, it's something I have the ability to make. Anyone with access to cutting and grinding tools could have done it. As I said, there was nothing sophisticated about it. However, it wasn't me. You can check out my workshop if you like. You won't find any indication of me making anything like that. Besides anything else, I don't have the appropriate materials."

"Thank you for being so candid," Alex continued. "I'd now like to discuss the more delicate issue of your relationship with your wife."

"Yes?"

Calum sat up straight and gazed at his brother, his utterance coming more as a splutter than any coherent speech. "How can you let them treat you like this?

You don't need to put yourself through it. You're the injured party here. You should be telling them to sling their hooks and get out."

Graeme looked tired and his voice sounded laboured as if talking down to a tiresome child to whom he'd repeated the same lesson several times before. "Why? Why should I be obstructive? My wife is dead and these men are here to help find who was responsible and bring them to justice. I want that to happen so I need to cooperate. Yes, it's painful and it's personal. Yes, I'd prefer to be doing something else, anything else. But this is where I am and what I need to do." Then turning back towards Alex, "Okay, Inspector, what do you want me to tell you about?"

"Let's start with the facts: how long had you been married, details of children, etcetera."

Graeme comfortably confirmed all the facts and statistics already known.

"Now I need to enquire about some more intimate matters," Alex said.

Graeme nodded, resignedly, but Calum had had enough. He jumped to his feet. "Maybe you're prepared to accept this, but I won't dignify it by my attendance. I'll wait in the kitchen."

"In that case, maybe you'll prepare a pot of tea for us all," Graeme proposed, intentionally adding salt to the wound.

Calum stormed out without saying another word. He had no intention of accommodating his brother's request.

"You were going to ask?" Graeme continue, displaying no emotion at his brother's tantrum.

"Were you and your wife faithful to each other?" Alex enquired.

"Is this really relevant?" Graeme asked. There was no passion in his question. No anger, no irritation, only tiredness.

"We don't know yet, but we need to ask. It could be the basis for a motive," Alex replied. "From information we've already received, we're aware that your wife could be... how shall I say, flirty, perhaps?"

"You have heard about the books she'd published?" Graeme countered.

"Yes, we've heard she was a successful author and she'd published a series of historical romances," Sanjay said.

"Well, yes, that's true and she was quite successful. But you don't know about the others?" Seeing only a blank expression, Graeme continued. "Sheila published her romantic fiction series under her own name and yes, she derived a modest income, but she made more money from her other titles. She wrote under different pseudonyms and some really quite raunchy stuff. Joy Thurley-Ridden and Fanny Fox for example, they made her a lot more in royalties. Fanny, in particular, sold very well until Amazon changed their policies and banned her books as being too explicit. They became a bit iffy about stories which had group sex or bestiality and deleted them from their listings. They still sell well through other channels, even better I suppose, because they now have the distinction of being banned by Amazon," Graeme added with a smile. "One of the best ways to market anything is to show that it has limited availability."

"Sex in suburbia?" Alex asked. "Not what you would expect to be coming out of a smart bungalow in Giffnock, I suppose. But how does this relate to my question about fidelity?"

"It doesn't. Well, not directly," Graeme replied. "It does, though, let you see that she wasn't a regular prim and proper middle class housewife. She's always preferred the company of men and, to use your words, she was always a bit flirty. At first I thought it was all only in her imagination until I read some of her raunchier stories and then I started to have my suspicions. I've no direct evidence of Sheila screwing around, but I've got little doubt that she has been unfaithful, as you put it. If I can be frank, her sexual appetite was greater than I was able to satisfy."

"Did she ever admit to it? Did you not ask her?" Sanjay questioned." He was truly shocked by what he was being told, but he tried to retain an impression of being impassive.

"It's not the sort of thing to come up in normal conversation and I never wanted to ask, but I knew and she knew that I knew."

"And you weren't angry, or upset?" Alex quizzed.

"Sauce for the goose."

"Sorry?" Sanjay looked confused.

"I've had my dalliances too," Graeme replied. "I used to travel a lot on business and there were occasions when I became lonely. I suspect it was the same for Sheila being left at home alone so she ended up looking for other company. I remember after one time I'd been away for three weeks, Sheila seemed different after I returned. She was more passionate and adventurous and I suspected she'd been with someone else. I didn't dare ask. I'd been with someone while I was away and I felt too guilty about that to quiz her. Neither of us said anything and I suppose it became harder to talk as time went on. I'm certain there were many other times for her and I know there were some for me."

"We need more details," Sanjay asked. "We need to ask you who and when."

"I'm sure I don't need to answer that," Graeme claimed.

"I believe you know better than that," Alex stated. "Under the circumstances, it's something we're entitled to ask."

"Everything I've told you has been offered freely and voluntarily and it's as far as I'm prepared to go for the time being. If and when it's necessary to tell you more, then I'll do so, but only in the presence of a solicitor."

"Okay, I'll accept that," Alex replied. "You've been most helpful and we can leave it there for just now, but I suspect we will need to come back to you and I expect sooner rather than later."

Not surprisingly, Graeme couldn't find the packaging but was able to locate the stamps and he printed the emails as requested. He then showed Alex and

Sanjay to the door and, once alone in the car, they started to compare notes. Sanjay shook his head, as if unable to comprehend the evidence they'd gathered.

"I never had you down as a snob," Alex said.

"What? Sanjay reacted.

"You imagine because we're in a posh area that everything is sweetness and light. Well let me tell you that nothing could be further from the truth. You'll find every bit as much crime and debauchery in Giffnock as you will in Easterhouse or Drumchapel, the only difference is that here they're better able to cover it up and they can afford better lawyers to protect them and keep their indiscretions under wraps."

Sanjay was still shaking his head but did manage to venture, "Yes, I know, Boss. I just found his openness quite extraordinary. Do you reckon we'll need to read all her books to see if there might be any clues?"

"If you're volunteering, I suspect it's not only to pick up clues about the case?" Alex countered.

Sanjay's face flushed. It was the first time Alex had seen him truly flustered, trying to mouth his explanation but no words emerging.

Chapter 8

"I'd like to detour into Sainsburys on the way back. Sandra and I are both going to be working late. We've already stocked the fridge, but I want to pick up some snacks and drop them into my flat."

Sanjay considered making another comment about who was wearing the trousers, but then thought better than to voice it.

"What are you smiling at?" Alex enquired, seeing his amused expression.

"Nothing, nothing at all," he responded defensively.

Having collected an assortment of tasty morsels, selected for flavour, simplicity and being easy to compile, Alex returned to the car. He lifted his stylus and sent a text a message to advise Sandra, muttering as he did about how he hated using the touchscreen because his fingers were too meaty to properly work the keys.

Within seconds his phone rang with her number displayed.

"Good idea, Alex. I'll enjoy that when I get back and it'll be a lot healthier than picking up a chippie. And you texted as well, are you getting over your phobia?"

"It's not a phobia, just an aversion," Alex replied. "I still hate doing it, but I didn't want to call in case you were in the middle of something. Anyhow, I got some dips and tortilla chips, sliced chicken, pate and one of those nice walnut breads you like. What's more, nearly all of it was reduced to half price because the date stamp's up today."

"Well done, you don't get offers like that in France. They'll leave the food on the shelf until it forms a mould, then they'll move it to the cheese counter, put up the price and sell it as a speciality," Sandra commented.

"You have to be joking?" Alex asked.

"Yes, of course I was joking, but there are one or two shops where it may not be too far from the truth," she replied.

"How's your enquiry going?"

"Slowly, and we're trying to look into both incidents at the same time. We haven't tracked down Carson yet, but we're now even more certain he was involved. We've also picked up some pretty interesting leads on who might have been behind it."

"Tell me more."

"He was defending a case last week and really cocked it up. His client, a guy by the name of Zennick, was accused of fraud. He was a landlord who'd used multiple false identities to borrow money to buy properties, then traded them between the different names to raise even more money. He collected rent from housing benefit tenants, often when they didn't stay in the flats and he didn't even service the loans."

"Sounds a bit complex."

"Yes, it was and sufficiently so that Hardy should have been able to muddy the waters, but he didn't. His defence was inept and his client went down."

"And you reckon Zennick holds grudges."

"Could be, or he could have some friends who might have been a bit upset."

"Sounds plausible. It's not like Hardy to miss an opportunity."

"We have some thoughts there too. Two alternative theories: one, Zennick was maybe treading on the toes of Hardy's more regular clients and he was under instructions to foul up. The other is that Hardy's developed a liking for white powder and maybe he was a bit under the influence when he should have been keeping a clear head."

"Either way, he's underestimated Zennick, assuming it was him responsible."

"Too true. I'm hoping to get in to see Hardy later on, but I don't hold out much hope. Even if he does know anything, it's hardly likely he'll tell me."

"Hardy hardly likely to tell you? Hardy har har," Alex mocked.

"Oh don't, Alex. Your jokes are getting as bad as Phil's," Sandra replied.

"Now that really wounded me," Alex countered, feigning being deeply affronted.

"And you deserved it. Besides, I have more than enough to cope with without you making fun. Have you got nothing better to do with your time?"

"Hey, just a minute, I was only trying to lighten the mood. I've got plenty to deal with too. After spending the morning at the Vicky, Sanjay and I have interviewed the victim's husband, Graeme Armstrong, and his pain-in-the-ass brother, Calum."

"Where do you go next?" Sandra probed.

"Back to the ranch and see what the others have and find out if anything's in from the techies."

"Sounds like a plan. I guess I'd best get back to my problems. I suppose we'll catch up sooner or later," Sandra continued.

"I guess with all that's happening, it will more likely be 'later' than 'sooner' for both of us. Now don't overdo it," he added, looking round furtively to ensure Sanjay wasn't eavesdropping.

"Don't worry, I won't. And don't fuss. It doesn't make it any easier." Sandra paused for a moment then added, "But thanks for caring," then disengaged and the phone went dead.

Alex stuffed the phone back into his pocket and turned to Sanjay. "Home, Jeeves."

"Everything okay?" he enquired, simultaneously turning on the ignition.

* * *

Seeing Donny and Mary at their desks, Alex signalled for them to collect coffees and gather in his
office. No sooner had they settled down than they
were joined by Phil and Steve.

"You're senior officer on this," he said turning to
Sanjay. "You lead."

Sanjay had to suppress his smile as he took the
floor and made them all aware of his day's efforts.
"Now what have you got for me? Mary, you first."

"Right, Sarg. Donny and I started with Lionel. We
went to his house in Whitecraigs. It's a large detached bungalow. He lives there with his wife, just
the two of them. He's retired now, but he used to be
a partner in an accountancy practice. That's how he
ended up as treasurer of the writing group. He's gone
from being seriously respected, carrying out high-
level finance deals in a very well paid position to being moaned at as an unpaid skivvy and bookkeeper
for the writing group. That's using his words."

"In that case, why does he do it?" Sanjay asked.

"Exactly what I asked," Donny interrupted. "He
said it was his penance."

"What did he mean by that? What does he have to
be penitent about?" Sanjay probed.

"He said it was after forty years in finance, he felt
he had to give something back."

"Please go on, Mary," Sanjay requested.

"Well, we ran through all the standard questions,
but we didn't really come up with anything new.
It gave us confirmation of what we've already been
told. Lionel said he hardly knew Sheila outside of the

group, they only met at meetings or to talk about committee business. He took us through to his conservatory and we were joined by Hannah, his wife. She brought in tea and had no intention of leaving us alone. She showed great concern and sympathy for the victim, but quite honestly, I think she was just looking to be near the centre of things so she'd have some tasty gossip to dish up to her friends. We did, of course, make it clear to them that we are at a crucial stage in our investigations and they were not to discuss anything about the case. She didn't seem too happy at that."

"Didn't you consider asking her to leave?" Phil asked sarcastically.

"We thought about it," Donny replied, tartly, "but we would have had no real justification. We were there to information gather, not to interrogate and, although present at the scene, Lionel isn't really considered a suspect. Asking her to leave would have put everything on a much more formal footing and could have made Lionel a lot more guarded in anything he told us."

"Maybe," Phil stated, "but from what you said before, you didn't get much from him anyway. Perhaps he was reluctant to tell you anything in front of his wife."

Donny shrugged.

"I'm not just being bloody minded," Phil continued, "but we interviewed Aaron this afternoon and he gave a somewhat different impression."

"Go on," Sanjay pressed. "Don't leave us on tenter-hooks."

"Steve and I went to see Aaron at his office," Phil continued. "He has an upholstery business in Finnieston, not far from the Exhibition Centre. It's quite successful, employs about twenty people. The workrooms look fairly basic, but he has a very plush showroom and his office is really quite lavish. He took us through and had his secretary bring us coffee, served in a cafetiere, no less," Phil added, winking at Mary to note his points scoring. "Anyway, he also told us all the things we have heard already, but there's more. When talking about the Committee, he gave us the distinct impression that Lionel and Sheila knew each other very well. In fact, he all but suggested there was something going on behind the scenes, so to speak, and that certainly doesn't tie in with what Lionel said."

"Did he actually say anything specific?" Sanjay asked. "Maybe there was just a bit of sibling rivalry and they'd been winding each other up."

"I'm pretty certain it was more than that," Phil replied. "I'm sure he wasn't planting the information. It came out more in response to when we were asking him about Sheila and what he knew of her relationships. His answers started off quite vague, but when pressed he suggested we'd be able to find out a lot more information from Lionel. It was more a case of the information being coaxed out of him and he seemed quite upset afterwards because he hadn't meant to say anything which would have caused any trouble for his brother. Once it was said, he couldn't take it back, but I'm sure he wished he could. He clammed up afterwards and hardly said any more."

"You're sure it wasn't an act to lure you in?" Sanjay asked.

"Yes, I'm positive," Phil replied.

"Me too," Steve added, contributing for the first time.

"Okay, it looks like you'll need to go back and see Lionel. When you were there before, did he give you any information about the knives?" Sanjay asked.

"No, just the same as everyone else," Mary said.

"Well, that gives you another reason to talk to him without drawing suspicion," Sanjay stated. "Graeme told us that he'd purchased the knives through a magic wholesaler in Las Vegas and that he'd claimed back the cost. Lionel's the Treasurer, he'd have made the reimbursement and he'll have the invoice which he'd paid the money out against. I want you to call Lionel and tell him you need to see him again. Say you need to see the original invoice from the supplier, Top Hat, Graeme said they're called. Tell him you need it urgently and ask him to look it out and arrange for him to bring it in A.S.A.P. No doubt he'll be on his own, but even if not, you can make sure you see him alone."

"Sounds like a good approach," Alex added.

"That makes a lot of sense," Donny said. "However, I've got a problem. It's my wee grandson's parents' night at school and I really need to be there because my son and daughter-in-law are away for a few days and I've been left holding the baby, so to speak. Could I maybe arrange for Lionel to bring the papers in first thing tomorrow morning?"

Sanjay was about to answer, but he was too slow.

"No, it can't wait," Alex said. "Don't worry, you go to your parents' night and I'll sit in the interview with Mary. It could work quite well for him to see an unfamiliar face." He was secretly quite pleased to have something to get his teeth into.

"That's settled," Sanjay followed up, asserting some control. "You go and make the phone call and get Lionel in now. Meanwhile, we'll continue to check whatever other information's come in." He spotted a suppressed smirk from Phil and quickly added, "As for you two, you can get back round to see Aaron again. This is a murder investigation, not a matter for gossip and innuendo. You need to properly question him and get the answers to the questions signed off as a formal statement. I'll grant you did gather some good information, but you were shoddy how you went about it. What's more, in this unit we support each other and work together as a team. I expect better from you."

"Yes, Sarg," Phil and Steve echoed each other, both staring at their feet, feeling a little chastened, particularly when they saw Alex looking on, nodding his agreement.

"Next, what else have you got?" Sanjay continued.

"I tried calling Top Hat this morning but couldn't get through," Mary started. "Of course, I hadn't taken account of the time difference. I did manage to get them about an hour ago, after we came back from seeing Lionel. I spoke to their International Sales Manager. It took me a while to convince him who I was and that I wasn't making a spoof call, but after I did he was very cooperative. He confirmed the order from Graeme and said there hadn't been any orders for single knives or indeed any other orders for the set to anywhere in Scotland within the last three months. I also confirmed that they have a customer fulfilment facility organised through a magic manufacturer in Birmingham."

"What the Hell does that mean?" Steve enquired.

Mary continued, "They each hold the other's stock and pack and arrange postage of orders to enable quick delivery at reasonable prices. Graeme's order was sent out using this system. The guy in Vegas offered to arrange stock audit to ensure there are no blades unaccounted for, but it will take a few days before we have the results."

"Good work, Mary. It's the best we can hope for under the circumstances, but keep on at them until you get answers," Sanjay said.

Donny re-entered the room. "I spoke to Lionel and he should be here in about an hour." Looking at his watch, he added, "I can hang on for a bit, but if I'm to make the school meeting on time, I'll be away before he gets here."

"Righto, who's next?" Sanjay asked.

Phil kicked off, "I've talked to our technicians, the ones who've been analysing Sheila's computer. They've checked for any email correspondence about the argument Sheila had with the American author but found nothing of value. They then checked out her Facebook account and that was a whole different story. They've been able to provide the complete chain of correspondence and there's more to it. To cut a long story short, Sheila was a member of a Facebook group which was designed to supply mutual support amongst its members. They would read each other's work and promotional material and give one another tips. They would also trade reviews to try to boost their books' presence on the internet sales sites. It seems they had an unwritten rule that they only posted reviews where they were giving four or five stars. If they thought the other person's book deserved less, then they'd send their comments privately to avoid causing damage. Anyhow, Sheila did a review of a book written by this woman in Texas – her name's Honey D'Lite – well, at least that's what she calls herself when she's writing. Sheila really slated her and awarded her book only one star. She was quite ruthless in her comments. To give you an example, one talked about how sickly sweet Honey was, except for the bitter aftertaste this one left.

"Honey was incensed, accusing Sheila of breaking all the rules of the group. She said Sheila had set out to sabotage her by ripping into her book with a really bad review which was especially damaging as she hadn't had a chance to get established. Honey had demanded Sheila remove or improve the review. Sheila not only refused, she posted it on every book sales review site she could find. Honey campaigned for her to be expelled from the group. When it didn't happen, she made all sorts of threats about how she'd get even. Then it all seemed to go quiet. But wait for the best bit. According to her Facebook page, she's on a month's vacation, touring Europe and the tour includes a visit to Scotland. She's here in Glasgow as we speak."

"Well there's one suspect with motive, but what about means and opportunity?" Alex enquired.

"Early days, Sir," Phil replied. "But we certainly need to talk to her. Obviously, Honey D'Lite's a nom de plume. First we want to find out who she really is."

"Or he, don't rule out that it could be a man behind the disguise," Alex said.

Phil paused, contemplating and then continued, "I hadn't considered the possibility, but I reckon it's unlikely because of the content on the website and Facebook page. I've been able to learn a lot about who she is on-line and I've asked our colleagues across the pond to help out too."

"When do you expect to have something more concrete?" Sanjay asked

"Hopefully within the next couple of hours, but I can't promise," Phil said. "I'll let you know as soon as I hear."

"Medical Examiner's report?" Sanjay enquired.

"The formal report's not in yet, but we've had a provisional from Duffie. It's only verbal so far," Steve offered. "Again, it's pretty much as we expected. Cause of death is stabbing with the blade puncturing her heart and death followed within seconds. The incision is consistent with the knife we have and there's nothing whatsoever to suggest any other cause. But just for completeness, he noted that she'd had a couple of broken bones, left femur and fibula, probably incurred two or three years ago. She had some deep scratches on her back and upper arms, fairly recent, and there were traces of barbiturates in her bloodstream."

"What had she been on?" Sanjay asked. "Was it prescription?"

"They don't know yet for certain and we'll need to confirm with her G.P. but first impressions suggest it was uppers," Steve replied. "He also said something about a tumour and he'll know more later. On another matter, I've been checking in with the 'scene of crime' and again, it's all been confirmation of what we already have. The only prints on the knife were from Bert, but they've been doing a comparison of the murder weapon with the other real knife we recovered, and so far, everything looks authentic. They've some more tests to do, but that's how it stands at the moment."

"This may count for nothing," Donny added, "but I've something here which may justify further examination. Apparently, Sheila and Graeme arrived at the school in separate cars and about fifteen minutes apart."

"Interesting," Alex commented. "Where did you get that from?"

"One of the interviews raised the question, but it was confirmed by the office register. All visitors have to sign in."

"There's any number of innocent explanations of why they arrived separately, but taken together with other things we've learned, it does give pause for thought," Alex replied.

The discussions continued as they analysed each statement and piece of evidence gathered with all brainstorming to develop new angles and ideas. Donny left to attend his meeting, and shortly afterwards, the call came through to advise them Lionel had arrived.

Enthusiastically, Alex leapt to his feet, addressing Mary as he made for the door. "Come on, Lass, back to business."

Chapter 9

Immediately following receipt of a phone call from the hospital to advise her Fergus Hardy was considered fit enough to receive visitors, Sandra called for Peter Lister to join her, then rushed out to her car. She'd first met Peter a couple of days earlier, but already she'd been impressed. His chubby, round face was topped by a mass of blonde curls and this look combined with his boyish charm made him seem little more than a schoolchild. However, he was sharp and enthusiastic and his youthful appearance could prove quite disarming to potential suspects.

Travelling from the Court building, they took the M8 in the direction of the Clyde Tunnel, turning off at the last moment towards Govan Road, Linthouse, and the entrance to the Southern General Hospital. The whole journey took a little over ten minutes. However, they wasted more time searching the sprawling expanse to locate the building they wanted and then seek a vacant parking space. In the end, they abandoned Sandra's Hyundai in a 'no parking' zone but took the precaution to display a 'police on duty' sign. Looking up, they could see the massive glass and metal structure of the new hospital, now nearing completion and designed to replace the ancient sandstone buildings. Dodging construction traffic on the way, they found their way to the ward and introduced themselves to the nursing staff, asking to see Fergus Hardy. They were signalled towards a private room but warned they'd only be allowed a few minutes.

When they entered, they could see the lawyer only partially dressed, lying flat out on a hospital bed. His eyes were tightly closed and he had dark blue coloured bruising to his face and upper torso. His left leg was almost completely covered in plaster and raised in traction and his left arm was similarly bound.

"Good afternoon, Mr Hardy. I understand you've been through the wars a bit," Sandra opened. She'd already agreed with Peter their approach: she'd lead the questions and he'd take notes, only entering the conversation if the need arose or he picked up on any angles which she may have missed.

Hardy's eyes flickered. "Ah, Sergeant McKinnon, and here was I thinking life just couldn't get any better. And you've brought your baby brother with you too. How sweet."

"It's been Inspector McKinnon for the last few months and this is Detective Constable Lister. I'm glad you're pleased to see us and I only wish I could say it was mutual, but I'm sure you'll not be surprised to learn it's not a social call."

"Oh, have you come to consult me for some legal advice? Maybe you need me to defend you on a police brutality charge."

"Come, come, Fergus. I thought you'd be able to manage better than to roll out all the old clichés. Do I need to make special allowances because you're not too well or maybe it's the effect of the medication you're on?"

"Okay, Officer. As you say, it's not a social call so enough of the banter. I'm glad you've acknowledged I'm sedated which confirms you also realise that you can't rely on anything I say."

"I'm not certain I could ever have relied on anything you told me, but that aside, I'm looking into your assault and I want to know what you can tell me."

"Very little, I'm afraid. One moment I was talking to a client and the next I was flying through the air."

"Did you recognise the boys who did this?"

"I'm sorry, no. All I could tell was they were young and slim and wearing hoodies. That's as much as I saw."

"What about your client? Who was he?"

"I don't have to say anything about him."

"From information we've received, we understand it could have been Patrick Carson. Can you confirm this?"

Hardy paused and his contemplative expression gave them the impression they were correct, but he took a deep breath before replying, "No comment."

"Come now, Mr Hardy. Surely you don't imagine he'll be calling on your services to defend him for conspiracy to murder you."

Hardy's eyes flickered a couple of times before he repeated, "No comment."

"Do you consider this was an attempt to kill you, or was it maybe just to put the frighteners on?"

"I really couldn't say."

"Couldn't or don't want to?"

"Listen, Detective, your guess is as good as mine."

"I think not, but nevertheless, we want to find out why you were targeted."

"I can see that."

"Well?"

"I don't know."

"You wouldn't like to maybe hazard a guess?"

"No."

"It's been suggested to us that perhaps Mr Zennick was unhappy about losing his case last week."

"I'm sure Mr Zennick was disappointed with the verdict, as, of course, was I."

"Could he have been more than disappointed and perhaps considered it to be your fault? Maybe he wanted to get back at you."

"You can hardly expect me to comment on that. It's just idle speculation."

"It's a bit more than that, Mr Hardy. Zennick was shouting and swearing as he was led from the courtroom. You were the main target of his comments. He was claiming you'd let him down and worked against him."

"You seem to have already made up your own mind, so there isn't any point in me commenting."

"I'm sorry if I gave that impression. I'd truly like to know your opinion."

"I don't have an opinion and I don't need to say anything. You seem to forget, I'm the victim here," Hardy said.

"No, I haven't forgotten, but there are other issues that need examination. There could be further criminal issues." Sandra fixed Hardy with a stare.

Hardy's face kept a blank expression and he returned the stare without comment.

Following a short pause, Sandra continued, "Well, let's try another approach, Mr Hardy. The suggestion has been made that some of your more influential clients had a desire for Mr Zennick to lose his case and perhaps exerted pressure on you, so you wouldn't represent him as effectively as you might have."

"Now that's an outrageous suggestion. You don't really expect me to give merit to it with a reply. I've already said more than enough. I think you'd better leave." Despite the severity of his words, Hardy remained composed and impassive.

"So be it," Sandra replied. "But just one last thing. What can you tell me about the hold-up of the Court's cash office, yesterday?"

Hardy visibly relaxed and a broad smile spread across his face. "Yes, I heard about it. Very embarrassing for the Court and for your people. I can't tell you anything about it though."

"The perpetrators were young, slim and wearing hoodies. In your opinion, could there be any link to the boys who assaulted you?"

"I've no idea. That's for you to find out."

Sandra nodded curtly then walked out of the door, quickly followed by Peter. They walked in silence until they reached the car.

"What did you make of that one?" Sandra asked.

"Hard to tell, he's a real cold fish. He didn't give anything away."

"I wouldn't say that. I reckon we can be fairly certain that he was set up by Patrick Carson and I now calculate it's odds on that it's been on Zennick's instructions."

"But he didn't say anything."

"He didn't need to."

"Should we go and talk to Zennick then?" Peter asked.

"Perhaps later, there's not much point now as we don't have enough evidence. We don't have any evidence actually, just 'idle speculation' was Hardy's expression. Zennick has a cast-iron alibi, sitting as he is at the moment in a cell in Bar-L. What we can do though is check to see what visitors he's received since he went inside."

"I'll get straight onto it as soon as we're back in the office."

"Good, we'll head back then. There's nothing further for us to do at the Court just now."

"Okay, Ma'am. Can I ask you something? You asked Hardy about a possible connection between the hold-up and the assault. Do you think it likely?"

"Not particularly. On first appearance, the two crimes are unrelated, but on the other hand, as I said to Hardy, they both involved young men wearing hoodies and they happened within a few yards of each other on successive days. It seems an awful lot of a coincidence. There were only two of them involved in the hold-up whereas it took four to throw Hardy over the wall, but we ought to learn more after we've examined surveillance tapes from the local area."

Their office in the Helen Street, Divisional Headquarters was a very short drive away and the return journey took only a few minutes.

Sandra settled at the desk recently assigned to her and began studying reports. Peter secured a desk close-by and immediately started working the phones.

After a few moments, Sandra selected some of the files and lifted them across to a large table in the corner of the room. She started to extract photographs and placed them in groupings to let her compare each set, carefully studying the detail.

"Bingo!" she called.

"Just a mo," Peter said, covering the receiver. "I'm almost finished, I'll be over when I complete this call."

A few seconds later, Peter replaced the phone. "What have you got?"

"Have a look at these. I've extracted this top set from the CCTV in the cash room and the second group were picked up from cameras the following day, from around the Courthouse, shortly before or after the assault."

"You can make out the weapon on the top ones, but I can't judge if it's real or a replica, or even a toy. The men are not very clear, you can't see their faces in any of the photos," Peter replied. "What do you see?"

"First of all, the size and shape of the gunman looks fairly close to this one in the other photos, and the wee guy with him could be the small one of the second group, but more to the point, look at what he's wearing." Sandra pointed to the taller of the young men.

"I don't see what you mean. The shoes and chinos look similar, but it's just a plain trackie top."

"Try using this," Sandra offered, handing him a magnifying glass.

He studied the photos again and shook his head.

"Look at the sleeve, near the top."

"I've got it," he yelled enthusiastically. "The Hugo Boss logo, it's on both of the photos. He didn't buy that in Primark or TJ's."

"More likely Fraser's and probably nicked it rather than bought it," Sandra replied.

"But there can't be too many of them around. Not enough to make it likely to be worn by two different people committing crimes in the same place a day apart."

"That was my thinking," Sandra said.

"You have your link."

"It's *a* link, not my link. Now all we have to do is work out what on earth the connection could be. Why should the same person be behind setting up an armed robbery which was only ever likely to yield a pittance and what looks like a revenge attack on Hardy?"

"Well, you said earlier that you thought Zennick was responsible for the attack on Hardy and, if so, perhaps it was motivated by revenge for him screwing up his defence," Peter suggested.

"Yes?"

"Maybe, he also felt aggrieved at the Courts and the Procurator and the Police and he staged the hold-up solely to cause embarrassment, a way of getting his own back a little."

"Okay, I can follow your reasoning, but is it really likely he'd go to all that trouble and put himself or his people at so much risk for so little return, even allowing for the embarrassment angle?" Sandra asked.

"Who knows? Perhaps he didn't realise how little cash was kept on the premises. In any event, it's a working hypothesis and, for the time being, we don't have anything better to go on," Peter replied.

"Fair enough. How did you get on checking on Zenick's visitors?"

"There's only been one, his brother, Karol. He went to see him twice, but Zenick's also made phone calls. Though I've not yet been able to find out to whom."

"Wait a minute," Sandra interrupted. "I've read his file. Zennick doesn't have a brother. Or rather he only has a half-brother who lives in Ukraine, no other family in the UK. This raises a number of new questions. Who came to see him? And what identification were they able to show to enable them to pass through security?"

"This could end up a long night," Peter said.

"Not for me, I'm afraid. I've been at it since first thing this morning and my brain won't function for much longer if I don't get some rest. I've not got back into a proper rhythm yet, since my holiday."

"I thought after a holiday, you're meant to come back bright and refreshed and raring to go," Peter challenged.

"Yeah, that's the theory."

Chapter 10

Lionel looked confident as he approached the interview room. Aged sixty-two, he was only slightly short of six foot in height and his full head of hair was a natural brown colour. His robust and muscular frame conveyed the impression of a military deportment and, supplemented by a Mediterranean tan, he could easily have passed for ten years younger.

Despite the inclement conditions, he had no jacket, was dressed in an open-necked shirt worn loosely over chinos, and he was carrying a pilot case.

"DC McAvoy said you needed to see the invoice for the knife set. I don't understand the urgency, but I suppose that's your business. I also took a photocopy and I brought it and the original along with the whole of the receipts file for this year and the cash book, in the event you wanted to ask how the system works," he added indicating his bag.

"Most thorough indeed," Alex replied. "I'm DCI Alex Warren and we'd like you to come through here for a bit of a chat."

Lionel blinked twice and looked a little bit shaken. "You're a chief inspector and you want to see me. Why? I already told the constables what I knew."

"I'm overseeing this case and I've been going through the evidence collected. There are a few matters from your statement where we require some further clarification. Nothing for you to worry about. Now that you're here, it would be a good time to get these matters settled."

Lionel nodded slowly, but the blood seemed to drain from his face, giving him a more ashen complexion. "Yes, I suppose it's best to get it out of the way," he mumbled.

After taking their seats and going through the preliminaries, Alex commenced. "In your earlier statement, given to DC's McAvoy and McKenzie, you reported that you didn't know Sheila Armstrong very well. Now, put simply, that isn't true, is it?"

Lionel gave a brief shake of his head then and making a limited show of bravado, he exclaimed, "Why? Who's told you different?"

"It's of no relevance to you where we get our information. What's very important is you've lied, and more to the point, you've been caught lying amidst a major crime investigation. This is a serious matter and you could be prosecuted." Alex's fierce expression intimidated and Lionel shrank back in his seat.

"You have to understand; I didn't mean to mislead you, but I couldn't really say anything while Hannah was there. I didn't have a free moment to talk privately to the officers and she wouldn't have understood."

"But you didn't voluntarily correct your statement afterwards," Alex pursued.

"No, you're right. I'm sorry," Lionel uttered in hardly more than a whisper. His eyes were heavy and he looked ready to burst into tears.

"Please speak clearly so you can be picked up on the recording," Alex continued, giving no indication of sympathy.

"I will tell you, but can we please keep this private? As I said, Hannah would never understand," Lionel pleaded.

"You are in no position to make demands. We don't know yet what you have to tell us; however, it will be your own private statement and, unless we find it necessary, there's no reason for the contents to be made public."

Alex's tone remained firm, but the reconciliatory nature of his words was reassuring enough. Lionel nodded his head slowly and replied, "Okay, what do you want to ask?"

"We need it in your own words. How well did you really know Sheila?"

Lionel looked down at his feet, unable to hold eye contact. "We'd been friends with each other for some years, seeing one another at the Group sessions and at the executive meetings. We used to have a good rapport, not just the two of us, but many within the group. It's not surprising, when you put together a number of people with sharp minds and a love for words, then that's what happens. There was lots of banter and sometimes it could become quite racy, full of double entendres, but all very innocent. Well, that's how it was." Lionel had attached emphasis to the word "was."

"And?" Alex pushed.

"I'm giving you the background," Lionel resumed. "As I said, we had become good friends, as had many of the writers, and then a few months ago..." Lionel halted for several seconds and Alex and Mary both knew better than to say anything, the silence pressuring him to continue.

When Lionel continued, his voice was barely audible, at first spoken in staccato fashion, with pauses punctuating each sentence, then gathering pace and volume as if desperate to purge himself.

"Sheila asked me over to her house to discuss some Committee business.

"It was in the afternoon and Graeme was out.

"We discussed the business and we drank wine.

"I'm not much of a drinker and certainly not through the day. I was feeling a little bit tipsy.

"We started discussing the Club's entry for the one act play. I told her I had one or two ideas but I hadn't started writing anything yet.

"Sheila told me she was hoping her application would be selected. She had it almost completed and offered to let me see it.

"She added that she was hoping for my support as I'd be one of the appraisers drawing up the shortlist. I suppose I felt a bit flattered, her being a talented, attractive, younger woman asking for my help. She said she'd get her entry for me to read.

"She topped up my glass then left the room and returned a few minutes later." Lionel's speech steadily became more fluid, almost as if he was reading a script. "She had changed what she was wearing and was dressed in a loose-fitting kimono style outfit. She started to read me her play. The air was heavy with the smell of perfume. I made a comment like 'something smelled nice' and she asked if I liked it. Before I could answer, she came over very close and pulled my head between her breasts. She wasn't wearing a bra and my face was touching her flesh. Then she asked if I liked it any better now.

"I was intoxicated by the wine and the perfume and the feel of her skin. I couldn't believe what was happening," Lionel paused.

"You had sex?" Alex asked.

"Well, not in the true sense. I remember Bill Clinton making the claim that the sort of intimacy he had wasn't sex. But yes, we had relations. She was amazing. She did things and let me do things Hannah wouldn't have dreamed of. It wouldn't have been kosher, if you know what I mean," he added with a weak smile.

"And was this a one off?" Alex asked.

"No, we met two more times, always at Sheila's house. By then she had my full support for her entry in the competition. I'd become entranced. I'd have done anything she asked, I wanted to see her again, but she said no. With the benefit of hindsight, I'm sure she only used me to get what she wanted and then she wasn't interested."

"And that was it?" Alex enquired.

"I tried to pressure her to see me again, but she refused and she threatened to say something to Hannah if I didn't leave her alone. It was then I woke up and realised how stupid I'd been. My marriage, my family, my life, I'd risked them all for a few moments of passion. I wanted to put it behind me and prayed Hannah would never find out. You won't have to say anything, will you?"

"We'll need to see," Alex replied. "What you've told us is a cast-iron motive for wanting to silence her and, what's more, you had advance knowledge of the contents of the play. I'm making no promises that the whole story won't come out. However, for the time being, at least, we have no reason to make anything public.

"Let me ask you something else," Alex added. "Do you have any interest in acting or performing magic?"

"No, none at all," Lionel answered. "I'm happy writing and even reading out my work, but the very thought of appearing on a stage or in front of an audience terrifies me. I'll help at Club events, but only with the backstage work. I sometimes had to do presentations at work and I always hated them. Why do you ask?"

"It's not important," Alex replied. "That's all we need from you for just now, unless Mary has anything." Mary shook her head. "In that case, you can go, but we may need to talk to you again."

"Thank you, Chief Inspector. I won't be far away if you need me for anything and please remember to keep what I've said private, if you possibly can," Lionel pleaded.

He left the room and Mary turned to Alex. She didn't say anything but raised her eyebrows in a display of mock amazement.

"I take it you didn't see that coming?" Alex asked.

"Didn't you see, I had to bite my lip so as not to giggle or appear unprofessional. I'll probably be bruised for a week."

"Just one of the perils of the job and don't go thinking you can make an industrial injury claim." They were both still laughing as they arrived back at their offices to be met by Phil, on his way out with Steve, having received notification of where Honey D'Lite was staying.

"Hi, Boss, I finally got word through. Honey's real name is Annabelle Ratcliffe. She and her partner are touring Europe and staying at the Malmaison, so she's certainly not roughing it. Obviously, she has plenty of cash. She's there at the moment and booked in for dinner. I've phoned ahead to say we need to meet her," Phil advised.

"Good, but just to ensure you don't get any wrong ideas, you're allowable expenses don't run to joining her for a meal," Alex replied, smiling. "Keep me posted on how you get on."

* * *

The Malmaison is a boutique hotel converted from a blonde-coloured, sandstone-fronted, Episcopal Church, set in West George Street, in the centre of Glasgow's Commercial district. It's only a short distance from the Central Police Offices in Pitt Street and close to Blythswood Square. Phil and Steve jogged up the steps and across the marble floor to approach the dark wood-panelled reception and asked for Ms Ratcliffe.

A call was placed to her room and the detectives took a seat next to a coffee table to await her arrival. Phil and Steve chatted distractedly, occasionally looking around them expecting the arrival of the petite young American lady, whose photo they'd seen on Honey D'Lite's Facebook page. They were completely wrong-footed when a shadow descended over them, created by the heavy-set frame of a figure standing close to six feet six inches tall and with shoulders which wouldn't have been out of place in a WWF ring.

"Detective Morrison. I'm Annabelle Ratcliffe," the voice boomed and a large meaty hand was proffered in introduction.

Phil looked round, then up and up further to see a heavily freckled but pretty face with long cascading curls, smiling down at him.

He jumped to his feet and raised his hand to complete the introduction. "Yes, I'm Phil Morrison and this is my colleague Detective Constable Steve Fleming," Phil stammered then unsteadily released his hand from the vice-like handshake. "As I said on the phone, there's something we need to talk to you about."

"Yes, I was most intrigued by your call, my husband too, but I've convinced him to wait in our room to give me time to find out what this is all about."

"I'm sorry, I wasn't able to say before and we were in a hurry to speak to you while you were available in Glasgow. Is there somewhere we can talk that's a little more private?"

"Okay, we can go downstairs to the bar. I'm sure we can find a quiet corner."

A few moments later they settled into a booth, having already rejected the offer of drinks or coffees.

"Please excuse me for staring, but you don't look at all like your photograph," Phil started. He was only beginning to come to terms with the size and shape of Ms Ratcliffe and her being so different from what he'd expected. He remembered Alex's suggestion that it could be a man and, despite being informed her husband was upstairs in their bedroom, he found himself staring at her neck, looking for an Adam's apple.

"My photograph? I don't understand. Now what is this all about?" Annabelle questioned.

"I'm sorry, I should have explained first. We understand that you're a writer and that you use the pseudonym Honey D'Lite."

"Why, yes, that's right, but how could you possibly know? I don't have many fans in Britain." It was now Annabelle's turn to look surprised.

"We're involved in an investigation and we wanted to find out more about 'Honey D'Lite.' Our enquiries revealed the person behind the name was currently in Glasgow and furthermore that it was you, Annabelle Ratcliffe."

"That's starting to make sense, but why on earth would Glasgow police want to know anything about Honey?"

"We can explain all of that in a few minutes, but to start with we need you to answer a few questions. First, can you tell us when you arrived in Glasgow, how you've got here and where you've been staying?"

"Yes, no problem. We flew from Rome to London last Wednesday and then travelled to Glasgow by train two days ago. I have copies of our itinerary and our flight tickets if you need them."

"Yes, that would be helpful," Steve replied. "Might you also have records proving where you went or what you did each day since arriving in the UK?"

"Are you serious? I thought this was a free country. Why should the police want to interrogate me about anything and everything I've been doing?"

"I think it's time for me to explain," Phil said. "We are homicide detectives, if I can use the terminology you'd be most familiar with, and we're investigating the murder of Sheila Armstrong. We have records showing some very harsh words and threats being exchanged between Sheila and Honey."

"Oh, Good God!" Annabelle cried. "Sheila Armstrong is dead? I can't say I'm sorry. She was a real bitch to me. I wanted her dead and my prayers have been answered. What happened?" After a short pause, Annabelle continued. "I'm sorry. I can't believe I said that. It's so unlike me. I don't really want anyone dead. It was just an unfortunate turn of phrase. I hated Sheila for what she did to me, but I didn't truly wish any evil, I only wanted her to correct the damage she did. Please tell me what happened."

"Not quite yet. First of all, we want to learn more about your grievance with her."

"Surely you don't really consider that I was involved with whatever's happened?" Annabelle asked.

"Whatever I believe or don't believe is of absolutely no consequence here. Now please, just answer our questions," Phil's response was firm and determined.

Annabelle's face flushed and her hand started to shake, nervously. "I'll tell you everything you want to know, but please trust me, I had nothing whatsoever to do with whatever happened to Sheila Armstrong." She then paused for a few seconds, to regain her composure before starting her report.

"I've always enjoyed writing stories, but it's only recently that I've started trying to do anything with them. A couple years ago, I attended a college course on creative writing and it gave me a lot of encouragement. Other students liked my work and told me I ought to do something with it. I then undertook further training and read everything I could get my hands on about self publishing. I found a group on LinkedIn which worked to assist authors in preparing and presenting their work and this gave me lots of support because there were other people like myself. We would exchange ideas and we sometimes helped by proofreading and editing each other's work. I wrote my first novel. It was a romance and I received a lot of help. I was able to encourage lots of other people too. Anyhow, having learned what to do, I managed to have it published as an ebook on Amazon. Sheila Armstrong was a member of the same group, but up until then I'd hardly come across her. I don't understand why she was there because she was already a published author through a big company and didn't need anyone else's help. The first I knew of her was when she offered to read and review my book. At first I was delighted. I thought she was being really kind and that I'd made a useful and important friend. I thought it would be a great boost to have my story reviewed by a known author. It was really naïve of me. When she wrote her review, she savaged my book. She didn't just criticise the writing, she became really personal. It was like being attacked. I felt I'd been violated. This was my own work, something very intimate, and she'd torn it to shreds. It was a horrible thing for anyone to do, but what made it worse was that she was meant to be a 'friend,' a close associate within a mutual help group. Worse still, the book had only been launched two weeks earlier and I'd put in loads of effort and spent a lot of money promoting it. At the time, she posted her review, I only had two previous ones, a five and a four star. But when her review came in as a one star, it destroyed all the good work I'd already done. No-one in their right mind would have considered buying my book after reading her review. All the effort was a write-off.

"I protested and appealed to her to ask if she would remove or change what she'd written. In response, she posted the same review everywhere. Rather than try to help, she made a deliberate effort to maximise the damage. That was when I really reacted. I wrote to everyone else in the group to complain and I asked for her to be expelled. They showed sympathy, but I'm sorry to say they didn't really do anything to help. I think they were all afraid of Sheila and didn't want to put their heads above the parapet. They were afraid if they made themselves noticeable then she might do the same to them as she did to me. I wrote to Sheila herself and told her what a bitch she was and probably said things like I'd like to see her dead, but I didn't mean it, not literally."

"Have you given up writing because of her?" Steve asked.

"No, quite the reverse actually. After what happened sunk in, I realised my book would never be a success as it was. There were a couple of small errors in it which Sheila highlighted in her review amongst her more general hateful remarks, but aside from that, the title and cover were both quite poor. I corrected the mistakes and I gave it a new title and a new cover and then re-launched. I abandoned everything I'd done to market it before and I used a different pseudonym, created a whole new identity, setting up new Facebook and Twitter accounts and this time it did really well. It actually won a couple of small competitions and has been selling internationally. I've since written a sequel and I'm part way through a third in the series. It's not made me a fortune but the royalties have helped to pay for this holiday."

"But we managed to trace you through your social network presence as Honey?" Steve enquired.

"Well, yes, I kept the accounts going to maintain contact with some of the better friends I'd made, but I never let anything link to the new edition of my book."

"And you don't bear any grudges?" Phil asked.

"No, what would be the point? It's really strange, but I suppose in some perverse way I owe my success to Sheila Armstrong. If she hadn't destroyed the first version of my book, then I'd never have had the incentive to change it."

"Thank you, you've been most helpful," Phil commented. "Now you said you had some documentary evidence to show your travel arrangements and where you've been?"

"No problem, please wait here and I'll go and get them."

Once Annabelle was out of sight and earshot, Steve shook his head. "What did you make of that?"

"Not at all what I expected, but nevertheless, I'm sure she had nothing to do with it and we're wasting our time. Irrespective, we need to go through the motions and make sure all the 'I's' are dotted and 'T's' crossed. We need to show the boss we've handled it completely and professionally, particularly after what was said about the talk we had with Aaron this afternoon."

"If what she's told us is true, then it sounds like our victim has been a true, Class A bitch. I can't get my head round why she'd be so cruel. There can't have been anything in it for her. After all, Honey D'Lite could never have been considered a competitor. So why do it?" Steve considered.

"Although Annabelle may have an alibi, it raises the question how many more people might Sheila have really pissed off, and which of them was angry enough and motivated enough to do something about it," Phil speculated.

"Yeah, if how she treated Honey is any indication of her character, then it looks as if she could have been capable of making enemies wherever she went. As always, the most likely person to do something about it is someone who is, or rather was, much closer to her. I think that's confirmed by the method of the murder. It had to be someone who knew her, and her story, well enough to set up the knives."

"Fair point," Steve replied. "Listen, I could really get used to a place like this," he added casting an appreciative eye over the well-stocked bar and the opulent surroundings.

Within a few minutes, Annabelle returned clutching a handful of papers. She sat and laid them out on the table between them and explained the contents, a printed itinerary prepared by their travel agent together with flight confirmations and hotel bills from their destinations. She then produced a digital camera. "My holiday snaps will let you see where I've been and in what order. Is that any help for you?" she asked.

Phil was mortified at the thought of having to work his way through her photos. "No, what you've given us with these papers is quite enough," he said and took out his notebook to list the significant details of where she had been and was going and her contact information. Having quickly extracted all the information he needed, he explained to Annabelle what had happened, referring only to information already in the public domain and suggesting she may wish to keep her eyes on news reports in the following days.

Chapter 11

Alex and Sandra both arrived back at his flat in the not-so-early evening having exhausted themselves and their enquiries for the time being.

They discussed their respective cases while they gorged themselves on the tasty selection purchased by Alex earlier in the day. He opened a bottle of Eisberg Cabernet Sauvignon and poured them each a large glass of the ruby-coloured liquid.

"Not for me, Alex, I mustn't drink alcohol as I'm planning to be very careful for the sake of our baby."

"It's okay, you're allowed this one. It's alcohol free, look at the label. I checked the website too and they claim it's perfectly safe to have during pregnancy. All the same taste as wine but without the risk, from what they say."

Sandra took a sip. "Hmmm, not bad, but there's no reason why you can't have the real thing."

"I'm fine with this for just now." Alex stood up then stretched wearily before taking Sandra's hand

and guiding her across to the sofa. He switched on the television and suggested they should have a lazy evening, clearing their heads of work and other responsibilities.

"Sounds good to me, but there's one thing I wanted to tell you first. I'm taking a couple of hours out tomorrow morning. I've made an appointment to see my G.P. at eleven, to get a check-up and confirm what we believe we already know. Then I've arranged to see Mum and Dad for a brunch so I can give them our news."

"Would you like me to come with you? I can juggle my appointments so I can be available. It's no trouble."

"No, it's better if I do this myself, this time at least. It could be safer too with my parents. Let's allow them to get used to the idea a bit before we expose you to them."

"Don't worry, Sandra. I can handle it. They'll need to get used to me at some time anyway."

"I've thought it through and it'll be better as I've planned. I need to see the doctor alone anyway. However, if he confirms everything's okay, then next we should tell your boys. It's best done in private. What do you say we ask them to come over for dinner tomorrow after school. As for Helen, I'll leave you to give her the news yourself if you don't mind. It's as well she's told sooner rather than later because she's bound to find out after we speak to the boys."

Alex looked pensive for a moment. "Yes, you're right, of course, that's the best way. I hadn't given a lot of thought to Helen or how she'd take it." Seeing Sandra's concerned look, he added, "It doesn't bother me what she thinks; she's history as far as I'm concerned, but I'd rather keep her sweet so she doesn't make things more difficult for me with the boys."

* * *

Alex's morning was uncharacteristically unproductive. Anticipating his attention would be distracted, he left Sanjay and the team to proceed with the active enquiries while he sat in his office with the door firmly closed, thumbing through reports and statements looking for leads and anomalies. Any interruptions were met by barked orders for him to be left in peace unless there was something desperately urgent. Sitting alone, he deliberated over Sandra's appointments while running all possible scenarios through his mind. His emotions alternated between elation and despair. His jumpiness was exacerbated by caffeine from the multiple cups of coffee he consumed to help pass the time. He couldn't remember when he'd last felt so nervous.

Every few minutes, he lifted his mobile, wanting to hear Sandra's voice and discover what news she had, but then he laid it back down realising he'd have to be patient. He stared at the words on the paper in front of him and realised he'd read the same report four times, yet still had been unable to digest its contents. However much he'd anticipated it, the incoming call didn't help. At 1.30pm, on hearing the familiar ringtone, he physically jumped from his seat. Reaching for the handset, his elbow upset a half full beaker of lukewarm liquid. Fortunately the coffee only dispersed over his blotter.

"Sandra?" the panic in his voice was palpable.

"What's wrong? Are you okay?"

"Of course I'm okay. It's you I'm worried about. What did the doctor say?"

Sandra had to stop herself from laughing hearing the emotion in Alex's voice, yet she was joyous realising this was an endorsement of how much he cared. "He told me I'm the fittest and healthiest he's seen me in years," then after a moment's silence she added, "and he confirmed I'm pregnant. Everything's great."

"Thank God!"

"You're not getting religious, are you?" she asked.

"Not unless you want me to. Did you see your parents?"

"Oh yes. Mum burst into tears and Dad was caught in a quandary not certain whether to be happy about becoming a grandfather again or wondering if he needed to find a shotgun to come after you."

Completely missing the intended humour, Alex continued, "Will he be okay about it? Should I speak to him?"

"Don't concern yourself, he'll be fine. He just has to come to terms with the fact that his baby girl is no longer a virgin. Mum's already started talking about knitting and buying a hat. I had to tell her, and Dad, that there's no wedding on the horizon. I made it clear that it's me and not you that needs to be convinced, so they won't be nagging you. We can all get together soon, once work quietens down a bit."

"Well the next step is seeing Craig and Andrew. I've checked and neither of them has afterschool activities tonight. I'll call Helen and tell her I want to see them and I'll text them as well. I won't give anything away, but I'll say we want to see them now as we're back from the holiday and we've brought them some gifts, which is true enough. I can set it up for six tonight if that's okay for you. I'll arrange to pick them up at quarter to. We can order pizzas -and that way, the food's taken care of."

"Yes, good idea."

After making the arrangements, Alex was keen to catch up on his work. Now feeling quite elated, he swung open his door, and seeing Mary standing at the far end of the office, he called her over.

"Take this," he said handing her a twenty-pound-note. "Nip round to the bakers and buy a selection of cream cakes for the squad."

A broad grin covered her face. "Yes, Sir. What are you celebrating? Don't tell me it's your birthday and you've kept it a secret."

"Nothing like that, not today, anyway. I only want to say thanks to you all for the hard work you're doing and the extra hours you've put in," Alex claimed lamely, belatedly realising he didn't want to give any hint of his real news.

Mary took the cash and set off, wondering as she went what might be behind Alex's sudden mood swing. She and the others could talk about it later and speculate on the cause, maybe even have a gamble and run a book to see who guessed closest to the truth, assuming they ever got to the bottom of the mystery.

Alex went out to the main office for an update on developments.

"There are a number of bits and pieces," Sanjay replied, lifting some folders and handing them to Alex to peruse. "You've already seen Phil and Steve's report on their interview with the American writer, but what she's said is reinforced by info we've heard back from the techies. They analysed Sheila's computer and have extracted her correspondence with D'Lite, but they've also traced several other times when she'd done the same or similar to other writers. She seems to have targeted new, self-published authors who'd been working hard to promote their first book and then she's done a hatchet job on them. They've found five others already but reckon there could be a lot more."

"I was going to ask the question, 'What kind of sick, perverse mind does something as cruel?' but there's no point. It would be rhetorical as we already know. In this bloody job, we get to meet every kind of sick preserve mind there is."

"Yes, Sir, but in this case, we only met the sick perverse mind after she was dead and our job's to find another even more perverse one that made her that way."

Alex chuckled and nodded his head without replying.

"Some other things to update," Sanjay continued. "We have a report back from the two uniforms who went to break the news to Sheila's mum and step-dad. The couple live in a large, semi-detached bungalow on the outskirts of Ayr. Apparently, he's a keen golfer and a member at Turnberry. From the report, they were really stunned by the news, but it seems they weren't a very close family. They hadn't seen Sheila for more than five years; there was some talk of a major fall out. Sheila had been much closer to her father and he died seven years ago in a boating accident. Her mother remarried within a year and the new man's a lot younger. Funnily enough, he seemed much more upset by the news than the mother was, so read into that anything you like. I don't know, maybe the mother was in shock, but in any event, she didn't appear overly distressed."

"Good police-work. It sounds quite a comprehensive report."

"Yes, Boss. You've got the file if you want to read the full details. It wasn't too different a story with her sister. We arranged for someone from Melbourne's finest to pass on the news in person. The sister's name is Dorothy Morgan, married with four children. She moved to Oz nearly twenty years ago, married out there and has never returned, nor has any of the family been out to visit her, even for the wedding. She last spoke to her sister at Christmas. They maintained some contact, but limited. We've done our duty, but no information or leads to go on."

"You only seem to be closing doors. Have you not managed to open any?" Alex asked.

"That depends what you're looking for. Going back to the technical reports we have some more information on the knives. Our people have stripped them down to the bare components and discovered something interesting. Hidden on the metal underneath the hilt there's a registration mark denoting the batch number. The set consisting of the real knife and the fake one which Graeme bought have the same number. It's the fake knife that we recovered from the bin and the real one that was used in the play before the on-stage switch. The same code is also shown as part of the reference number on the invoice Lionel gave us and that's what we would have expected. But what's really interesting is the second genuine knife, the one which ended up as the murder weapon, also had a registration mark."

"And what does that tell us?" Alex asked.

"The number corresponds to a much earlier batch. It means it was part of a set manufactured about six years ago. Whoever planned the murder must have already had or been able to get hold of an old set of knives, and they've known how to match it up with the ones Graeme bought so they could carry out the crime. I'm guessing it's something the murderer already owned, and when they found out about the play, they put their plan together."

"I see what you're getting at, Sanjay, but I think you might be going too fast in jumping to conclusions. What you suggest is a feasible explanation but it's not the only one. After hearing about the play, the killer could have found out what props were going to be used and then set out to find copy knives. They may already have known someone who had them or where they could get them. Because they were manufactured several years ago doesn't mean they were sold then, they might have been held in stock by the manufacturer or by a retailer and only sold recently. There's also the possibility that it could have been owned and kept in store by a theatre group or a magic club, or even a magic performer. Then our killer, perhaps already aware of them and where they were, pilfered the weapon. There's even another explanation going back to the possibility that the murder weapon was manufactured as a copy by the killer. If he knew about the registration number, he could have stamped one on to make his copy appear even more authentic."

Sanjay looked despondent, "So we're no further ahead."

"I wouldn't go that far," Alex said. "It gives us confirmation of some of our suspicions. The murderer was either involved in magic or stage-work or had some link to it to be able to identify and get their hands on the murder weapon. They only had a limited window of opportunity as well. They've come up with their plan at some point after learning about the play, but not only that, they'd have also needed to know about the type of knife being used for the act to be able to arrange the copy. Graeme will have been aware first as he ordered the props. However, anyone else would only have learned about the mechanism, and known how to copy it, once he'd told them what it was or shown the ones he'd purchased. It doesn't give them much time to have put it all together."

"There's something else which bothers me," Sanjay continued. "The murderer must have gone to an awful lot of effort to set this all up, but he'd have absolutely no certainty that it would work. Sheila could have turned away from the knife instead of into it. Bert might have realised the knife was wrong before using it, or he may not have lunged with sufficient strength to harm, let alone kill, Sheila. There are so many things that could have gone wrong."

"You're right. Perhaps the intention may not have been to kill her, maybe only to cause injury or even just to frighten her," Alex speculated. "Has anything come out of the other interviews?"

"Not a lot. They mostly say the same things. Everyone who saw the stabbing has the same story. All the members of the writers' group confirm that Graeme brought the knives to their last meeting and explained in detail how they worked. They've all known the plot of the play for weeks. The teachers and admin staff at the school were all told the play was going on, but none of them admit to having been told any more. Some of them, your pal Brian Phelps among them, were quite indignant about the writers bringing blades onto the premises and particularly without giving advance warning. Unlike many of the comprehensives across the country, they're proud that they haven't had a serious problem with knives in the school before and they want to keep it that way. None of them admit to seeing any of the blades or knowing they were going to be used."

"Now give me some good news," Alex pleaded.

"I'm afraid it's in short supply. The embossing on the knives was the only really bright spot and you've put that into perspective. We can start making enquiries with theatre groups and conjuring clubs and, of course, any suppliers we can find. We want to see if they have any knives unaccounted for or else any information about who might own them, but that's pretty much it.

"Wait a minute, I just thought, you weren't about when the update on the M.E. report came through, were you?"

Alex looked perplexed. "No, was there something unexpected?"

"Kind of, although it's probably irrelevant to the murder. Duffie found an abnormality with Sheila Armstrong's brain. He ran a scan and found a large tumour. He spoke to her G.P. and confirmed that it had been diagnosed. It was considered inoperable by her oncologist. More precisely, the percentages of success were too low to make it a realistic option."

"Was the diagnosis terminal?"

"It was, but there was no indication of whether it might have been weeks or years. She was able to continue as normal and was having regular check-ups. She was on medication but the doctor knew she also dabbled with recreational drugs. She reckoned she didn't have a lot to lose and said she wanted to make the most of her time."

"Do you think that may also explain some of her erratic behaviour?" Alex enquired.

"I asked the same question. Nobody has any idea."

Alex took the files back to his room to pore over the reports until it was time to leave.

Chapter 12

Exactly on schedule, Alex arrived at the house to collect his sons. They were both ready and waiting with Helen too preoccupied talking on the phone to delay their departure.

The boys quickly left the house and closed the door. Craig, the eldest jumped into the front while Andrew opened the back door; all this time Jake, their Labrador, was barking and jumping up at the lounge window.

"Sorry about the rushed plans," Alex started. "I'd hoped to see you as soon as I came back from holiday and I've brought back a couple of things for each of you, but I was dragged into an investigation as soon as my plane landed, so I haven't had a moment. Sandra's been really busy too," he added as an afterthought.

"Are you involved in the incident at our school?" Craig asked. "One of my pals was standing outside, on the evening after it happened, and he said he thought he recognised you arriving."

"I do have some involvement, but as you'd expect, I can't tell you anything about it."

"We were all sent home early on Monday and everything was still a bit chaotic yesterday morning. Other than what's been on the news, nobody will tell us anything," Craig continued.

"They can't tell you what they don't know," Alex replied. "It's a police investigation, and as such, it has to be kept confidential. The school staff have no idea what's actually going on. No, I'm being a bit harsh. They know what's happened because some of them were present before we arrived, but we don't keep them informed of developments."

"What developments have there been?" Andrew persisted.

Alex smiled but said nothing.

"A number of the staff seemed really upset," Craig said, "and of course, we've been given all the regurgitated lectures on the dangers of carrying knives in case someone gets hurt. It's as if they think we're all stupid. After all, we're not still at primary school. Saying things like don't carry a sharp stick or sharpen your pencil too much in case you or someone else accidentally falls and knocks their eye out.

"I mean to say, how often have you come across someone losing an eye because they've fallen onto a pencil?"

Alex looked over questioningly.

"Alright, maybe I'm exaggerating a bit," Craig replied to the unasked question.

"A bit?" Andrew added.

"You shut up," Craig yelled at his younger brother.

"Okay, just calm down and be kind to each other," Alex commanded. "We're almost there. Let's have a nice pleasant evening together: the two of you, Sandra and me."

A few minutes later they were all seated in the flat. Alex and Sandra produced three packages, the first they handed to Craig. He ripped open the outer wrapping and unfolded sheets of white tissue paper to reveal a fist-sized, grey-coloured rock, a line drawn down the middle. As he held it in his hand, it fell apart into two halves bisected where the line had appeared to be. His jaw dropped in surprise as each half revealed what looked like a cave filled with amethyst crystals.

"It's a geode and it's beautiful," he exclaimed, turning the pieces over and over in his hands for closer inspection. "This will take pride of place in my rock collection."

Andrew looked expectantly before being handled the second package. Unlike his brother, he carefully removed the outer sticky tape to unwrap the gift paper undamaged. He too removed tissue paper to reveal a highly polished, slate-black plate about twenty-five centimetres in circumference which had embedded fossils.

His eyes widened. "They're orthocera," he said excitedly. "It's a type of ammonite."

"We were told it was baculites," Alex said. "Is that different?"

"Not very," Andrew replied, knowledgeably. "Both are cephalopods and they look similar but baculites are from the Cretaceous period around the time of some of the dinosaurs whereas orthocera are much older, back in the Ordovician times, that's about three hundred million years earlier," he added smugly.

"Dork," Craig mouthed and was met by a stern expression from Alex.

"We have something else for you," Sandra interrupted to change the subject. She lifted the third parcel, a polythene bag, and extracted two blue T shirts, handing one to each boy. As they pulled them open they saw the letters "L'INDEP" spelled out vertically in white. In tandem, their brows furrowed, awaiting an explanation.

"We thought you might like them," Sandra stated.

"But Dad, I thought you were against Scottish Independence?" Craig questioned.

"Wrong on two counts," Alex answered. "First of all, the message on these T shirts has nothing whatsoever to do with Scotland and its politics. The message is 'L'Indep' and they are distributed by and to promote *L'Independent*, the regional newspaper. It's only a coincidence that their colours are blue and white, the same as the Scottish flag.

"On the second count, I'm not actually against Scottish Independence, but it's true to say I do have many reservations, as I expect any thinking person should when there's so many uncertainties."

"What do you mean?" Andrew asked.

"With this upcoming referendum, there's been too much information passed about, too many claims and counterclaims, but little in the way of clear facts. One side is as bad as the other. Both setting out to rubbish each other. There's no doubt Scotland has substantial assets, not just oil but exports of whisky and salmon, but what about the liabilities, and is there political capability? A large percentage of the population have a benefit culture engrained in them, sometimes where three generations of the same family have never worked. There's uncertainty over Europe, will Scotland be admitted to the EC and what about NATO? There's no doubt Spain would oppose because they don't want Catalonia and the Basque Territory to follow the example. What would happen about currency, would we keep the pound, would we even want to? Will we inherit a share of the National Debt? What will it cost to set up a completely independent civil service? None of these questions have been properly answered by either the Yes Campaign or Better Together, and without having a clear idea of the answers, how are we meant to make a decision?"

"So, are you not going to vote?" Craig asked.

"For me, that's not an option either. I treasure the fact that we live in a democratic country which holds honest and free elections with every adult having a say. I consider it my duty to exercise my vote. It's my opinion that I have an obligation to become as well informed as I can and then to make a decision. It may not be easy and maybe I won't decide correctly, but it's something I believe I have to do."

"Surely your one vote won't make any difference?" Craig asked.

"Not on its own, no. But if everyone thought that way then we wouldn't have a democracy."

"Why should it only be adults who vote?" Andrew asked.

"It's a difficult question, but a line has to be drawn somewhere because, to be democratic, each person should have only one vote and it would be too easy for adults to influence how their children voted."

"In this referendum, for the first time, the voting age has been lowered to sixteen," Craig stated.

"I suppose that's fair. In Scotland, you can get married at sixteen, so why shouldn't you be allowed to vote?" Sandra contributed.

"Yeah, but the effect of a vote can last for a very long time while most marriages these days are short term arrangements," Alex said. He was about to make an even more flippant remark when he thought better of it, considering how the boys had been affected by his divorce from their mother, together with the risk of him down-valuing his proposal to Sandra.

"Listen, enough of this for now," he continued. "Sandra and I have some really important news to tell you."

"What, more important than the future of our country?" Andrew challenged.

"We'll let you be the judges," Alex countered. "How would you feel about having a little brother or sister?"

"What? What do you mean?" Andrew asked.

"What we're telling you is that you're going to have a new brother or sister. Sandra's expecting a baby."

Craig's head turned back and forward, looking in turn from Alex to Sandra's face and then her belly.

"Eeeu," Andrew said. "That means you've been doing it. Are you not too old?" he continued staring at his father.

"Don't be stupid," Craig admonished, punching Andrew on the arm. "People have sex at all ages."

"Craig's correct," Alex agreed. "In fact, Charlie Chaplin became a father when he was over seventy years of age."

"Who's Charlie Chaplin?" Andrew asked.

Alex shook his head in despair wondering whether it was worth the effort to explain, but he needn't have worried.

"Never mind Chaplin, did you hear the story about the eighty-year-old man who married an eighteen-year-old girl?" Craig asked. "Before the wedding, he went to see his friend, a doctor, to ask for advice. The doctor told him the best advice he could give was for him to take in a young attractive lodger. A few months later, he met the doctor and joyously told him that his wife was pregnant. 'Ah, you took my advice about the lodger.' the friend asked. 'Yes,' he replied, 'and I've got her pregnant too.'"

"Very funny," Alex said. "Now if we can get back to reality."

"I'm just thinking how unfair it was for you to have lectured me about safe sex when I started going out with my girlfriend," Craig accosted. "It seems like you could do with taking some of your own advice. Just consider, how would you have reacted if I'd come home to tell you that Jenny was pregnant?"

"It's not the same thing, we're adults," Alex defended. "You're still a teenager. You have your whole life ahead of you with all its opportunities. It would be a mistake to restrict your potential by starting a family so young."

"And how will it affect Sandra's job opportunities to have a career break. She's only just won her promotion. What will it mean for her to stop work to have a baby?" Craig retorted.

Alex's face reddened, realising the truth in Craig's words and not too certain how to handle the situation until Sandra took over. "Your father and I care very deeply for each other and we've decided to make our future together." Alex looked up relieved not only at being rescued but even more so by Sandra's declared statement.

"But Jenny and I are happy together too."

"Maybe, but are you ready to commit your entire future?"

Craig thought for a second and then decided to change tack. "Will Jenny and I get to babysit?"

"I don't see why not, when the time is right. I take it you two are still an item?" Sandra asked.

"Yes, we've been going out for months now and it would appear we've got a clearer understanding than you two about contraception," he added with a grin.

Realising his son had previously denied that his relationship had progressed to such an intimate level, Alex was immediately aware of the significance of the statement. However, he knew now was not the time to question him further. Besides, given his own situation, he was too embarrassed to answer.

The moment was broken by Andrew. "So, are you going to get married?" he asked.

"We haven't decided yet about a number of things, but be assured you'll be one of the first to be told," Alex answered.

"What will Mum say? Have you told her yet?" Craig asked.

"It's really got nothing whatsoever to do with your mum," Alex defended. "I've not said anything to her yet as I wanted you both to know first, but I'm planning to talk to her when I take you home, later."

Being a school-night, Alex didn't want to keep the boys out too late. A couple of hours later, he dropped them back home. Instead of driving off, he followed them up the path and rang the bell, even though the boys had keys and let themselves in.

"Can I have word with you?" he asked, when Helen came to the door.

"Yes, of course," she ushered him into the lounge. "Is there a problem? Come and sit down. I'll put the kettle on."

"There isn't a problem. Don't bother with tea, I won't take long," Alex said, while lowering himself into an armchair. Helen sat on the couch next to Colin, her partner, and looked enquiringly.

"I've some news to tell you. I've already said to the boys, but I wanted to tell you myself."

"Uh-huh?"

"Sandra's expecting. Craig and Andrew are going to have a baby brother or sister," he said without preamble.

A dazed expression came across Helen's face. "And you're keeping it?"

"Of course."

She froze for a few moments before jumping to her feet. "How could you do this to the boys? How could you do this to me? It's madness, it's cruel. It can't be allowed to happen. I won't let it."

In response, Alex quickly stood, his face reddened as his blood pressure rose. He made a supreme effort trying to keep his words dispassionate. "What are you talking about? This has absolutely nothing to do with you. Yes, it's relevant to the boys because they'll have a new sibling, but it won't affect them in a bad way. I won't treat them any different to the way I've always done."

Colin grasped Helen's arm, holding her back. "He's right. Why are you getting so upset?"

She pushed him away. "Why are you taking his side?" she challenged, then she darted from the room while slamming the door, tears already wetting her cheeks.

"I think I'd better leave," Alex said.

"Yes, probably a good idea. She'll get over it. I reckon she's just a bit shocked by your news. She'll no doubt be really embarrassed when it all sinks in," Colin said.

Alex nodded and quietly let himself out of the front door. He sat in his car breathing deeply, trying to seek an explanation for Helen's reaction and making no attempt to turn the ignition. He'd expected her to be surprised, but her reaction was wild and unreasonable. He'd seen her act strangely many times before, although not recently, and he was stunned. Trying to rationalise her behaviour, he realised the news was unfortunately timed, with Helen now reaching a stage where childbirth was beyond her. Although she hadn't wanted more children after Andrew's birth, the choice had been hers. Sandra had certainly made a good decision allowing Alex to pass on the news alone. Nevertheless, he needed to warn her, to avoid her being upset or hurt if she suffered the sharp edge of Helen's tongue.

Chapter 13

Alex slept restlessly, tossing, turning and waking frequently. Helen's reaction and bitter words left him feeling uneasy. Although their years of marriage had left him well acquainted with her tantrums, he was not immune. Although he felt no concerns for himself, he feared any potential repercussions from her behaviour. He was aware of Sandra lying beside him and he wanted to avoid his restlessness disturbing her. At 5.00 am he rose, lifted a blanket from the hall cupboard and lay down on the lounge sofa.

It took some time for him to doze, and no sooner had he drifted into his first sound sleep of the night than he was awoken by Sandra enquiring what was wrong.

"What's the time?" he asked.

Sandra yawned, pulled up the sleeve of her dressing gown and mumbled, "Ten past six. What are you doing here?"

"I couldn't sleep and didn't want to wake you too," he replied.

"Come back to bed, we can manage another hour's shut-eye before we need to get up. I'm cold and need a hug."

Alex followed her back to the bedroom; however, before they'd properly settled, Sandra's mobile rang.

"What now?" she reached for the handset.

"Yes... Say that again.... Where? .... Who? .... Any signs of foul play? .... How long? .... Who reported it?" Alex was now wide awake hearing the staccato questions and he patiently waited to find out what was going on.

"A body was found in the Clyde. It was washed ashore a little bit north of Erskine to be more precise," Sandra informed him as soon as she hung up.

"Why you?" he asked.

"Identification hasn't been confirmed yet, but he was carrying a travel pass with the name Patrick Carson."

"What, the one who set up Fergus Hardy?"

"So it would seem. They don't know yet how he got there, but the body's been in the water for some time. I'm no gambler, but after the Hardy incident, putting two and two together, it looks odds on we're now dealing with a murder."

"Early days but have you suspicions as to who or why?" Alex asked.

"Well, if it is Carson and if he did set up Hardy, then we have two possibilities. One is that Zennick, or whoever arranged for Hardy to be attacked, saw

Carson as a weak link and silenced him. The second is that one of Hardy's allies found out about Carson's involvement and did it out of revenge."

"Either way, you may find the organised crime specialists might want to muscle in."

"Yeah, that could be a problem. This is my first big case – the first I've been in charge of. I don't want anyone taking it from me, not now, especially not the Gartcosh boys. I won't let them have it without a fight. If I can make as much progress as I can before they catch on, then I might manage to keep control."

"What's your next step?"

"If I leave right away, I'll be able to get to the scene before the body gets moved. I'd like to see the M.E. while he's on-site and find out what he can tell me."

"He may be able to give you an idea of how long Carson's been in the water. Then if you can get someone to study the tides and the current, you ought to be able to calculate approximately where he went in and when."

"Yeah, I'll need to take expert advice."

"Some tea and toast before you go?"

"I'd love to, but I don't have time."

"Make time," Alex answered. "You need something in your stomach, even more so because of your condition. You don't want to have to live down retching at a crime scene and damaging the evidence. You go and get ready. I'll make you some breakfast."

* * *

Sandra donned her wellington boots while sitting in her car before wading across the muddy sands to join the team already surrounding the body.

Although not unfamiliar with death and crime scenes, she hadn't previously had to deal with a body newly recovered from the river. Sandra had to breathe deeply and swallow to stop the bile from rising after catching the smell and sight of the hideous, bloated corpse. She silently mouthed a thank you to Alex for making her eat something before leaving.

"Judging from the state of the body, he's been in the water at least twenty-four hours," the doctor advised. "I'll be able to tell you more after I open him up."

The mental image of a postmortem made Sandra feel even worse and she picked up her phone, turned away, and bluffed an imaginary call, hoping to avoid her discomfort being too obvious.

Peter left the others to join her and waited for her to replace her mobile. "Are you okay, Ma'am? You're looking a little green around the gills if you don't mind me saying. There's nothing more we can do here. Can I suggest a cup of tea to revive us? There's a place I know a couple of miles along the road."

"Good idea," she replied.

A few minutes later they were sitting facing each other across a table in a traditional transport café, complete with plastic chintz table cover, drinking tea from builders' mugs. Sandra was feeling much better.

"Can we be certain it's Carson?" Peter asked.

"It's yet to be confirmed, but he was carrying his ID, he's the same size and shape and the naked lady tattoo on his arm is enough to eliminate any doubt I might have had."

"I guess. Well, without him to point the way, how can we link Zennick to the Hardy assault?"

"There's more than one way to skin a cat," Sandra replied. "Besides, Carson's murder, assuming we can prove it was, takes priority. Who knows, we might be able to roll it all up in one case."

"Positive thinking, I like that. Where do we go next?" Peter asked.

"I'd like to start with Carson's brother. According to reports, he's been completely unhelpful in recent days since we've been trying to find Carson. Maybe when he hears what's happened, he might feel guilty. Who knows, he may even be cooperative."

"Sounds rather optimistic given the short shrift he gave our boys last time. I guess you have to hope and we don't have anything better to start with."

They detoured past Helen Street police station without going in, but deposited Peter's vehicle to enable them to travel together. A short while later Sandra pulled her car to a halt in South Street a short distance away from the First Bus, Scotstoun depot.

"I do a double take every time I come here," Peter said. "It's strange to see two rows of mock Tudor terraces surrounding what can only be described as a village green and set right in the heart of what was one of Glasgow's most industrial areas."

"Yeah, I suppose. Are you aware of the history? It dates back well over a hundred years. When Harland and Wolff set up their shipyard and brought workers up from down south, they couldn't get used to the traditional Glasgow tenements and didn't want to move. To get round the problem, the shipbuilders built these houses for their managers and artisans to make them feel more at home. The company only built the structure and let the employees design the internal layout themselves. There's no two the same," Sandra advised.

"How do you know all this?" Peter asked.

"I only came across it by accident, a short while back. I was looking for a flat to rent and saw one there. I fell in love with it but I was too slow and someone else got in first. But not before I learned about the history; my father told me. He knows about these things because he was a surveyor before he retired."

Arriving at the main door flat, Peter rapped heavily. He waited several seconds then repeated the action.

"What are you wantin?" A sleepy voice replied.

"Police. We need to talk to you," Peter stated.

"I've already telt you, I know nuthin'."

"Please open the door, Mr Carson. It's very important that we speak to you and it would be better done in private," Peter said.

The sigh was audible through the thickness of the heavy wooden door. This was followed by clanking metallic noises as two bolts were pulled back and then the click of a key turning. The door opened a few inches, revealing a barefoot Joseph Carson dressed in pyjama bottoms and a string vest. The attire reminded Sandra of the actor Gregor Fisher in the guise of his TV character Rab C Nesbitt. Joseph's overall appearance wasn't too dissimilar either. He was heavy set with a large beer belly. A round, pudgy face was shadowed by two days' growth and his head was intermittently thatched by long, greasy curls. Sandra found it difficult to believe Joseph was Patrick's brother, as Patrick was small, slim, dapper and always without a whisker of hair on either face or head.

From earlier research, Sandra was aware Joseph Carson was aged mid-forties and had never done an honest day's work in his life. He rented this flat, his rent paid directly out of the benefit system. Alike many of nature's parasites, Carson had an inbuilt defence structure. The stench from his body odour was overpowering and only superseded by the noxious odour of his halitosis when he opened his mouth to speak.

"What are you doin' gettin' me out o' bed in the middle o' the night?" His words were belied by the cigarette which dangled from the edge of his lip, seemingly a permanent fixture, and it flared with each breath.

"It's hardly the middle of the night; near enough nine o'clock already. We've come about Patrick," Peter replied. "Can we come in and talk to you?" Without awaiting a reply, they both squeezed past, breathing in before they passed him to avoid any physical contact, and walked through to the lounge. They remained standing, finding a space as far away from him and any of his furniture as they could.

Although not small, the room was cluttered, every surface covered in an assortment of debris: jars, bottles, cans, old newspapers, fast-food carry out containers and overfilled ash trays.

"I'd worked that out mysel'. You're wastin' your time though. I've telt you already, I've no' seen or heard from him in days."

"The reason we've come is we believe we've found him," Peter said.

"How come you're here then?"

"Please take a seat, Mr Carson," Sandra suggested

Carson perched on the arm of a settee. "What are you after?"

"I'm sorry to tell you, Mr Carson, but a body washed ashore in the Clyde, near Erskine. We understand it to be your brother," Sandra advised.

"Oh, no you don't. You're no' catchin' me out like that. This is a trick to get me to talk."

"I'm afraid not," Sandra replied. "Our code of practice wouldn't permit us to do that. This is for real. The body we have fits your brother's description and was carrying his ID. You're his next of kin. We have to ask you to confirm the identification."

"You're no' jokin' here, are you?" Carson's tone turned serious and his face looked grim. He slid back into the chair, squashing some of the debris as he went.

"When did you last see your brother?" Sandra asked.

"No' since last week, but I spoke to him on Monday mornin'. He telt me he had a job comin' up an' he was goin' to be quids in."

"Can you tell me who he was going to be working for?" Sandra pursued, hoping to find out everything she could while Carson was being cooperative.

"I dinnae know for sure. He didnae say at the time, but over the last few months, he'd been talkin' about doin' work for some big Russian guy. I'd tried to tell him he should stay clear, it was too dangerous, but there was no tellin' him."

"Can you tell me his name?" Sandra asked.

"I'm no' sure. I think he mentioned somethin' but I cannae remember."

"Please try," Sandra pushed.

"I'm no' sure. It was foreign soundin'. Sandor or Sendy or somethin' like that."

"Could it have been Zennick?" Sandra prompted.

"Zennick, Zennick, sounds familiar, yeah, that might be it."

Sandra turned to Peter and they exchanged wry smiles. "Did he mention any other names?"

Carson shook his head in response. "What do I do now?" he asked.

"We can arrange for you to view the body, but I'll need to check first with the Medical Examiner when he can arrange for you to view the body. In the meantime, is there someone you want to be with you? A

friend or family member or we can arrange for a social worker."

"No, I'm fine. My son's meant to be comin' over
this mornin'. I can give him a call mysel'."

Sandra called the M.E. and provided him with Carson's number to call when he was ready.

They then reluctantly waited while Carson called
his son who, fortunately, arrived within a few minutes.

* * *

A short while later, having recently arrived back
at her office, Sandra squealed, "Yes!" after perusing a
report which analysed communications Zennick had
made or received while in prison.

Peter called over, "What is it?"

"We've a positive ID on Zennick's contact. He's
been recognised from the CCTV at the prison. His
name's Andrei Devosky. He's the one who visited
him in the clink, claiming to be his brother. There're
also phone records showing communication from
Devosky's mobile to the Bar-L."

"A damn good start, but we've no proof yet; nothing the fiscal can use," Peter replied.

"Maybe not, but we're building up the picture and
we've enough to bring in Devosky and lean on him
pretty hard. That's if we can find him. From what I
can gather, he's been in the country for three years
and he's been fighting deportation for the last two.
He's lost every hearing and now he's gone under-

ground, making himself invisible. There's no current address on record for him."

"Shit! It couldn't have been easy, could it?" Peter uttered.

"Let's try another angle," Sandra suggested. "Devosky only managed to get in to see Zennick in prison by using a false ID. It must have been approved by someone to let him in. I have the name of the screw who allowed him entry, one Norman Gilchrist – his friends call him Norrie. I think Mr Gilchrist has earned himself a visit."

Peter was quickly able to establish that Norrie Gilchrist would be working backshift and was currently at home, a semi-villa in Cumbernauld. He phoned ahead and arranged to see him.

Sandra parked at the kerb. The house looked relatively new and appeared substantial, with a large, well-stocked garden. A new Audi Four series sat in the driveway.

"Not short of a bob or two," Peter whispered. "I didn't know prison officers were paid so much."

Sandra responded with a raised eyebrow and a terse nod.

The door was opened to welcome them when they were only halfway along the path. Gilchrist stepped forward in greeting. He was well-tanned, tall and muscular, with the physique of a body builder. His handshake was firm and confident.

"Hi. You said on the phone you wanted a word. You thought I might be able to help you out with some information. Come on through to the kitchen, I've just made a fresh pot of tea."

Sandra and Peter followed him along a hallway and through to a large dining kitchen with views over a tidily landscaped garden. Sandra couldn't help herself comparing the fresh, clean, open spaciousness to the smelly, oppressive, claustrophobic atmosphere of Carson's flat. It seemed several light years away, but in fact was less than twenty miles and a couple of hours earlier.

"Tea?" Gilchrist asked, then without waiting for a reply, he poured what looked to be a strong brew into three chunky, Denby mugs. "Help yourself to sugar and milk," he added pushing forward matching containers.

"A nice place you have here," Sandra noted.

Gilchrist looked around him and smiled, "Thanks, and before you ask, I could never afford this on my salary. My wife's an accountant, a manager with one of the big four. She earns twice as much as I do. What's this all about?"

Sandra nodded. "We want to talk to you about one of your charges, a Mr Zennick."

"Oh yes, he's only been with us for a few days. What do you want to know?"

"We understand that you were the one who approved him being visited by his brother."

"So?"

"Mr Zennick doesn't have a brother in this country. The person who actually visited him was an Andrei Devosky."

Gilchrist paled slightly. "Oh really, I can't understand that, I must have made a mistake."

"Come now, Mr Gilchrist. There are strict procedures for approving visitors and checking identification. This must have been more than an ordinary mistake," Peter said.

Gilchrist stepped back a pace and held on to a worktop for support. He paused then inhaled a deep breath. "I don't want to say any more. I'm entitled to have a solicitor present if you want to talk to me."

"Why have you gone defensive?" Sandra asked. "We're trying to get some information for our investigation and we hoped you'd want to help. We can, of course, go down the formal channels, but that will take a lot longer and might give you some problems at work."

"I have nothing to say to you," Gilchrist asserted.

"If that's how you want to play it, we can take you into custody now and wait until we get the answers we're looking for, with or without your solicitor," Sandra replied.

"You can't do that. This is a prison matter. You have no jurisdiction," although speaking forcefully, Gilchrist had lost a lot of his confidence.

"That's where you're wrong. Crimes have been committed, crimes we understand have been set up by Mr Zennick and organised through Mr Devosky. We have clear evidence to show that you facilitated the communication between these gentlemen. One of the crimes was the serious assault on the lawyer Fergus Hardy. We don't yet know how the fiscal will pursue his prosecution. He might go for attempted murder or he may settle for GBH, that's his business. But irrespective, we now have a body from what we've ascertained is a related crime. We're now looking at premeditated murder and you're involved."

"This has got nothing to do with me," Gilchrist defended.

"Once again, I have to correct you," Sandra claimed. "Have you ever heard of the concept of 'Joint Enterprise'?"

"What are you talking about?"

"It's a legal doctrine that's being increasingly used to prosecute each of the people who've been involved in carrying out a crime, as if they were the ones who committed it. In this case, a murder has been carried out and you've been an essential ingredient in enabling it to take place. This leaves you liable to be prosecuted for murder."

"What? You can't be serious. There's nothing you can pin on me."

"You hang onto that thought if it makes you feel better, but don't get too comfortable," Sandra challenged. "In fact, you should check it out with your solicitor when you speak to him. By the way, you do realise you could end up sharing a cell with some of the inmates you've previously been looking after. I hope you've not made too many enemies."

Gilchrist struggled to maintain his composure. All colour drained from his face and his hands trembled. "I had no part in any murder. I never intended any harm to come to anyone. I didn't mean any wrong. I can tell you what I know, but you must promise that you'll never let on that you got anything from me."

"It's up to the fiscal who and how he plans to prosecute, but it'll stand you in much better stead if you're seen to cooperate. I can't make any promises though," Sandra added.

"It's not only prosecution I'm worried about, it's what he'll do if he finds out I talked. You have to realise I did what I did out of fear, not greed."

"I think you'd better tell us all about it," Sandra said. "We want your information and we'll do what we can to keep the source confidential. The safest thing for you is if we catch the ones behind this and put them away."

"It's a long, complicated story," Gilchrist started. "Let's sit down and I'll tell you what I can.

"The first I heard of Zennick was less than two weeks ago, when he came to Barlinnie," Gilchrist started. "The very same day, I received a phone call from my sister, Angela, telling me she'd been contacted by one of Zennick's men. I hadn't come across him before, but the man turned out to be Devosky. Angela's husband is Ukrainian but he's the only one of his family who's been able to come here. Devosky told Angela that he needed a small favour and this turned out to be pressuring me to allow him in to see Zennick."

"And what was he offering you to give you encouragement?" Sandra asked.

"I wasn't bribed, if that's what you mean. Devosky told Angela if her husband ever wanted to hear from his family again then she had to make me comply. She didn't believe him at first, but when they tried to call her husband's parents and brothers they couldn't get an answer. They managed to speak to cousins, but no one could tell them where the immediate family were or what had become of them. Angela and her husband were frantic. I didn't want to do anything, but I had to help."

"You should have come to the police," Sandra said.

"Yeah, and what would you have done? What could you have done? You can't control the foreign gangsters over here, what chance would you have in their own country?"

Sandra went to answer then stopped. She realised he was right. She couldn't offer Gilchrist effective protection against Zennick's gang in Glasgow. How could she claim any influence to protect his brother in law's family in Ukraine? Instead, she decided to pursue a different approach. "How did you communicate with Zennick and Devosky?"

"I've had no contact with Zennick at all. Yes, I knew he was in the prison, but I've not had any direct dealings with him and I haven't spoken to him at any time. My instructions came from Devosky and, once I found out what I was becoming involved in, I kept as far a distance as I reasonably could from Zennick to avoid drawing any suspicion."

"And what about Devosky?"

"After he'd spoken to Angela, he gave her time to contact me and then called her back to confirm I'd play ball. He then phoned me with instructions. The call came in from an unlisted number; I noted that at the time. He gave me a mobile number to call him back on once I'd put everything in place for him."

"And did you use it?" Sandra asked.

"Yes, it was someone else who answered though, and passed the phone to him. So, it was either his phone answered by someone else or the phone belonged to someone he was with."

"You called him only once?" Sandra probed.

"Yes, just the one time."

"Do you still have the number?"

"Yes, I have it on a pad. I didn't save it on the phone. Wait a minute and I'll get it for you."

Gilchrist fished about in a drawer then handed over a yellow post-it pad.

Sandra and Peter looked at it. "Very odd; this isn't the number we have for Devosky. It's not the one we have registered to him, the one Zennick used to contact him," Peter explained.

"Something else we need to know," Sandra said, then she addressed Gilchrist again. "Can you give us Angela's details so we can check out what you've told us?"

"I really don't want you to do that. She's already worried sick about her in-laws and I don't think she can take any more. These are dangerous people. If they find out I've shopped them, then it's not only my life that's at risk. If Angela learns what I've told you then it could knock her over the edge. Word could get back to Devosky and then we'd all be in danger. And don't think you're safe; he's not afraid of the police.

In fact, I wouldn't put anything past him. No, I don't want her to find out."

"I understand your concern, but it's not down to you to decide," Sandra replied.

Gilchrist looked dejected, his former confidence had ebbed away, his head bowed and his shoulders slouched.

"I guess I could lose my job over this," he said.

"I reckon that to be more than likely," Sandra stated. "You were in a position of trust and you betrayed that trust. I can fully understand your reason, but it doesn't change the facts. It's not a matter we have any say over in any event and it may depend on the way the procurator fiscal choses to proceed."

"What do you mean? I told you everything I know so I wouldn't be charged," Gilchrist replied forcefully.

Although understanding his predicament, Sandra had limited sympathy. "You only told us what you know because you were caught. You didn't come to us to volunteer information. Maybe you've forgotten but we already have one body on a mortuary slab and another in the infirmary and this is as a direct result of the assistance you gave Zennick. I don't think you have anything to be proud of. Fair enough, you were forthcoming with information once we cornered you, and for that I'm prepared to put in a word on your behalf, but it's not my decision whether there will be criminal proceedings against you.

"We'll leave it at that for now, but rest assured you will be seeing us again. It's up to you to consider whether to own up to your bosses or to wait and see whether we take action."

"What should I do now?" Gilchrist pleaded.

"Maybe you should consult your solicitor," Sandra suggested.

"If you don't already have one, I hear Fergus Hardy has a good reputation," Peter added, without any attempt to hide a smirk.

* * *

Once settled in the car, Peter and Sandra compared notes.

"It's been a most productive morning," Sandra said. "We've now a confirmed relationship between Zennick and Devosky with a more tenuous one to Carson and Hardy. We have enough to hold Devosky if we can find him although his immigration problems would give us grounds to detain him anyway. If we could just find the hoodies too and a link to Carson's little swim then that would give us the full picture."

"You're not asking a lot," Peter commented.

"Well, why not? You have to be optimistic."

Chapter 14

Alex spent much of the morning in his office studying witness statements. He had a niggling feeling, believing something had been overlooked. He read reports over and over hoping to find a pattern or an inconsistency which hadn't already been identified.

He called Sanjay, wanting to discuss the reports and subsequent actions.

"You explained your system to me. Have you now spoken to everyone you wanted to?" Alex asked.

"Everyone identified at the start has been interviewed by at least one of our team."

"Mmm, all the teachers and school staff?"

"Yes, I think so."

"I've come across three separate interviews with the writers who mention someone who brought them tea at some point in the morning, a slender, fair-haired woman. I haven't seen anything that shows she'd been identified and interviewed."

Sanjay's brows furrowed. "I remember something. Yes, Bert made mention. I asked Donny to check it out, but you're right, I haven't seen any follow-up. She was mentioned in other interviews too, you say?"

"Yes, look here," Alex replied. "You need to keep better control when you set tasks to make sure they're completed, particularly where Donny's concerned. He can be a lazy son-of-a-bitch if you don't stand over his shoulder."

Sanjay stared at Alex, surprised at his words.

"I'm warning you for your own benefit. I may be overseeing, but you're the senior investigating officer. Your staff are accountable to you and you're responsible for their actions or inactions. If you handle this well, and maybe have a lucky break or two, then you've a chance to make a name for yourself and it could help your career path. On the other hand, if you're sloppy or allow your subordinates to be sloppy, then it's you who'll get hung out to dry."

Sanjay nodded. "Point taken, thanks for the advice. I guess I need to toughen up my people management skills."

"Sanjay, you're recognised as very competent; the upper corridors are well-aware of your potential, but you're also a nice guy. You want to be liked and to be one of the boys. You're naturally gentle by nature. There's nothing wrong with being that way, but it doesn't always work when you're in a position of responsibility. It's nice to be liked, but it's far more important to be respected. You need to be listened to and, more importantly, if you give an order, it needs to be followed."

Sanjay nodded again but looked uncertain.

"I'm not saying you have to shout and scream. That's not how to get results. But you have to make it clear to your team what you expect from them. Give them credit when they produce and let them know in no uncertain terms when they don't. Most staff will respond well, although it's harder with the likes of Donny. He's close to retirement and basically marking time whenever he can get away with it. He's resentful of authority because he never had any success with his own promotion attempts. As a result, you need to keep a close eye on him and stay on his case."

"Yes, Sir. Good advice. I'll be a lot more careful in future."

Sanjay returned to his desk and immediately called Donny over to ask what he'd discovered. In reply, he was treated to the start of what promised to be a lengthy monologue with detailed descriptions of anything and everything he might have been doing. Sanjay had to interrupt the presentation on three occasions within the first couple of minutes, insisting that Donny stick to the point and answer the direct question of what he'd done about researching the woman who'd brought tea to the writers' group.

"As I've been trying to tell you, Sarg. I've not had time," Donny eventually conceded.

"That's not good enough," Sanjay replied. "If I give you a direct instruction, you do it. You don't question it and you don't do something else first. If there's a particularly good reason why you can't do it, then you tell me, and by that, I mean right away, not days later when I have to chase you up for an answer."

Donny was peeved but tried to retain a bored expression. "Okay, okay, if that's what you want, then I'll head straight over to the school and try to get an answer."

"No, you won't, you've wasted enough time already," Sanjay said forcefully. "The first thing you'll do is collate the best description you can and then get on the blower to the school's office and see if they can tell you who she is and what she was doing there. Once you bring me that answer, then I'll decide what's to happen next."

Donny moved back to his own desk while Alex looked on from a distance. Although too far away to follow the conversation, Alex was confident using his interpretation of the body language, Sanjay had learned an important lesson and wouldn't allow Donny to take advantage.

Within minutes, Donny returned to advise he'd spoken to various admin staff and there appeared to be a consensus identifying the young lady as Yvonne Kitson, a drama instructor who worked part-time at the school. Further enquiry revealed she had not been scheduled to be at Eastfarm School on the day of the murder.

Sanjay instructed Donny to track her down for her to be interviewed, and then advised Alex of the new development.

"Let me give Brian Phelps a call to see what background I can find," he suggested.

Brian was taking a class when Alex phoned, but his call was returned within the hour.

"Hi, Alex, how are you? No doubt being a workaholic as usual."

"You'd better believe it."

"And what about the beautiful Sandra? How's she? I trust you're not neglecting her," Brian joked.

"You think I overwork; well, in the last few days, I'd be considered a slacker compared to her. She's been at it nearly flat out since we came back from holiday. Because of staff shortages, she was called back early and given a case which has now turned into three. Although they look to be related, each on their own could be a full-time job. I'm busy enough supervising the incident at your school."

"Are you able to tell me any more about what's going on?" Brian asked.

"Quite the reverse, I was hoping you'd be able to give me some information. There's nothing I can tell you that you've not already heard or will have read in the papers. We're going through all the motions, interviewing everyone in sight and eliminating possibilities. We have some interesting lines of enquiry but we've yet to come up with anything concrete. The reason I was calling was to take forward one of those lines; I reckoned that you might be able to help."

"Sure, I'll do anything I can," Brian offered.

"What can you tell me about Yvonne Kitson?"

"Yvonne Kitson? The name's familiar but I can't place it."

"I understand she's a drama assistant," Alex prompted.

"Ah, Vonnie, of course. It didn't ring a bell at first. What can I tell you about her?"

"Anything and everything you have," Alex answered.

"She's a lovely girl, always willing to help and very popular with the staff and pupils. She's employed directly by the Education Authority, not through the school, so I don't have a personnel file. She's allocated to us for one or two days a week and helps with projects and productions, predominantly with the English department. Why are you asking?"

"It's probably nothing. We're just trying to tie up some loose ends, so we can speak to anyone who was in the school the morning Sheila Armstrong died."

"There's nothing unusual there. As I said, she's allocated to the school part-time."

"Maybe so, but she wasn't meant to be with you on Monday. In fact, I've just been handed a note saying her personnel record shows she was scheduled to be at a school in Barrhead but she phoned in saying she was sick."

"Sounds very odd. Why would she do that?" Brian mused.

"You can see why we'd want the answer to that question."

Alex could only hear Brian's breathing while he considered. "I can't believe she could be involved. She's just a wee lassie."

"I'm not claiming she was involved, only that her story doesn't add up. And just for the record, what do you imagine someone involved in a murder does look like? There's no standard image. I wish to God there was because it would make my job a lot easier. No, you can't pick out a murderer on the basis of appearance. It can be a child or it can be a geriatric."

"Sorry, I suppose it was a stupid thing to say. It's just that she always appeared to be gentle and kind; I've never heard her raise her voice, not unless you count her acting on stage."

"How good an actress is she? How convincing can she be when playing a part?" Alex asked.

"Fair point. I'm in an area that's outside my comfort zone. I suppose it's something you have to deal with all the time. From anything I know of her, I find it difficult to accept she could be capable of a cold-blooded, premeditated murder," Brian said.

"Maybe you're right and the job's affected me. After what I've had to deal with over the years, I've become dispassionate and callous and I've learned there isn't much that that the average 'normal' human can't do if given the right provocation. Every one of us is capable of the most ruthless, brutal actions if the circumstances are right, or wrong, I suppose. Trust me. To get back to the matter in hand, I need to find out everything you can tell me about Yvonne. Is she married or single? Has she a partner?

Who are her friends? Where does she live? etcetera, etcetera. Anything and everything you know."

"I might not be the best one to ask," Brian replied. "She isn't working here today. She's scheduled to be at the Academy. From what I've heard, she lives alone and has a flat in Cathcart. She gives the impression of being a bit of a party animal, but as I said, I'm not the best one for gossip. You'd be better speaking to the girls in the office."

"Okay, thanks, we'll do that," Alex replied.

"Hey, while we're on the subject of gossip, what can you give me? The staff know we're friends and they keep pumping me for information. They assume you must have told me something. Is there anything you can tell me? Anything I can drop in conversation at coffee break which might improve my street cred? It doesn't have to be anything meaningful, just something I can use."

Alex thought for a moment, not certain if he should rebuke his friend for asking or whether it would be better to offer him some useless titbit. Finally, he decided to yield. "You can't say you got this from me but the victim had a reputation for cutting down new independent authors. She wrote some really cruel reviews and posted them on the internet. I can't say it's yielded us any relevant suspects but she'd certainly made a lot of enemies. This isn't privileged information because anyone could find it on the web if they knew where to look."

"Thanks, Alex, I'll be able to do some background research to support it, then I'll be able to dine out on that for a week."

Alex shook his head. "Fine, I'll go now and try to get some work done."

Alex pressed the button on the phone to disengage but didn't hang up. Instead, he keyed Sanjay's number and passed on the new information.

Sanjay had wasted no time in tracking down Yvonne, finding her as expected at the Academy. He sent Donny and Phil there to collect her and bring her in for questioning.

When they returned, he asked Phil to join him as he went to conduct the interview.

They entered the room to find her pacing the floor. "Miss Kitson, please sit down. I'm Sergeant Guptar and I'm investigating the death of Sheila Armstrong. Now we understand you were at Eastfarm School on Monday?"

Kitson nodded her head but didn't speak.

"Please speak clearly for the recording. Now you nodded an agreement but please audibly confirm you were at Eastfarm at the time of Sheila Armstrong's death."

"Yes, that's correct." Kitson's voice was quiet and hesitant.

"Thank you. Now this raises a couple of questions. First of all, the school's records show you weren't due to be on duty, and secondly, why did you not come forward to advise us you'd been there?"

Kitson drew a deep breath. "I don't know where to start," she said, her whole body shaking. "I wasn't meant to be there. I should have been at the Academy on Monday but I didn't go. I'd been invited to audition for a professional production at the Kings. The audition was to take place late afternoon, but I decided not to go into the Academy in case I got caught up and couldn't get away. Instead, I phoned them to say I was sick. In the morning, I went to Eastfarm. I didn't own up as I didn't want to get myself into bother."

"You could be in a lot more bother because you didn't say," Sanjay replied.

"Yes, I see that now. I quite often switch around my schedule so I can be where I'm most needed."

"That may be understandable but shouldn't you report back to your employers when you make a timing change?" Sanjay challenged.

"Yes, of course, you're right, but it's impractical. I've tried before. Whenever you want to make a schedule change, it takes hours and needs to be signed off by a dozen people. I didn't want to go through all the hassle, not for what was only a simple switch of timings."

"Maybe you thought it wouldn't be approved?" Sanjay asked.

"No, it wasn't that."

"I can understand if the Education Authority wasn't too happy about employees thinking they could ignore their schedules and just turn up where and when they wanted," Sanjay pursued.

"No, really, it's not an issue. Because of the type of work I do, I'm given a lot of latitude to be where and when I'm needed as long as I achieve the desired result. They get a good deal too. I put in considerably longer hours than I'm paid for," Kitson defended.

"That's hardly the point. Your bosses expect you to be where you're assigned or they'd have no control. Maybe it suits to allow some flexibility, but surely they'd expect you to report whenever you make changes. As a case in point, you didn't only change your schedule, you lied about it too. Why else would you have called in sick?" Sanjay asked.

Kitson became flustered. "I wasn't cheating. I only juggled my timetable, switching one day for another. As I had to be away early, it was more practical for me to leave from Eastfarm, and besides, I wanted to be there because I knew the writers' group would be performing their play and I wanted to see it."

"Oh yes? Maybe now we're getting closer to the truth." Sanjay looked at her quizzically. "Tell me more."

She bit her lip nervously, realising she'd said more than she'd intended. Kitson resumed talking slowly, trying to be cautious with her words. "I enjoy watching theatre of all types, whether amateur or professional. I heard the writers were going to be rehearsing and I wanted to take the opportunity to see them. They can be really entertaining; I've seen a lot of what they've done in the past."

"The entertainment didn't go quite as expected on Monday," Phil said.

Kitson looked down at the floor, not trusting herself to answer.

"And what did you make of the performance?" Sanjay continued.

"I didn't see much. I took in a trolley with tea and biscuits while they were rehearsing. What I saw looked very well done, but they stopped to have a break not long after I arrived. As I had no excuse to stay, I left before they restarted."

"Are you telling me you weren't there when the stabbing took place?" Sanjay enquired.

"That's right. It wasn't long after I left, maybe half an hour, certainly no more. I'd gone through to help out in the English department. Mr Grimes can verify if you like; I was with him and his class when the hullabaloo started."

"Did you see the knives?" Sanjay asked.

"Knives?" Kitson looked up.

"The ones used in the play," Sanjay said.

"Not that I can remember."

"It's hardly something you're likely to forget. Now come on, I need a more definite answer," Sanjay pushed.

"I've tried to think it all through. I have no conscious memory of seeing them. They must have been there but I didn't notice. No, I didn't see them."

"So, you knew there was more than one?" Sanjay asked.

"Yes, I've come across this type of prop in other productions."

"Thank you. Tell me more," Phil continued.

"Yes, I'm sure I must have. I've been involved in a lot of theatre work in the past. I've used all sorts of props. I will have seen similar, but I don't know the specifications of the knives in question to be able to say more."

Sanjay and Phil shared a questioning look, as if to confirm their mutual suspicions, before Phil continued. "Do you know any of the group's members?"

"I've met a couple of them."

"Who in particular and how well do you know them?" Sanjay asked.

"I've met several of them at performances, but we're no more than nodding acquaintances. However, I'm better acquainted with Graeme and Sheila."

"You're not telling us everything," Sanjay admonished.

Kitson's face was flushed and she appeared increasingly nervous. "I've met them several times, Sheila invited me to their house on one occasion."

"Okay, but isn't it true you're a lot closer to Graeme?" Sanjay had a hunch and thought he'd try his luck.

Tears ran down Kitson's cheeks and she raised her hands to cover her face. "How did you find out? Did Graeme tell you?"

"No, we haven't spoken to him on the subject yet. We suspected, but you just confirmed our suspicions," Sanjay replied. "Tell me about your relationship with him."

Kitson lowered her hands, her face was drawn and she seemed to have aged in the few minutes they'd been talking. "We've been friends for some time now. We met at the South Caledonian Amateur Players, it's an am-dram club we're both members of. Graeme's really into it, on the management side as well as performing. Sheila sometimes went along as well which was how we met. Sheila and I socialised together sometimes and got along really well."

"Was she aware of you and Graeme?" Sanjay asked.

"No, to start with we were all friends and there was nothing more to it. Then some months ago, Graeme and I were cast as lovers in a play. After the first rehearsal, he asked me out for a drink and told me he'd been the one to set up the whole thing because he wanted to get closer to me. He said he and Sheila had an open marriage, which wasn't really news to me as I'd seen what she could be like around men on more than one occasion. What's more, she'd hinted to me she was bisexual too, but seemed to back off when I showed no interest.

"On that first night, Graeme said he could book us a hotel room and suggested that if we could get closer to each other, then it would improve our performance. It was a really cheesy line, but it worked because I'd fancied him for some time. I thought he'd set me up for a one night stand, but I went along with it anyway. I expected he was only there for a quick shag and then he'd leave, but to my surprise, we spent the night together and we met regularly afterwards – once, sometimes twice a week. We discovered we loved each other and wanted to be together. Graeme promised he would leave Sheila and we could set up home together, but it never happened. There was always some reason why he couldn't tell her."

"So, Sheila wasn't told about the two of you?" Sanjay asked.

"I'm not so sure. I think Graeme may have said something, but he didn't have the courage to actually leave her. Sheila was different to me when we met. She never said anything, but she was a lot frostier, as if she tolerated my presence but didn't approve of it."

"Well, now that Sheila's dead, there's nothing to keep you apart," Sanjay stated, carefully looking for a reaction."

"I don't ...," Kitson stammered through a flood of tears. "I haven't heard from him since it happened. I tried calling and I left messages, but he hasn't called back."

"Now that you both may be under investigation, maybe he doesn't want to be associated with you anymore?" Phil enquired.

"No, he's not like that."

"Then maybe you think he had something more sinister to do with Sheila's death?" Sanjay asked.

"No, he couldn't."

"Oh really?" Sanjay said. "It seems awfully convenient if the two of you really wanted to be together and the only impediment was Sheila, and now she's been murdered."

Kitson froze, looking in turn from Sanjay to Phil. "No, no, it wasn't like that. Of course I wanted to be with Graeme and I wanted him to leave Sheila, but I had nothing to do with her death."

"So, are you telling me you think Graeme may have killed his wife?" Phil asked.

"Definitely not," Kitson blurted then paused considering her answer. "Graeme couldn't have killed her. He wouldn't hurt a fly. He's kind and loving and caring. Although he no longer loved her, he was still very fond of Sheila. He would never have hurt her."

"Well, if it wasn't Graeme, it must have been you," Phil countered.

"No," Kitson cried, shouting out the word. "It wasn't me either. It must have been someone else, someone who Sheila had annoyed or upset. She did have a tendency to rub people up the wrong way."

"So we've heard," Sanjay replied. "But it's still the case that no-one else had a stronger motive to see Sheila dead than you and Graeme. If you believe someone else was responsible, then you need to tell us who and why."

"If I knew, I'd tell you, but I don't have a clue who it could have been. I'm just sure it wasn't Graeme and it wasn't me."

"Why should we believe you?" Sanjay probed.

"Because it's the truth."

"Very convenient," Sanjay challenged. "You expect us to trust what you're telling us, but we already know that you're an accomplished liar and a cheat."

"What do you mean?" Kitson asked.

"You're a drama teacher and a professional actor. You've already admitted you lie to your employers whenever it suits because it's too much work to tell the truth. You're skilled at putting on an act, so we have no basis to accept anything you say to us. You're only telling us things that might help you and saying what you think we want to hear. The truth takes a very poor third place under these circumstances."

Kitson looked ready to start crying again but held back the tears, fearing any demonstrative display would be put down to another attempt of her trying to manipulate her audience.

"Truly, I haven't done anything wrong and neither has Graeme. It needs to have been someone else."

"We heard you the first time," Phil said.

"But there's nothing more I can tell you. Can I go now?" Kitson pleaded.

"No, it wouldn't be appropriate. For the moment, at least, you're the best suspect we have and we don't want you to be too far away. We're finished talking for just now, but we'll need to detain you for a bit longer while we make some further enquiries. It will give you some time to think; you might even come up with some useful information while you're waiting," Sanjay said.

"I think I ought to contact a solicitor," Kitson said.

"Yes, you're entitled to do that, and it's probably a good idea," Sanjay responded before walking out the room, followed by Phil.

Chapter 15

"Well done, lads," Alex greeted Sanjay and Phil as they left the room. "I was following the interview from the observation area and you've made some excellent progress. I've taken the liberty of sending Steve and Donny out to pick up Graeme Armstrong for a follow-up chat. After what we've learned from his girlfriend, he has an awful lot of explaining to do."

"Thanks, Boss," Sanjay replied. "Exactly what I had in mind."

"Yeah, well, there's more. Maybe we're getting all our Christmases at once, if you'll pardon the contra-multicultural expression. I had a word with Donny about what he'd actually been doing. He was rather contrite about the rollicking you gave him and was keen to prove he'd been working effectively."

"Really, has he actually stumbled onto something?" Sanjay asked.

Alex smiled but didn't comment. "He's been managing the enquiries into magic clubs, theatre groups, magicians and theatrical suppliers and, from what I can see, he's done a good job."

"You mean he has actually come up with something useful?" Sanjay asked.

"He was trying to find out who had knives like the ones used for the murder and he has made a lot of progress. It seems very few magicians use this type of prop as they prefer a different method. They use a single knife, it has a similar sort of retractable blade, but with a lock, so the blade can be held firm when demonstrating that it's a real knife. It has the advantage of being a single instrument but the disadvantage that whoever's using it needs to know what they're about to avoid accidents. The two-knife variety, which we're dealing with, is considered to be a lot safer but requires the act to be a bit more contrived so the blades can be switched."

"Well, it didn't turn out to be safer for Sheila Armstrong," Phil interrupted.

"When someone has sufficient motive, they'll find a way to use whatever tools they have to do the job. But getting back to what you've said, Boss, I suppose it means there'd be less of the double blade variety about than we might have previously expected and they'd be more likely to be used by theatres than magicians," Sanjay surmised.

"Precisely what I thought and, to be fair, so did Donny. He concentrated on theatre groups to ask if they used such a prop and if they owned their own. Where they did, he enquired if it could be properly accounted for at the time of Sheila's death. Several didn't understand what he was talking about, a few did but didn't have their own props. Very few actually had one of their own and even less maintained proper records. In the end, there were only two which really stood out. One's a group in North Kelvinside who confirmed that they own one set, but don't keep good enough records to be certain if they still have them, nor do they have the first idea where they might be or who might have borrowed them. They said they'd make enquiries and come back to him, but at this point in time, we have no idea. The second is far more interesting. They're a very professional club and keep impeccable records with every item having to be signed out and back in. Their stock accounts show they ought to have a set of knives, which 'coincidentally' are the same generation as the ones we're looking for. Donny found out who their supplier was and checked it out with Top Hat. Each batch with the same number has one hundred sets of knives. With the particular batch in question, only eight were sold into the U.K., two of which went through this one supplier. In any event, the knives are missing. No-one signed them out and no-one could tell him where they are." Alex smiled, holding them in suspense.

"And?" Sanjay pressed, realising the best was yet to come.

"And this group is the South Caledonian Amateur Players, the very same group Yvonne and Graeme are members of," Alex announced.

"It's all circumstantial, but even so, it's really damning," Sanjay stated.

Phil burst out laughing and they each stared at him questioningly. "Have you worked out the acronym? South Caledonian Amateur Players. S.C.A.P. Perhaps they're not really guilty but just the SCAPe goats?"

"Maybe it should be Members and not Players," Sanjay joked. "That way the whole thing would be a SCAM."

"Very droll," Alex replied. "Anyway, you've quite a lot to work with. I'd like to sit in on the interview with Graeme, but in the meantime, I'll give Sandra a ring and see if she's getting anywhere with her cases."

* * *

"Hello, Love, how are you getting on?" Alex asked.

They each exchanged news of their successful mornings, enthusiastically sharing their contentment at the advances they'd respectively made.

"Have you seen this evening's paper?" Sandra enquired.

"Is it that time already? No, I try to avoid the media unless necessary. It's too depressing to hear the amateurs, who don't have a real clue about what's going on, lecture the world about what a terrible job I'm doing."

"You shouldn't take it so personally," Sandra replied. "Sometimes they can have their uses. Anyhow, in today's issue, we're sharing the front page."

"What! Good God, what are they saying?"

"It's not all bad, Alex. They're headlining the number of suspicious deaths hitting Glasgow and they have a special column devoted to you. They mentioned the previously reported death of famous author Sheila Armstrong having progressed from being considered a terrible accident to something more sinister. The usual hackneyed expressions about her death matching the mystery of her writing, truth stranger than fiction and such-like. They obviously haven't done enough research to check she writes Romances and not Thrillers but, in any event, it should turn her into a posthumous bestseller. Because they've picked up on it being you and your team investigating, they've jumped to the conclusion it must be murder. Full of speculation and a bit light on the facts."

"Nothing unexpected then," Alex commented. "You said we were both featured. What have they got on you?"

"They were quick off the mark on this one. They've a photo of me amongst the huddle of investigators at the scene in Erskine this morning. The body's not shown, fortunately enough, or they'd have put their readers off their tea, but they have commented saying he'd been identified as petty criminal, Patrick Carson. The rest is all conjecture.

"Further on in the paper, there are items on the two incidents at the Court and the usual criticism about how safe the streets are if the authorities can't prevent crime on their own home turf. No different to what we'd expected and, if anything, a bit later and less critical than we might have predicted."

"Who knows, maybe the top brass have called in some favours," Alex postulated. "Back to business, though. Have you any leads to try to track down Devosky?"

"He really doesn't want to be found. We can't be certain he's still in Glasgow. We're following all the usual paths, but so far, it's drawing a blank. I've got the techies trying to do a trace on his mobile and I'm about to go down to see if they've come up with anything. Hang on a sec, Peter's signalling me, looks like something urgent, I'd better go."

"Okay, I'll leave you to it. Good luck. See you back at the flat, sometime I guess."

* * *

"What's happening?" Sandra asked.

"We've got a problem, a really serious one," Peter replied.

"Why? What is it?"

"We may have just come up with a motive for the robbery at the Court."

"I don't like riddles, Peter. Out with it, what are you talking about?"

"We've received word about a case being tried today. The defence lawyer made a special request for a dismissal. The claim was based on his allegation of there being improper custody of evidence. He cited the robbery in the cash office with armed robbers looting the safe which held the trial evidence."

"Is it true? Was evidence kept in the same safe?" Sandra asked.

"Apparently, although there'd been no report of anything going missing or being tampered with. The fiscal nearly blew his stack. He demanded the defence lawyer told him where he had got his information. He all but accused him of being part of, or even orchestrating the crime so he could get his client off. The Sheriff wasn't amused. He told the fiscal to withdraw his accusation or he'd face a charge of Contempt."

"Bloody Hell! What happened about the trial?" Sandra asked.

The Sheriff called an adjournment. He asked for a full report on all and any evidence which had been held in the safe before the robbery, together with an inventory of what was there afterwards. It turns out all but one of the items is accounted for. The one from the case held today was exactly where it should have been. The missing item was fairly trivial as it was one of many which relates to a breaking-and-entering trial scheduled for next week. However, the fiscal's shit-scared the Sheriff could rule there's been a breach of integrity and disqualify every item that had been in the safe at the time. If that happens, there could be as many as thirty cases affected and the loss of usable evidence could be critical."

"Did the lawyer or his client have any connection to Zennick or Devosky?" Sandra asked hopefully.

"Nothing obvious. The case appears totally unrelated, although there are two known associates of theirs due to be tried over the next few days and their trials are amongst the thirty which could potentially be dismissed.

"The lawyer claimed he'd received a text advising him of the evidence trail problem and suggesting he might want to make use of it. I reckon Zennick has been behind it, as we'd already suspected, and that he's used this lawyer as a stooge to do his work for him. If he gets a result, then Zennick's men will almost certainly go free."

"Damn, damn, damn," Sandra swore. "Why didn't I see it? I knew the robbery didn't make sense in its own right. I suspected there had to be another motive. Why didn't I check the safe contents more thoroughly? I should have realised. If only I'd worked it out, we could have done all the checking first and mitigated any damage."

"Don't beat yourself up over it," Peter replied. "No-one else saw it coming either, and anyhow, you wouldn't have been able to do much anyway. Besides anything else, after the attack on Hardy, most of your attention was diverted in that direction and as from this morning, even more so onto Carson's death."

"You're being very kind, but it doesn't alter the facts. I should have done better. However, we are where we are and need to go forward from here. Let's see how cooperative this lawyer really is. If he did get a text to tip him off, then we need to find out where it came from."

"It's worth a try. The last I heard, he was leaving court and going back to his office. We ought to be able to find him there. His name is Pryce and he has a suite in one of the buildings in St Vincent Street, near Charing Cross."

Thirty minutes later, Sandra and Peter alighted from the elevator on the fifth floor and introduced themselves at Pryce's reception.

The receptionist looked to have stepped out of an earlier era. She was a matronly lady, dressed in a medium-length, black dress, her grey hair tied back in a bun, and she wore two strings of perfect-looking pearls around her neck.

"I guess he's won his bet then," she uttered quietly as if speaking to herself.

"Pardon, bet did you say?" Sandra asked,

"Yes, he was only joking but he said you'd be round within the hour. When I say 'you,' he wasn't specific, but he did predict a visit by two officers, and here you are."

"Can we go through now?" Sandra asked.

"No, wait, I'll buzz through and see if he's free to meet you."

"I thought you said he was expecting us," Peter queried.

"He is, but that doesn't mean he has the time to sit around waiting. He's busy working. You'll need to wait until he's free."

Peter was ready to resume his challenge but Sandra gave him a sharp look and diverted him to a chair in the waiting area. It was a full fifteen minutes before they were shown through to Pryce's office.

"Inspector, Constable, please come in and sit down."

"I believe you already know why we're here," Sandra started. "Time is short and we're all very busy, so I'll dispense with pleasantries and come straight to the point. I understand you received a text suggesting you raised the issue in court about the chain of evidence. We need you to tell us who sent it."

Pryce smiled slowly. "And why do you think I'd want to help you? The person who provided the information did me a favour. My client believes I'm a miracle worker."

"You may be a solicitor, but you're a law-abiding citizen as far as I'm aware. Whoever sent you the message must have had a close association with the armed robbery; furthermore, them sending you the text is a clear case of Perverting the Course of Justice. I doubt you want to be involved in a criminal prosecution sitting at the defence table and not in your role as a lawyer," Sandra offered.

"Any communication between a lawyer and his client is privileged," he replied.

"That's not a relevant argument unless he is your client and was at the time of the communication," Sandra retorted.

"You're right; however, I still can't help you. Before you ask, I'm not withholding evidence. I don't have any to withhold."

"What about the phone?" Sandra asked.

"Look for yourself. Here's the log. It shows the text came in as an undisclosed number," he offered.

"Yes, I see that," Sandra acknowledged. "Now can I take note of your number and service provider so we can try another route?"

"Be my guest," Pryce offered and supplied the requested information.

"Is there anything else you can tell us?"

"No, I'm afraid not."

"And you've had no previous contact?"

"Not that I'm aware of. It's difficult to tell when I don't know where it came from."

"How did they get your mobile number?"

"It's no secret; it's on my letterhead and my business card. Anyone could have found it."

"Why do you think they chose you?" Sandra asked.

"I have no idea. But I'm not ungrateful," Pryce replied. "My client doesn't have a strong defence, but without use of their evidence the prosecution doesn't have much of a case. I was hardly going to look a gift horse in the mouth."

"Isn't your job supposed to be about getting justice for your client?" Peter asked.

"Ho, ho, ho," Pryce laughed theatrically. "What idealistic planet did you descend from? Are you really that naïve? My 'job,' as you put it, is to use every legal device and tool available to me to secure a 'not guilty' verdict for my client, whoever he is."

"But don't you have a conscience? How do you feel knowing you sometimes help criminals keep their freedom?" Peter continued, undaunted.

"It's not my problem. If a client of mine is guilty, then it's your job and the fiscal's to find and present evidence to prove the fact and secure a conviction. If that's beyond your capability, then it's your failing and not mine."

Sandra knew he was correct but wasn't prepared to give him the satisfaction of acknowledging it. "In the case of your client, we have done precisely that, and you've already accepted that to be the case. If it wasn't for one of your friends criminally tampering with evidence, your client would have been tried and sentenced by now."

Pryce smiled and shrugged. "He may have done me a favour, but he wasn't a friend of mine. If you really thought he was, then you'd hardly be leaving me in peace to enjoy my liberty. So, if there's nothing else?" Pryce stood and beckoned them towards the door.

Sandra and Peter silently left the building. Although neither one had expected any different, they inwardly raged at Pryce's complacency.

Once back in the office, Sandra collapsed into her chair. She was tired. A restless night followed by an early start had taken its toll. A pile of reports sat in front of her and she was anxious to scan them, hopeful of finding a new lead or at least some development, but she couldn't face it straight away.

She closed her eyes for a moment's respite only to be roused by a sense of movement very close.

"Sorry, Mam, didn't mean to startle you. I thought you could do with this," Peter announced, pointing to the freshly brewed mug of tea he'd placed in front of her.

Sandra blinked a couple of times bringing her vision into focus, "Thanks, just what the doctor ordered. I'm going to have to keep you around, I'm getting used to having a P.A."

"All part of the service," Peter smirked. "Have you found anything interesting?"

"I've not been able to check them yet. Pull up a chair and we can split the task."

Time passed as they each worked through the paperwork, intermittently broken by expressions of interest or consternation together with scribbling on notepads.

"Okay, there appears to be a pattern," Sandra said. "The ones I have here match up quite well. I have a reported disturbance on Tuesday night on the riverside, not far from the Finnieston Crane. There seems to have been a group of youngsters up to no good and reportedly something was thrown into the water. There are a number of different statements which don't match exactly, but close enough to sound promising. The bottom line is, somewhere between three and six lads wearing hoodies were apparently scuffling with an older man. Big splash and then the boys legged it with no further report of the adult. Tuesday was the day Hardy was attacked and the last time Carson was seen or heard of. It also ties in with time of death from the M.E. What we need to do next is get someone to check the reports we have on currents and tides. We need to see if it's consistent for a body being dropped in the Clyde at Finnieston on Tuesday night and coming ashore at Erskine this morning. We also want to pull any CCTV footage to see if we can identify anyone. Check out if Constable Fitzpatrick's available. He was brilliant studying the films on a case I worked on with Alex a year or so ago. When it comes to this type of work, he'll always be my first choice if I can get him."

"Great, I'll get on to it in a moment," Peter replied. "But before I do, I think you'll want to see these. First, the bad news, there's been no activity on Devosky's mobile all week and traces to locate it haven't found anything either. They're going to try to search further afield, but even if we get a positive, it doesn't mean we'll find him in the same place as the phone. The number Gilchrist called him on is more promising. The account's been active with calls made to numbers in Scotland and England, also internet activity on Facebook and a gambling website. It's located near Glasgow, mostly in and around the Greenock area. No-one's tried calling it yet as they didn't want to risk tipping him off. On the downside, I suspect it hasn't been Devosky, but it could be someone who can take us closer."

"I agree. Let's pinpoint where it is before doing anything else."

"Okay, will do. Now I've saved the best 'til last. We've pulled everything on active hoodie gangs and we've a prime contender. It's a group of lads from Castlemilk: two are from the Valley, the other three from the Dougrie Road area. They all have form, but nothing serious. Some car crime, some petty theft, a couple of assaults, carrying concealed weapons, but nothing where firearms were used."

"You said 'the best,' – that didn't sound too impressive," Sandra said.

"You're too impatient. They have a known associate, a sixteen-year-old by the name of Kevin Speirs, a kid from a wealthy family. He lives in Clarkston and goes to Eastfarm School. Wait for it, he's in the habit of wearing a Hugo Boss hoodie. The kid's got no record, but by all accounts he's pretty much out of control. There was an incident a few months back where he allegedly took a firearm into a youth club, but it was all hushed up. No-one was prepared to give evidence and it's understood his father bought off anyone who knew anything and the authorities had nothing to work with."

"Okay, I get your point now. Sounds very promising. Eastfarm's the school Alex's boys go to and it's where Sheila Armstrong was murdered. It would be too much of a coincidence for Speirs to have any connection there, but we'd better check, just in case. I'll speak to Alex too because we don't want to get under each other's feet."

Chapter 16

"Alex, we need to talk,"

"That's a very intimidating way to start a conversation," Alex replied.

"I'm sorry, Love. My head's full of this case – cases, actually. I should have thought to ask first how you were and how your day has been. It's because we've built up a head of steam and I was trying not to lose momentum. I wasn't thinking. Can you forgive me?"

Alex chuckled. "Of course, but a word of advice if I may. Stay calm and don't stress yourself. If you're making good progress, then there's no reason for it to change. It's far more important to keep everything under control to make sure you don't miss anything relevant. Now, what was it you wanted to ask me?"

"Don't worry, I'm not getting carried away, at least I don't think so. I'm just being a bit over-enthusiastic. I want to hear about your day, but first I'd like to tell you about some developments which overlap our cases and see how we can best handle them and help each other."

Sandra continued to explain about what she'd found and, in particular, her concerns about Kevin Speirs.

"I can't see him having any impact on our investigation, but it's a loose end and he needs to be checked. You continue the same as you've been doing, but I'll have a word with Brian Phelps and see what he can tell me or what might be on school records, on an unofficial basis. There's also one of my informants I'd like to sound out. He's an ex-con who keeps his ear to the ground. I can't put you on to him as he'll only talk to me, but I'll pass along anything I pick up for you to take forward."

"I'd appreciate anything you can do to help. We're badly understaffed. I've asked for reinforcements, but with so many people off sick at the moment, I doubt if it'll come to anything," Sandra said.

"Well, I don't want to tempt providence but we've had a bit of a break on this one. I hope if our luck holds then we might have a result before too long. If that happens and if I'm not assigned anything else significant, then you might be able to poach some of my team for a while."

"I'd like to take you up on that, just as long as you don't dump Donny on me on one of his lazier days."

"Don't be too quick putting him down. I'll be the first to admit he can be an awkward sod anytime he can get away with it, but he's been quite effective today and provided some research which could be crucial," Alex said.

"You may be right and I recognise he does have ability, but he's more responsive to you. As you're already well aware, he's not happy working for a female, or anyone who's not male, white, Anglo-Saxon and Protestant for that matter. To go with any of his other failings, he's a racist, misogynistic bigot."

"I won't argue the point. But right now, I'd better press on and we can talk later," Alex concluded.

For the second time in one afternoon, Alex called Brian, and this time he got straight through.

"It's always a pleasure, Alex, but it's starting to become a bit of a habit. Did you forget something or are you on to give me some nice, juicy titbit?"

"Neither, it's something new and I'm being a message boy for Sandra, most like, but what can you tell me about Kevin Speirs?"

Alex heard a deep intake of breath before Brian replied, "What's the wee bastard done now? For the last couple of years, that one's been the bane of my life."

"Tell me more. If he's as bad as you're suggesting, how come you've never mentioned him before? In fact, how come I haven't heard his name come up from my own people?"

"I've not had any reason to discuss him. True, he's nothing but trouble, and always has been, but we haven't ever had cause or evidence to turn it into a police matter. Any time we've come close, his father's intervened, complaining about us being heavy-handed and pulling strings at a high level. It's left us fighting a rear-guard action."

"Who's the father?"

"Mr Speirs, what did you expect?"

"Very funny, Brian, your sense of humour hasn't improved. Now quit the clowning and tell me something meaningful. How come he's got clout?"

"Sorry, Alex, I couldn't resist it, particularly as you were being so serious. The whole story is that Kevin's an only child and brought up by his mother. The parents separated when he was a toddler. She has her own problems, depression and nerves I've heard, and she can't cope. As a result, Kevin has almost total freedom to do what he wants and takes full advantage. Of course, his behaviour has a negative effect on the mother, which becomes a vicious circle with him behaving more and more outrageously. His father's a businessman, I'm told, very wealthy and with influential friends. I say friends, but according to rumour, he's more of a puppet-master. His name's Richard Speirs and he's alleged to pull the strings of quite a few politicians, including members of the Education Board. He hardly ever sees the boy and showers money on him instead of attention. He doesn't and never has exerted any discipline, and what we're left with is an out-of-control kid. He doesn't believe any of the rules apply to him, and whenever he comes close to being caught, Big Daddy steps out of the shadows and bails him out."

"And what sort of misdemeanours have you been unable to pin on him?"

"Nothing's ever been pinned on him, but we know he's guilty of all the usual things: bullying, petty theft, intimidation, assault and, of course, swearing and smoking are a given. We've often had complaints, but then any witnesses seem to have memory lapses and can't remember seeing anything. That's not just the kids; it's teaching staff as well."

"Why was it never reported to us?" Alex asked.

"There was no point. The complainant had usually withdrawn their statement and there was no-one or nothing to corroborate the incident."

"I understand, but our people are far more experienced at finding out the truth and extracting evidence where it's needed."

"We had nothing to give you and we had old man Speirs, or his lackeys, breathing down our necks."

"Okay Brian, I'm not having a go at you; I'm just frustrated that all this has been going on without us having the chance to do anything about it. What about friends? Who does he associate with?"

"He doesn't. There used to be some lads he hung around with, but that was a couple of years back before Kevin became as radical. No doubt he scared them away. There isn't anyone we'd consider his friend, not within the school. He quite often has some of the junior pupils running his errands for him, but I doubt it's out of friendship; more likely, it's out of fear or else he's paying them. I've heard stories he associates with some other lads from outside of the district. They've been spotted meeting up at the school gates on occasions."

"Do you know who they are?"

"I'm afraid not. I can put out some feelers if you like."

"Yes, please. Now, you said they meet at the gates. Does that mean he's a diligent pupil?"

"It's not how I'd describe him. He's intelligent enough and he's very good at English; a gifted writer, actually, but he chooses if and when he's prepared to make any effort. If it's something he likes or wants to do, then he's filled with enthusiasm and very often excels. However, when it's not what he wants to do, he makes no effort and very often doesn't even turn up."

"You said he liked writing," Alex said. "Did he have any connection with the writing group?"

"Now you mention it, yes. The group judges our short story competition and Kevin was the winner last year."

"Really, did he have any interaction with Sheila Armstrong?"

Brian thought for several seconds. "With the competitions, the entries are made using code names so the judges have no idea whose work they're evaluating. However, once the judging has been done, members of the writing group come in to the prize-giving. They read out their critique and they award the prizes. It was Sheila who did it last year. She must have met Kevin."

"And did they meet at any other time?"

"Not as far as the school was concerned, but I couldn't tell you about anything out-with."

"If you're going to do some fishing anyway, see if you can find out if anyone else has any useful information. Witnesses, hearsay or rumours, I'll take the lot and then try to sort the wheat from the chaff."

"Okay, Alex, I'll see what I can do."

Before the receiver reached the rest, Alex started yelling instructions to Phil. He wanted every record pulled and every piece of information searched to find anything they could about Richard Speirs. Not waiting for a response, he picked up his car keys and was out the door within seconds.

Twenty minutes later, he drew to a halt in the car-park of a Lidl supermarket in Pollocksheilds. He locked his vehicle and walked for a short distance, past the Shawbridge Arcade, then he stepped through the door of a traditional watering hole. It was a compact pub with a long timber bar. Although clean and fresh, it had the feeling of an old-style, spit and sawdust, working man's pub. Indeed, had it not been for the wall-mounted, wide-screen television, permanently tuned to Sky Sports, it could have been transferred straight out of the nineteen-forties. Alex quickly scanned the room and found his target sitting at a booth in the corner – a small man with rat-like features. Even though he was indoors, he was wearing a cap and a fawn coloured trench-coat buttoned up to the neck. A quarter-full, pint-sized, glass tankard was in his hand containing bright orange liquid.

Pleased to see he was sitting alone, Alex sidled into the booth and moved close, leaning over to whisper in his ear, "Hello, Shuggie, long time no see."

The man had been half-asleep and jumped, roused by the interruption. "It's you, Mr Warren. What are you wanting?"

"Now come on, Shuggie, you don't sound very happy to see me. You needn't get upset, it's not you I'm after."

"It wouldn't matter if it was. I've done nothing wrong, so there's nothing you can get me for," he answered defiantly. "I've made my mistakes over the years, but I've served my time and all I want now is a quiet life."

"Let me get you a top-up, Shuggie. What are you on?"

"Very kind of you, Mr Warren. I'll have another orange juice and soda," he replied and drained the remaining liquid from his glass.

"You don't want a chaser to go with it?" Alex offered.

"No thanks, I've been off the hard stuff for a good while now. In fact, no alcohol has passed my lips for close on four years and I'm healthier for it."

"Well, how come you spend every afternoon of your life in a pub?"

Shuggie shrugged. "Where else is there for me to go? I know most of the folk that come in here. I come here for the companionship. We meet here to discuss what's happening and watch whatever game's on the box," Shuggie said, indicating towards the big screen.

"Well, although you hardly ever leave this place, you somehow seem to hear a lot about what's going on, so I'm here to find out what you know."

Shuggie raised his eyebrows. "And precisely what do you want me to tell you?"

"If I knew precisely that, then I wouldn't need to ask," Alex answered cryptically. "On a more serious note, I want to hear anything you can tell me about a young lad from Clarkston, his name's Kevin Speirs."

Shuggie sat impassively until Alex reached into his pocket, unfurled a twenty pound note and placed it on the table. He snatched the money at lightning speed then began, speaking in hushed tones, "I've heard of him, Mr Warren, but I've no wish to meet him. He's a nasty piece of work from all accounts. He's done some muggings. I've heard some stories that he and a couple of mates go about the town when the pubs come out and pick on anyone they think is, let's say, 'under the influence.' They don't just take money though. They give the poor sods a good kicking as well. They've also picked on beggars, rolled them over and taken anything they could."

"How come we've not had any reports?"

"Come on, Mr Warren, most of the beggars are illegals, or of the few that aren't, many have no reason to be begging in the first place. The police are hardly going to be their first port of call even if they do have a legitimate reason for complaint. As for the drunks, someone turning up at A&E complaining about being ripped off, when they were too steamin' to tell them what had happened, wouldn't be given top priority by your lads."

"Yes, that's a fair comment," Alex answered. "But there has to be more to it."

"Yeah, maybe that's the more interesting bit. He's still just a kid and he and his mates have been treading on other people's toes but nothing's been done about it. I can't be sure of the reason, but it's reckoned someone's bought off the opposition, paid for him to be given space, something like that."

"And do you have any idea of who?" Alex asked.

"Not exactly, but there's some talk he's involved with an Eastern European unit."

"Now we're getting somewhere. Tell me more."

"There isn't any more. There may be nothing to it. I don't know anything else and I don't want to. I don't need to tell you what it's like with these people. They don't have any rules. They'd stick a knife in you as soon look at you. You don't get involved, not if you want a long and happy life. You certainly don't talk about anything they do and, if anyone else is stupid enough to, then you don't listen."

Okay, Shuggie. Can you tell me anything about young Kevin's old man? His name's Richard Speirs."

Shuggie mused over the name, repeating it to himself a few times. His nose twitched, increasing his rat-like expression, then shook his head. "The name means nothing, that's it, Mr Warren, I don't know any more. Richard Speirs doesn't ring any bells."

"It's a start," Alex replied. "Okay, thanks anyway," Alex stood and lifted a card from his wallet and slipped it across the table accompanied by a ten pound note. "Here, take this. If you think of something else or if you hear anything, anything at all about Kevin or Richard Speirs, then I want to know, and I'll make it worth your while."

Alex was feeling exhausted as he walked back to collect his car. It was a good exhaustion; he felt he'd achieved a great deal but he felt physically drained. He remembered he'd sent Steve and Donny to bring Graeme in for questioning and he'd told Sanjay he wanted to be present. Alex rushed back to the office, hoping he hadn't held anyone back by his absence.

More by good fortune than judgement, he arrived at the same time as Graeme was being escorted towards an interview room.

Chapter 17

Opening her email, Sandra examined an item newly in from the M.E. It was his preliminary report and she confirmed the findings were consistent with the initial indications. Water was in Carson's lungs and the cause of death was drowning. There was a severe gash to the back of his head and considerable bruising to the torso. The report made it clear that the injuries had been sustained prior to death and they would almost certainly have completely incapacitated the victim. The head wound was profound and, left unattended, it would likely have led to death, but in this instance it hadn't killed him. Being immersed unconscious in the flowing waters of the Clyde had taken its toll first. The overall impression corroborated the theory of Carson taking a beating on the Tuesday evening, then being dumped in the water to drown, with his body washing ashore where he had been found that morning.

'My God, that was only this morning,' she thought. 'It feels like a week away. Only a few days ago, Alex and I were lazing on a Mediterranean beach, now look at us,' she mused. 'Two murders, a serious assault and an armed robbery to deal with, not to mention a baby on the way.' She smiled openly at the thought of her pregnancy.

"Is that some good news for a change?" Peter asked, seeing her apparently looking at the screen with a happy expression.

Sandra quickly brought her thoughts back to the here and now.

"We need to pin down these hoodies," she replied, avoiding the question. "I want to hold off going after Speirs until we have some more to go on. Have you found out anything for me?"

"Working from our database, I've pulled out all the likely suspects who're the right age group and type and have a link to the Castlemilk area. To start with, we want to talk to these two." Peter handed her a sheet of paper with the profiles of two brothers, Sean and Thomas McGuire, aged seventeen and fifteen respectively.

Sandra cast her eye over the document. "Bring them in," she instructed, "and send two cars, I want them kept apart."

"Would it not be easier to go out to them?" Peter enquired.

"Easier, yes, but less effective. I'd like them picked up and brought in, before they see us or find out any details of what it's all about. It'll give them a chance to sweat a little before we start. Reading between the lines of what's in your summary, they're pretty full of themselves, the younger one in particular. I'd like to shake that confidence a bit, and having the discussion on our home territory and not theirs is a good start. Just to be on the safe side, have an appropriate adult in attendance. I don't want to risk any a claims of coercion."

"Righto, Ma'am, I'll get it organised. The only problem might be finding them. This time of day they could be anywhere and up to any sort of mischief."

"Just do what you can. The sooner the better."

It was three hours before the McGuire boys were tracked down and persuaded 'to help the police with their enquiries.'

"Let's start with the young one, Thomas, isn't it?" Sandra asked.

"That's right, we have him in room four," Peter replied.

Sandra walked into the room, started the recorder then introduced herself and Peter and explained his rights. "Do you understand what I've just said?" she asked.

"Yeh, perfectly clear, but I'd like my brother to sit wi' me."

"I'm afraid that won't be possible. We have questions to ask him too, so my answer has to be no. You are entitled to have an adult present. We can bring in one of your parents if you'd like."

"You'd be lucky, you wilnae get them out o' the pub at this time."

"We can arrange for another relative, a teacher, or an approved responsible adult or a solicitor if you'd prefer," Sandra offered.

"Nah, I dinnae want some stranger listenin' in. It's either Sean or no-one."

"Well, it can't be Sean, as I've already explained," Sandra repeated

"So, it'll be no-one then," Thomas said smugly.

"Now we'd like to ask you some questions," she started.

Thomas leaned back in his chair and placed his hands behind his head leisurely. "I don't need to say anythin', you've already telt me."

Sandra exhaled heavily, unable to hide her frustration. "You are correct that you don't need to say anything, but if you've done nothing wrong, then why not help us. Even if you have done something wrong, then any cooperation you give us will be taken into account when we decide what happens next."

"Ha Ha. You must think my heid buttons up at the back if you believe I'll do anythin' to help you stitch me up."

Sandra suppressed a smile, aware of the boy's mixed metaphors. "You've been watching too many bad movies and TV programmes. We're investigating a series of crimes and we're looking for information to help us to understand what's actually happened."

"Aye, right. You just keep talkin' and I'll just keep listenin'. I'll tell you nothin'. Now if you let Sean sit in wi' me, maybe I'll think again."

Sandra realised she'd get nothing from him as things stood, but wondered if he might be less uncooperative if left for a while. She indicated to Peter to leave the room and instructed a P.C. to remain in attendance. "I'll be back to see you in a short while," she said, moments before the door closed.

"A right tough wee bugger," Peter said, once they were on their own.

"He is that. He seemed awfully keen to be with his big brother and I don't reckon it was anything to do with his own lack of self-confidence. It's more likely he's afraid of what Sean might tell us and he wanted to warn him off first. Let's try working on Sean. You never know, we might hit it lucky."

They walked a few yards and entered another interview room. They went through the same process of introduction, but not before realising they were dealing with a completely different animal. Sean was much taller and broader than his younger brother. Lank, thin, bleached-blonde hair sprouted from his head and his face had a dark uneven shadow showing he had yet to master the art of shaving. He had a crumpled look and appeared in age to be well in excess of his teenage years. He sat with his arms crossed and his feet together on the floor, legs rigid, gently swaying back and forward, his eyes darting around the room nervously.

He seemed almost relieved when Sandra and Peter entered the room, anxious to get whatever was to happen over and done with.

"Okay, Sean, I've explained your rights, are you happy to keep talking to me?" Sandra opened.

"Aye, aye, whatever."

Sandra glanced at Peter and gave a barely imperceptible nod. Her normal interview technique was first to try and put her suspect at ease hoping to eke out the information she wanted. However, seeing Sean's anxiousness, she thought it better to go straight in hoping to give him the opportunity of unburdening himself.

"We understand you know Kevin Speirs," Sandra stated

"Aye, that's right, he's one o' my mates."

"And you've spent quite a bit of time with him this week."

"Well ..." Sean became pensive.

"We'd like you to tell us where you were on Monday afternoon around 2.00pm," she continued.

"I was at school."

"And 11am on Tuesday morning."

"Same thing."

"It's not what your school records show," Sandra asserted. She hadn't pre-checked, but took the chance making her challenge.

Sean looked panicked. "Kev said he'd sort it," he blurted.

"Kevin would sort what?" Sandra asked.

"Oh shit, shit, shit," he mumbled looking down at the floor, his whole body trembling.

"What is it Sean?" Sandra asked gently.

"I cannae say anythin' else."

"What is it? What are you afraid of?"

"I cannae say. He'll give me a good kickin' for sayin' anythin'."

"Who, Kevin?" Sandra asked

Sean sat rigid but Sandra saw a slight nod of his head.

"You don't need to worry about Kevin. With what we have on him, he'll be going away for a long period of time. He won't be able to hurt you."

Sean looked up, his eyes were watery. "But how? He said he'd take care o' everythin' and nobody would ever be able to get anythin' on him."

"Because he said it doesn't make it true. You don't need to be afraid of him," Sandra replied. She was treading a dangerous path knowing what she'd told Sean had no substance, but realising it was what he needed to hear for him to trust her.

"I did what Kevin telt me. I registered into school each day and then skipped out to meet him. He telt me it would be okay."

"Was Tommy there with you too?"

Sean nodded.

"And the three of you went to the Sheriff Court," Sandra prompted.

"Aye. You know about that?"

"You'd be surprised what we know," Sandra answered honestly, thinking in truth the reverse was more accurate.

"And Kevin brought the weapon," Sandra again prompted.

"I never saw it, but Tommy telt me about it. Kevin said for me to wait around by the Theatre on Gorbals Street. He said he might need me later, then he went away with Tommy. I was just standin' about. It was really borin' 'cos they were away for nearly an hour. They were laughin' and gigglin' when they came back and Kev gave me a tenner."

"Do you know where they'd been?" Sandra asked.

"I'm no' sure exactly, but it was somethin' to do with the Court."

"Did they not tell you any more about it?" Sandra pressed. "Maybe they mentioned a name or said what they were doing or why."

Sean's expression was blank. "Nah, nothin' I can think of. They were laughin' when they came back though. They were very happy."

"What happened then?"

"We went for a walk, ended up at Macdonald's. Kevin bought the food; he got me a Big Mac meal. I wanted to pay for my own. It wisnae fair for him to pay when he'd already given me money, but he insisted. It was a really good day."

"And was he still carrying his weapon?"

"I dinnae know."

"Let's move on to Tuesday. You met up with Tommy and Kevin again."

"Aye, that's right. There was someone else as well."

"Who was it?"

"I dinnae know. I hadn't seen him before and he didnae want to talk to me. He telt me to shut up whenever I asked anythin'."

"He wasn't someone from your school?"

"I dinnae think so."

"Okay, what happened this time?" Sandra asked.

"Kevin said we were going to play a game. He said he had somethin' planned. We all stood at the corner of the building and, when Kevin gave the word, we were to run forward an' follow him. We were to grab a man and make him run wi' us down the path."

"Is that what he said?" Sandra asked.

"Aye, it was. He said he wanted us to give him a fright."

"What actually happened?"

"Well, just like I said, Kevin said, 'Go,' and we all ran forward and rushed him away. It worked, he looked really scared. Then Kevin said to chuck him on the top of the wall. I lifted him and Kevin and this other boy pushed. The man was screamin' and then he disappeared. I think maybe he jumped over the other side to get away. Anyhow, Kevin said let's run and we ran away."

"What was Tommy doing?"

"Tommy was too wee to do much; he was wi' us at the start, but he stood back when we lifted the man up. I remember now, I dinnae know why, but I think he was callin' for us to stop."

"What happened then?" Sandra asked.

"Well, we ran over the bridge and into town. Tommy was annoyed about somethin' and said he had to talk to Kevin. They went away, leavin' me wi' the other boy, but he turned his heid whenever

I wanted to talk. Then Tommy and Kevin came back and we all went hame."

"What did Tommy say about what happened?"

"He telt me he didnae want to talk about what happened and I wisnae to say to anyone else. It was to be our secret. Aw naw, Tommy'll be angry; I've spoilt the secret."

"It's okay, Sean. What you've told us is very good. It's not the sort of secret that you're meant to keep. Now tell me, did you go out with Tommy and Kevin that evening?"

"Aye."

"And what happened?"

"I've no' to say." Sean pursed his lips and looked adamant.

"You went down by the river, didn't you?"

Sean looked up, surprised, his involuntarily nod confirming the answer, but kept his lips tight closed."

"It's okay, Sean, you don't need to say anything because we've already got it worked out. I'm going to tell you what I think happened and I want you to nod your head if I'm right. Would that be okay?"

Sean nodded.

"You met up with some other boys." Sean nodded again.

"Then Kevin said you were to give someone else a fright."

"Na, it wisnae Kevin, it was Tommy." The words were out before Sean realised, and a panicked look went across his eyes as he clamped his hands over his mouth.

"It's okay, Sean. I got it wrong and you corrected me. You're doing very well. Now, after Tommy explained what you were going to do, you all grabbed a man. It was a man that had been at the Court earlier on, wasn't it. Not the same one who was on the wall but one who'd been with him."

Sean nodded enthusiastically.

"When you found him, he was given a bit a beating." Sean nodded sombrely.

"Then someone walloped him on the head." Another nod.

"Was it Tommy who hit him?" Sean shook his head.

"It was Kevin then." Sean indicated agreement.

"Was it Kevin's idea to drop him in the river? Sean nodded and smiled.

"There must have been a big splash." Sean nodded again, enthusiastically.

"Then you all split up and went home." Nod.

"Did you know any of the other boys?" Sean indicated a negative.

"Then Tommy told you it was all to be a secret and you weren't to say anything. What reason did he give when he said you mustn't talk about it?"

"He said we'd done a bad thing and we had to say nothin' so it'd go away."

"And did Kevin say anything about it?"

"No, he wisnae there after we split up. Tommy said we wouldnae see him again, not for a lang time."

"Thank you, Sean. What you've told us is very important. You've done very well. We're going to go now and I'm going to ask someone to bring in some photos for you to look at. They'll tell you more about it, but I want you to tell them if you see anyone who was with you on Tuesday, either the other boy at the Court or any of the people who were with you at the river. I'll see you later."

When they stepped out of the room, Sandra breathed an enormous sigh.

"That was amazing," Peter stated. "You've cracked all three cases."

"Not quite," Sandra replied. "We now understand what happened and we can try and use what he's told us to find out more, but none of the evidence is admissible. I didn't realise in advance that he had learning difficulties and by the time I was sure, we were already in the middle of things and there was no point stopping. By rights, I should have stopped as soon as I realised. We shouldn't have been interviewing him on his own. We should have made sure he had a family member or an advisor or a lawyer, but in any event, nothing he's said can be used in a court of law."

"But you read him his rights and repeated several times telling him he didn't need to answer the questions."

"I'm afraid that isn't the point, as any good lawyer can argue that he didn't have the mental capacity to understand the question being asked or the consequences of giving the answers he did. What we can do is use what he's told us to try to draw out information, or even better still a confession, from Tommy or from Kevin."

Chapter 18

Sanjay joined Alex in his office planning their interview with Graeme Armstrong when Phil knocked on the door and called in, "You're going to want to see this."

Alex invited him in and Phil passed over a report, but not content to leave it to be read, by way of explanation, he added, "I've been to see Sheila Armstrong's oncologist."

"I'm heading into an interview. Save me time studying this, what does he say?" Alex requested.

"Sheila's tumour was first diagnosed more than two years ago. She was warned it would be terminal but at that time they had no way of knowing if it would be months or years. She was informed that, in the meantime, if she was careful, she could lead a normal life.

"Sheila had no wish to be careful. 'If it was going to happen, it would happen,' she told the doctor, and she didn't want the diagnosis to be made public. The only concession she made was to have regular check-ups every three months."

"I suppose it was her right," Alex responded.

"Her last appointment was little over a week ago. The doctor advised her that the tumour had grown and was pressing on her brain; she needed to make plans. The end might only be days away and certainly no more than a month."

"How did she take the news?" Alex asked.

"The doctor said she was very pragmatic and showed no emotion. He offered to get her help or counselling but she refused. She said she'd hoped for longer but she was ready. She'd already settled her affairs but needed to make some final adjustments."

"Had the doctor been surprised?" Alex queried.

"I asked, he said it was uncommon but not unheard of. He'd had to pass on similar news to many, many people over the years and the range of reactions was enormous, from denial to acceptance, defiance to resignation. Sheila had been unusual, but he'd half expected it as she had a very controlled and controlling personality."

"Very interesting," Alex said. "Now let's see what her husband has to say."

* * *

"Good afternoon, Mr Armstrong, thank you for coming in to see us," Alex held out his hand.

Graeme ignored the gesture and remained seated, looking considerably peeved. "What was so important you had to see me straight away? I had plans for this evening. Have you found who was responsible?"

"We've made a lot of progress," Alex stated, curtly. "Please sit down, we have some more questions for you."

"Now come on, I've been interviewed twice already. You surely don't consider me a suspect, do you? Maybe I should have listened more to my brother and not have been as cooperative."

"I'm sure you know better," Alex replied. "You've been most understanding up until now. There are many people we're interviewing, and it's true that you must be considered a suspect, but as I'm sure you're already aware, the immediate family are the first people we have to look into and eliminate from suspicion. Now, as you've commented yourself, you've already been interviewed, so I must remind you the caution you've already been given still applies."

Armstrong nodded and confirmed audibly when requested.

"You're familiar with the routine; let's get down to business," Alex started. "We've now gathered a lot more information and we're aware you haven't been honest with us."

"What do you mean?" Armstrong asked. "Every word I've told you is true."

"You've been withholding important information," Alex pushed.

"What do you mean?" he repeated.

"About your mistress."

"How can you say that? Our conversation already touched on it and I said I'd rather not say. I might not have told you everything but I didn't hide anything," Armstrong defended.

"Maybe so, but you gave us no indication of her significance."

"How do you mean?" Armstrong asked.

"You didn't tell us she was a teacher and more particularly you didn't advise us that she was in the school and actually saw Sheila on the morning of her death."

"What! What are you talking about? She wasn't there on Monday. She was working in a different school. We'd talked about it when I told her the group were going to be there."

"Now come on, Mr Armstrong, surely you're not expecting us to believe you didn't know she was there and that you didn't see her."

"That's precisely what I am saying," Armstrong claimed, his voice almost at shouting level. "I didn't see her. I don't remember her being there. Why should I believe you when you say different?"

"We already have three separate confirmations, not to mention her own admission. She brought in the tea, for God's sake."

Armstrong's eyes looked wildly from face to face. "I didn't know. I must have been out of the room at the time. I had to go to my car to bring in some equipment. I wasn't there when the tea trolley was brought in. I do remember seeing it though."

Alex and Sanjay exchanged glances. They were taken aback by Armstrong's denial and were trying to assess the credibility of his claim.

"She told us she'd been scheduled to be at another school on Monday, but she'd rearranged her plans so as to be at Eastfarm to see the writers perform, but also because she had an audition in one of the theatres."

"She did mention something about an audition," Armstrong conceded.

"On that particular day," Alex stressed.

"If you say so, but I didn't know she'd be at Eastfarm on Monday," Armstrong reaffirmed.

"You don't deny having an affair with Yvonne Kitson?"

"We were in a relationship," Armstrong confirmed.

"She told us you were planning to leave Sheila and it was your intention to set up home together."

Armstrong said nothing, his head dropped, and he stared downward.

"She said you wanted to get a divorce, also that you had asked Sheila and she'd refused," Alex prompted.

"It isn't that simple."

"Okay, then tell us," Alex pressed.

"I told you before about Sheila, how she'd become increasingly promiscuous. I said I didn't know about actual relationships but that wasn't completely truthful. She'd asked me to do things. This started a while ago. She wanted to be voyeuristic and for me to do the same. She wanted me to watch her having sex with another man. I think her real intention was to have a threesome. I refused, the idea revolted me. She also wanted to watch me with someone else. I didn't want to, I thought the idea was really weird. But she kept on about it. She said she'd try to set me up with a woman, someone she fancied as well. Now that really did throw me. Imagine your wife wanting to match you up with another woman and for her to watch and then join in. I had no idea she'd had any lesbian or bisexual tendencies before. I said no again, but I started thinking about it and imagining what it would be like."

"So, you agreed," Alex queried.

"Not exactly. I didn't say yes, but I didn't refuse outright either."

"Go on." Alex prompted.

There was silence for several seconds before Armstrong continued. "Sheila told me she'd met someone she thought would be suitable. She hadn't discussed anything with her but it was her opinion she'd be right. She said she knew the sort of woman I'd go for. I was amazed. I told her not to be so daft. She said I should meet the woman and get to know her and then decide. I thought what harm can come of meeting her. It was then she told me it was someone I'd already met, Yvonne Kitson from the am-dram group. Although I'd seen her before, I didn't know her well, but she was young and pretty and the thought of having a fling and doing it with my wife's blessing thrilled me in a strange sort of way, even though I knew what she was planning."

"And what say did Ms Kitson have in all of this?" Alex asked.

"She knew nothing about it, still doesn't as far as I'm aware," Armstrong answered. "I'm guessing Sheila had some previous conversation with her and gauged that she might have been attracted to me."

Before Armstrong could continue, there was a loud hammering on the door. Alex held up his hand to indicate a pause and pointed for Sanjay to see the cause of the interruption.

Sanjay left and returned a few minutes later. "It's Calum Armstrong out there creating hell about us bringing in Graeme without his say-so. He has a Mr Pettigrew, their family lawyer with him. I explained we had no reason to seek Calum's permission. Fair's fair, the lawyer tried to help me calm him down, but they both insisted Pettigrew be allowed to speak to his client and I have no justification in refusing, not unless Mr Armstrong here doesn't want him."

Alex nodded his agreement.

"I suppose as long as he's already here, I should speak to him," Armstrong said.

Alex suspended the interview and said he'd send Pettigrew in to speak to Armstrong. No sooner was he out the door than he was subjected to a barrage of abuse from Calum. Alex pointed the way for Pettigrew then firmly led Calum away. "You have no reason to be here. You can, of course, wait for your brother, and if you wish to do so, then there's a seating area you can use. However, I warn you, it could take some considerable time. You can rest assured Mr

Pettigrew will have full access to your brother and attend any discussions, but only if it's your brother's wish. Now, if you'll please step over there and let us get on with our jobs."

"It's not good enough. I want to make a formal complaint and I know all the right people to present it," Calum threatened.

"Everything has been handled correctly and professionally. It is, of course, your prerogative if you chose to complain. You can go to the front desk and see the duty Sergeant to get the appropriate forms. All complaints are fully investigated, but for the reasons I've stated, you'd be wasting your time and our resources," Alex added caustically.

Calum stormed away.

Following a thirty-minute recess while the client discussion took place, Alex and Sanjay returned to the interview room. Armstrong told them his lawyer had advised him to say nothing further, but as he had a desire to see the matter resolved, he was prepared to continue the interview, albeit conceding it would be best to keep Mr Pettigrew in attendance.

"If we can pick up where we left off," Alex started. "You were telling us about how Sheila wanted to set you up with Yvonne Kitson."

"Yes, indeed," Armstrong replied. "Sheila had the idea of having me act opposite Yvonne in a play, and between us, we managed to set it up. It was a steamy love story which brought us close together on stage, very close in fact. I met up with her privately. Sheila knew, of course, but it was only the two of us. Sheila had picked well but not for the reason she'd thought. Quite unexpectedly, we found a real closeness. We felt perfectly matched. It wasn't only sex. We were comfortable in each other's company in a way I couldn't be with my wife. Of course, I wasn't prepared to go through with Sheila's plan. It was really strange because we felt right together and all the time I knew it was Sheila who'd been the matchmaker and I couldn't let Yvonne find out how it'd come about. Nevertheless, we started seeing each other often. Yvonne wanted me to leave Sheila, and to be honest, I was attracted by the idea, but I couldn't go through with it."

"Why not?" Alex asked.

"I don't know. I suppose if I'm brutally honest, I'm set in my ways and I like the comforts in my life too much. If Sheila and I were to have broken up, it would have caused so much disruption. I don't have any assets in my own name. The house is owned jointly and I don't earn all that much now, not enough for the decent lifestyle I've got used to. I couldn't go back to living in a pokey flat and having to watch every penny."

"So, Sheila would have got her way?" Alex tried.

"No, I couldn't have done that either."

"That was why you had to kill her?" Sanjay now asked.

"No, no!" Armstrong cried out. "I could never have done that. I loved her. It may have been a strange relationship, but I did love her."

"So, what were you going to do?"

"I really don't know. I didn't have an answer but I could never have hurt Sheila."

"Maybe you believe Yvonne did it then," Alex asked.

"I'm sure she didn't," Armstrong defended.

"How can you say that? You weren't aware she was at Eastfarm at the time of Sheila's death, or at least that's what you've claimed," Alex challenged.

"No, you're twisting what I've said."

"I think we should have a recess. I want to talk to my client." Pettigrew leaned forward; he had, until then, seemed entranced listening to the story and was suddenly alerted by the prospect of his client being charged.

"Not now," Alex dismissed. "You had your chance earlier."

However, Pettigrew had achieved his purpose of breaking the flow and allowing Armstrong to realise his predicament and become more circumspect and acerbic with his answers.

"How well do you really know Ms Kitson?" Alex asked.

"I believe my client has already answered that," Pettigrew said.

"Maybe you're wanting all the lurid details of what happened in our bedroom. I don't see how it would be relevant. If that's how you get your kicks, just go and read some of Sheila's books," Armstrong retorted.

"Mr Armstrong, it's a legitimate question. You're purporting to be a character witness for Miss Kitson. You've told me …." Alex referred to his notes. "You've told me you're 'sure she didn't do it.' What qualifies you to make such a statement? How well did you really know her? You've told us in what capacity, at least in part, but are you really qualified to comment on her character? The things we already understand for sure are that she seems comfortable having a relationship with a married man and she manipulates her working timetable to suit herself and lies to her employer about it. Lied to you as well, it appears."

Armstrong paused before answering. "She didn't lie. She just didn't tell me she'd changed her plans. As far as knowing her, we first met about three years ago, but only as much as to recognise each other at meetings. The play we were in was performed in January, the rehearsals started much earlier, must have been October or November of last year. By that reckoning, we first got together about six months ago."

"And the two of you had been stringing Sheila along all this time?" Alex asked.

"I suppose, when you put it that way…it sounds bad. But Yvonne wanted me to be with her. She wanted me to leave Sheila, but she didn't wish her any harm. She never once said or implied anything of the sort."

"Let's put this into context, Mr Armstrong. You and Kitson have been having an affair for months. She wants you to herself. She asks you to leave your wife but you refuse. Whether it's because you care for Sheila or because of the money you'd lose if you left could be relevant, but Yvonne believes you want to be with her and Sheila's the only one standing in her way. Can you tell me a better motive for killing her? This way you get to keep your money and she gets to keep you."

"Oh my God, it's not like that. I don't know how to convince you. Yvonne and Sheila were friends before I was even involved. They cared about each other."

"That doesn't really help your argument, Mr Armstrong. You've already explained Sheila's motivation for that friendship. In fact, if she'd tried to take it further, then that could even give Yvonne further motivation to get rid of her."

"No, no," Armstrong looked defeated. "She's kind, she's caring. She's a teacher, an educator, for God's sake. She cares. She's charitable. She loves people, loves life," Armstrong blubbered in a quiet mantra.

"Let me change direction for a moment," Alex stated. "I want to go back to talking about the murder weapon."

"Yes," Armstrong replied hopefully, pleased to change the subject.

"We are now fairly certain that the knife used to kill your wife was an authentic one manufactured by the same company who made the prop ones," Alex started.

"Well, that's good news, if you've ruled out the theory that I fabricated a copy."

"We've not completely ruled it out, but as I said we're fairly certain. You may not consider it good news when I tell you the reason. The markings on the murder weapon indicate it came from a particular production batch and we have therefore focussed attention on where knives from that batch might have gone. We have discovered that South Caledonian Amateur Players were one of very few organisations throughout the world who owned one and, even more intriguing, their set of knives can't be found and their records do not identify where they might be. We understand that both you and Yvonne Kitson are members of the players. What's more, you told us a short time ago that you came together as a couple after you played opposite each other in one of their productions. We've spoken to some of the Committee of 'The Players' and they've also confirmed very few people had access to their prop stores. Amongst the list we have of those who did, both your name and Yvonne's appear. We don't have any faith in coincidence, so you'll understand why you're under suspicion."

"But, but …" Armstrong struggled to find words. "I don't believe it. You're trying to stitch me up. You, or someone else, are out to get me. There must be another explanation. There must be.

"It's true I do have access to the props room but I can list another dozen people who also have. They'll be plenty more too. You're jumping the gun if you think it was me. Show me some evidence, some real evidence. You can't, which is why it's clear I'm innocent."

"And Miss Kitson will be one of your dozen people. This is nowhere near as simple as you're making out," Alex replied. "We've established you and Miss Kitson both had a strong motive to end Sheila's life.

We know you had access to what now appears to be the murder weapon, which gave you the means. You were both at the scene, which means you had the opportunity. A full set, so by my reckoning we have you banged to rights. Now are you ready to confess?"

"Certainly not. I've done nothing wrong."

"It may well be a jury who has to make that call."

Armstrong looked bleak.

"We'd also like you to tell us about Sheila's illness," Alex probed.

Armstrong looked confused. "What illness?"

"You mean she had more than one?" Alex asked.

"No, what's this all about? I've no idea of what you're talking about." Armstrong became agitated, his face flushing bright red.

"Tell me about her brain tumour," Alex demanded.

Armstrong banged his hand on the table. "What are you talking about? Is this some sick joke? Or is it some perverse strategy to confuse me, to make me say something stupid or incriminating?" His frustration turned to anger. As he began to stand, Pettigrew placed a restraining hand on his arm. The move sufficiently settled him and he sat back in his chair breathing heavily.

Alex stared directly into Armstrong's eyes. He held the gaze, saying nothing. It was close to three minutes with the room so silent you could have heard a pin drop, but for those sitting, it felt like hours before Alex continued. "Are you honestly trying to tell us you knew nothing about it? We have Sheila's P.M. report showing she had a massive tumour. We've checked her medical records and found it was first diagnosed more than two years ago. She knew about it and was aware it would be terminal."

Armstrong's jaw dropped and he shook his head spasmodically, as if trying to ward off the information. "She said nothing. I didn't know. It can't be true; she'd couldn't have hidden something like that from me."

"She could and she did, if this is truly news to you," Alex replied.

"But why? Why would she not tell me?"

"Perhaps she didn't trust you with the news. Maybe it was a very bad mistake. After all, had you known, then you wouldn't have had the same reason to murder her. You could have just waited and left her to die."

Armstrong's eyes were watery. "I didn't kill her. I swear I didn't. You have to believe me."

"We think otherwise. Either you or Kitson or the two of you working together are responsible and you're going to be charged. Why not make it easy on yourself and everyone else and tell us the truth."

"I have," Armstrong pleaded. "I have been truthful, but how can I prove I didn't do it? How can I convince you?"

* * *

Sanjay and Alex compared notes following the interview. "We'll need to get Kitson in and charge her, but let's leave it until the morning. I'm knackered. We also need to arrange search warrants for both their houses," Alex suggested. "Now, would you like the fun job of advising his brother?"

"No, I'm going to pass," Sanjay smiled. "I'll leave it for Pettigrew; after all, he has to serve some useful purpose. He had such little impact on the interview he'd have been better not being there."

"Better for his client maybe," Alex said. "He did okay for us. He fulfilled the suspect's right to have a solicitor present and succeeded in being totally ineffective. I love it when we have a family lawyer to deal with. Technically, they're qualified, but they don't have a clue how to handle a criminal investigation or to look after their client's interests. It plays straight into our hands."

"What do you make of Armstrong? Do you think it credible for him really to know nothing about Sheila being at death's door?" Sanjay asked.

"He appeared very convincing. What purpose would there have been for him to lie, after all, why would he have killed Sheila if he'd been aware? Unless he wasn't prepared to wait for her to die. Having said that, do you believe the murder could be down to him? We have no shortage of circumstantial evidence, but we really want something more tangible. Let's see what we get from Kitson and the searches."

"I think Kitson may be the more likely one," Sanjay replied. "Of course, it might be an act, but Armstrong seemed too weak and indecisive to be the killer. Whoever did this didn't only want to murder Sheila, they wanted to make a show of it. The whole set up was a piece of exhibitionism and Kitson's the drama expert. What do you reckon?"

"You do have a point," Alex said. "There's the other possibility the two of them could have been working together. But I still can't get over the whole performance thing. Even if she, or he, or they, were turned on by the idea of the showmanship, they were taking one helluva chance of it not working. It could have failed entirely, or else only cut Sheila without causing serious damage and then where would they have been? There's a whole lot more we need to unearth if we're to get to the truth and if we're to have any chance of getting a conviction."

Chapter 19

Sandra and Peter walked back into the first interview room. Tommy was sitting where they'd left him and was trying to look nonchalant, but it was clear to them he was unnerved.

"Let's start where we left off, you're still under caution, but now we'd strongly recommend you have a solicitor sit with you before we progress. We can arrange for a duty solicitor to attend if you or your family don't have one you choose to use."

"I telt you before, I dinnae want a stranger listenin' in. Nothin's changed and I can look after mysel'," Tommy asserted.

"Okay, fine with me," Sandra said. "Just so long as it's understood that you were offered representation and knowingly declined."

"Aye, it's understood," Tommy answered, bowing theatrically after saying it.

"We've found out a lot more since we last spoke to you and you're in a lot of trouble. We have evidence to show that you were involved in a whole series of crimes. If convicted, then irrespective of your age, you're likely to go down for a very long time."

"I've done nothin' wrang that you can get me for," Tommy replied.

"I wouldn't be so hasty making assumptions," Sandra stated.

Tommy looked less confident but kept up his display of bravado. "I'm sayin' nothin'."

"That's up to you. We can't make you talk, but in the absence of you saying anything to defend yourself, then the buck stops with you. To start with, we'll call your parents and see if they want to appoint a legal representative and then we'll be charging you. We don't need to hit you with it all to start with, just enough to justify keeping you in custody. Peter, ask one of the lads to make the call."

Peter held the door open as he called out the instruction, adding he needed to arrange a warrant to search their house.

"I telt you, I didnae want my parents involved. I think you're bluffin', you don't have anythin'," Tommy said.

"As you're not prepared to talk to us, you've given us no alternative," Sandra said.

"Why should I talk? You'll only twist everythin' I say," Tommy challenged.

"As I said, it's up to you. We're already fairly certain about everything that's happened, so we don't need your evidence. We'd like more information about Kevin Speirs' involvement, but that would be bonus. As it is, our bosses will be happy we've cracked the case and you're in for a fall."

"Wait a minute, you already know about Kev. I thought he was bomb proof," Tommy said.

"I'm sure that's what he'd like everyone to believe. The truth is he's not as smart as he thinks and he's going to have a lot of time At Her Majesty's Pleasure to consider that. You'll not be short of company."

"What are you talkin' about? I've maybe been in the wrang place but I've no' done anythin'. What do you think you have on me?"

"We don't think, we know," Sandra was keeping the pressure on. "Where do you want me to start? Shall we do it chronologically? That would be easiest. Okay, to kick things off, we have truancy, but I'm not getting too excited about that one, more a community policing matter, isn't it? I'm more interested in your crimes than your misdemeanours. Let's see, we start with armed robbery, followed up quickly by a serious assault. We'll need to see how the fiscal wants to handle it, he may want to go for attempted murder, or settle for G.B.H., who knows? To crown it all, you go right to the top of the heap with a murder in the first degree. Oh, and mixed in with all the rest let's throw in trying to pervert the course of justice."

"Wait a minute, that's no' me, none of that's me."

"None of it?" Sandra contested.

Tommy looked down at his feet. "I didnae do it. None o' the bad stuff."

"It's all bad stuff," Sandra replied. "And we have you down for all of it. We've witness statements, camera footage and, after a search, I'm confident we'll have forensic back up as well."

"You've got it wrang; it wisnae me, I tell you. Okay, maybe I was there, but I didnae do it."

"You'll need to give me more. Tell me what happened."

"The hold-up was meant to be a bit o' a laugh. Kev said we'd go in and put on balaclavas, act as if it was bank robbery, somethin' like that. It surprised me as much as anyone else when Kev pulled out the toy and pretended it was a gun. It did look real, mind you."

"What makes you think it was a toy?" Sandra asked.

"Well, it had to be. Where would he 'ave got a real one?"

"Did you handle it?"

"Nah, he wouldnae let me."

"So, you really don't know what it was. Get on with your story." Sandra's arched eyebrows and intonation on the word 'story' showed her lack of belief, but Tommy gave no indication he'd picked up on it.

"Everyone was really scared. They opened the safe and the cash drawers and then backed away. They did exactly what they were telt. Kev went to the safe and telt me to empty the drawers."

"Did you see what he took?"

"Money of course."

"Nothing else?"

"I didnae see anything else. If there was other valuables, he never let on."

"What did you do with the money?"

248

"We ran off, and once we were safe, we divvied up. Kev kept most o' it but gave me two hundred quid."

"Tell me about Fergus Hardy?" Sandra probed.

"Who?" Tommy asked

"The man at the court on Tuesday. Did you not know who he was?"

"Kev said he had a job. He was to put the frighteners on some bloke and we'd all get paid. There was four o' us, Kev, Sean, Big Mal and me."

"Who was the job for?"

"Ah dunno, some guy Kev knew."

"And why was he wanting to scare Hardy?"

"Don't ask me. It was nothin' to do wi' me. All I was telt was we were to get paid to do it, but it all went wrong."

"How do you mean?" Sandra asked.

"The idea was to give him a bit o' a scare. We did that okay, but Kev thought if we pushed him up onto the wall it would give him a real fright. It was only five feet high, maybe no' even as much. The problem was Sean didn't realise his own strength and pushed too hard. The guy went right over the top o' the wall and there was a big drop on the other side. It was an accident, really it was. We didnae mean to hurt him bad."

"Did you check what happened?" Sandra asked.

"Shit no, we heard his scream and legged it before anyone else came alang."

"You don't seem too upset by it all," Sandra commented.

"No' a lot o' point. It had already happened, there's nothin' we could have done. Why risk gettin' caught?"

"How much were you paid?"

"No' a bean. Kev said we'd screwed up and he'd be in bother, so we weren't gettin' anythin'."

"How did you feel about that?"

"It was right enough. Sean had blown it. I'd no reason to complain. Big Mal wisnae happy though."

"What did Devosky say?" Sandra asked, dropping the name hoping for a reaction.

"Who's Devosky?" Tommy replied, without as much as blinking.

"The name means nothing to you?" Sandra continued.

"I dinnae recognise it. Who is he?"

"Never mind, we can leave it 'til later. You said Mal wasn't happy."

"Aye, he claimed he'd done everythin' asked o' him and was being penalised for someone else's mistake. Kev calmed him down, telt him he'd have plenty o' opportunity to make up his lost earnings."

"And how was he planning to deliver?" Sandra enquired.

"Kev said he'd sort him out. He had mates who'd be able to use him on some jobs he knew about."

"Who were the mates and who else was in on all of this?" Sandra tried.

"I dinnae know. All this was between the two o' them. I wasnae meant to hear any o' it, but from what I saw, Mal seemed happy enough."

"What happened with Carson, the man who set up Hardy?"

"Later that day, Kev and I talked about him. We realised he could identify us and we were worried he might turn us in. We decided to track him down and have a word. We found out he was stayin' in a flat near the river. Kev set up lookouts to watch for him.

"They tracked him down. We wanted to warn him off. After we found him, we tried speakin' to him, but he'd have none o' it. He wouldnae listen to a word, so we gave him a bit o' a kickin' to get his attention.

"In the end, he said he'd do or say whatever we wanted him to, but the more he promised the less believable he sounded. Kev said we'd never be able to rely on him and I agreed, but I'd no idea what he had in mind. He picked up a big bit of pavin' stone and walloped him on the heid. Carson collapsed onto the road and he wisnae moving. I had nothin' to do wi' it. Then Kev said we needed to drop him in the river. He said it'd waken him up and then he'd get away. But he'd learn a lesson. There's no way he'd cross us an' he'd be too feart to say anythin'. Anyway, that's what we did.

"We heard the splash and then there was nothin' else. We thought with him out o' the way, they'd be no way of tying anythin' to us."

"But you were wrong," Sandra said.

"Yes, I see that now. But as I said, it wisnae me. Sean made a mistake which ended in Hardy gettin' hurt. Kev is the one you should be speakin' to about the assault on Carson."

It was an effort for Sandra and Peter not to show their amazement at the cold, callous account. The boy showed no emotion and gave the impression he considered his actions justified. It was all someone else's fault and he was an innocent bystander only doing what he had to.

"It wasn't only an assault, it was murder. Carson was badly injured but he was still alive when he was thrown in the water and left to drown. Which means you're party to the murder."

"I telt you, it was Kev, it wisnae me. An' I've telt you everythin'. You cannae blame me. It wisnae my fault."

"Thank you for your help," Sandra answered, a distinct sarcastic note in her voice. "You can be assured we'll advise the fiscal how helpful you've been."

"Just make sure you dinnae let Kev hear. Ah wouldnae give much for my chances if he were to get hold o' me."

Outside the interview room, Sandra and Peter congratulated each other on a job well done. They agreed they had enough to charge both Sean and Tommy, but it was Kevin Speirs they most wanted to go after. Sandra felt they had more than enough to bring him in and charge him but decided it would be better left for the morning, when they'd be fresh. With both Sean and Tommy detained, there was little chance of him being forewarned.

"Not a bad result," Peter said. "We have enough to take them both down and we'll be able to get Speirs too. If only we could prove the link to Devosky, then we'd have the whole lot."

"Let's see if anything further has come in while we were tied up. I'll check while you write up the reports on these two."

"You're all heart, Boss. It was an early start this morning and it's been non-stop ever since. I've a feeling tomorrow will be the same, so I'll happily call it a night once this is done. You're looking pretty shattered yourself."

"You say the most flattering things, you certainly know how to make a girl feel good about herself," Sandra scowled, jokingly.

Peter's face flushed bright red. "I'm sorry, Sandra, I didn't mean..."

"Got you! Tired I may be, but my brain's not dead yet," she replied with a chuckle.

Peter shook his head while settling down to start his paperwork at the desk facing Sandra.

* * *

A tall stack of documents was waiting on Sandra's desk. Within moments, she'd leafed through them, binning several on the way and discarding the non-urgent in a filing tray, retaining only the most critical to her current work. Picking up the first folder, she perused the contents and was gratified to see the Sheriff had ruled on the claim for dismissal of evidence affected by the hold up. He'd been completely pragmatic in his approach, declaring no item stolen from the safe could be used or alluded to. However, for all items which hadn't been removed from the safe, he was satisfied the chain of custody was complete and declared that he'd permit them for use in their respective cases.

"If it's true, Speirs was working for Devosky, then might he have lifted the wrong package?" Peter asked.

"It could well be that he did, or else maybe they did it by design and thought they were being clever, if they didn't want there to be a direct link. Do you see what I mean? He took the evidence relating to a case Zennick and Devosky had no connection with, thinking it would make the evidence in their case inadmissible. I hope that's what happened, because if it is, then they've outsmarted themselves and they'll have achieved nothing. Good, isn't it?" Sandra had a broad grin.

"Zennick's not going to be too happy," Peter surmised. "It's a shame for him, isn't it? But with a bit of luck, it might force Devosky back into the open."

"No sign of it so far," Sandra replied while her eyes scanned a document, "According to this, there's been no activity on Devosky's mobile since Tuesday and it hasn't even been switched on to pick up a trace. The second number, the one Gilchrist connected to him on, is registered to some guy by the name of Campbell located in Greenock. It hasn't moved out of the area and seems to have had fairly normal use making only local and national calls. We can pick him up and see what he can tell us. Another job for tomorrow."

"I'm nearly done here. I've noted all the important stuff and I can flesh out the report in the morning. I'm off home for some beauty sleep. I need it even if you don't," Peter grinned.

"You're learning, boy. You're learning."

Chapter 20

Both totally exhausted, Sandra and Alex collapsed into bed. Neither one had been very hungry after an arduous day. They'd drunk piping hot tea and snacked on warm buttered toast followed by short-bread biscuits. Deciding there was nothing worth watching on television, they both felt too tired to start watching a DVD. Although physically drained, their minds were racing. They each had matching Kindles lying on their bedside tables, but each sat untouched, as they lay alongside one another discussing their days, delighting in their own and each other's progress.

"Tomorrow could be a big day. What's your plan?" Alex enquired.

"No plan as such. I don't want to be wrong footed when something unexpected happens. It's inevitable that it will and, if I'm blinkered by following a plan, I'll be thrown."

Alex was amused but shook his head in a mocking fashion. "Come on, no-one said you had to wear blinkers, and besides, what you've described, being prepared for the unexpected is a plan in itself."

Sandra punched his shoulder playfully. "Yeah, fair enough. My first priority is to bring in Speirs and get his version of events. From what I've heard already, I'm fairly certain he's the one I need to get for all three crimes. I'm hoping I'll be able to break him and get a link back to Devosky and Zennick, but I'm far from optimistic. Have any of your contacts come up with anything useful I can use?"

"Only what I've already told you. I'll give them a chase first thing to see if they have anything new for me, but I reckon it's a waste of time. They'd have come back to me themselves if there was anything significant."

"Yes, I suppose," Sandra replied. "I'm aiming to visit this man Campbell. I'm really wanting to tie in a link to Devosky before the organised crime team come a-calling."

"I understand, but from what you've told me there isn't much reason for them to show interest. There may be friction between different groups, and I'm not trying to say there's not more to it, but on the face of it, Hardy's injuries were caused by Sean being over-enthusiastic and Carson's death was caused by the other lads trying to cover up. It wasn't gang related. It's not like war breaking out on the streets. Mind you, there's always the possibility of Speirs having different connections and motives. Hopefully, you'll learn a lot more after you talk to him."

"I've ordered a check on his phone records, but it hasn't come through yet," Sandra advised.

"Don't hold your breath," Alex said. "Everything you've told me suggests he's too smart or at least too aware to give anything away."

"You're probably right, but he's arrogant too. I'm hoping he'll be complacent enough to have made a mistake."

"Good luck. I might need some myself too," Alex added.

"Why would you need luck? You're already home and dry. You have your evidence against Graeme Armstrong and Yvonne Kitson. All you're looking for now is a confession."

"Dream on. It's not likely to be so simple. I can't see either of them confessing and although I have two suspects, both of whom as individuals have the motive and opportunity, there's also the distinct possibility they could be working together in concert."

"I can't get my head round it. I can understand them wanting to kill Sheila. And from what you've told me about her behaviour and eccentricities, I can imagine lots of people would have wanted to kill her. Graeme and Yvonne had the strongest motives. They'd probably had to deal with a lot more of her strange controlling ways and, as she was also the one in their way of a future together, they had everything to gain. They had everything to gain financially as well, as it seems Sheila held the purse strings and was the main earner. They also had access to what now appears to be the murder weapon. Yeah, I get all that. What I don't get is the whole theatrical bit. Why would anyone choose such a contrived way to kill her unless they were every bit as strange as she was? Have you checked it out with a criminal psychologist? Was it some sort of demonstration of power? Did they hate Sheila that much they had to make an exhibition of her death? There can't have been anything in it for them other than some perverse gratification. There must have been a hundred more subtle and effective ways to kill her and bring less attention to the incident and to themselves. That suggests to me they wanted the attention, they craved the limelight so much they were ready to risk getting caught. With her medical prognosis, they would have been easier and safer leaving her to die. They wouldn't have had to wait very long and it would have been risk free," Sandra offered.

"Thanks for the complete rundown of my case; I'll maybe get you to do the report too," Alex jested. "Although you don't have it all. You're presupposing they knew about Sheila's medical condition. Graeme claims it was completely news to him and his reaction seemed genuine enough. I accept we're dealing with thespian types and they're no doubt very good at faking their reactions, but even so, they're comparative amateurs to some of the villains we normally deal with. What you were saying before has got me thinking. I will ask a psychologist for a professional opinion, but in the meantime, I see a lot of sense in what you've said. Most criminals want to hide from attention, but in this case, the murderer or murderers wanted to shock everyone. They wanted them to see and talk about the result of what they'd done. Kitson is used to being on stage and looking for attention. However, Armstrong is normally behind the scenes and gets his satisfaction from people appreciating his work without being aware of his contribution. Yes, you might be onto something. I had been feeling really uncomfortable about charging him. I couldn't accept how or why he'd kill Sheila that way, but this theory might just fly."

"While you're speaking to a psychologist, you might want to ask for his opinion on Sheila's behaviour. This whole tumour thing has me wondering if it could explain the way she treated people, her aggression and her promiscuity. From what you've told me, she has changed over the years and become more and more extreme. Is it likely the change might have been caused by a growing tumour affecting her brain?"

"I really don't know, Sandra. I've heard of criminal defences claiming a head injury had changed the person's character, but I've never put much store in it. I put it down to smart lawyers coming up with improbable excuses to try to get their clients off. Perhaps there is something to it, but I can't imagine how something like that can change a person. I would imagine it could cause a change of emphasis or a loss of inhibitions. I understand that's not uncommon with dementia or stroke victims, but it seems illogical to me for a person to change and become evil if the tendency wasn't there in the first place."

"I suppose you have a point, but I really don't know about these things. It might be best to talk to an expert. In any event, I don't see it makes much difference. The facts are, Sheila Armstrong was a nasty piece of work. She upset a lot of people and perhaps she upset someone enough to take her life in the most outrageous way. Does it really matter why she was the way she was?" Sandra asked.

"You're right, of course, it's for my own satisfaction. I want to understand why things happen the way they do. If I can come to terms with people's motivation, then I feel a lot happier doing my job."

"And what's your motivation at the moment?" Sandra laughed as she snuggled close allowing Alex's powerful arms to envelop her.

"Right now, my only motivation is to get some sleep. It's been a long, long day, it's late and we have another early start," he said, kissing her brow then manoeuvring their position to rest her head against his shoulder.

Despite their best intentions, anticipating the day ahead filled their heads and neither managed much restful sleep. By 7am they were both up, fed, dressed and anxious to face their respective challenges.

While waiting for Kitson to be brought in for interview, Alex checked the results of the search on Armstrong's house which Steve and Phil had attended. Full forensic tests would take some time to come in, but the preliminary report made interesting reading.

Alex was curious when he learned of a vault in the basement where Sheila kept a stock of each of her published titles. There was also a stack of lever arch files with copies of all her royalty statements and bank records and a bookcase with first edition copies of all her books. Tucked away on the lowest shelf was a stack of very raunchy magazines, not illegal, but more explicit than those you'd usually find on a newsagent's top shelf. Alex wondered whether she read them for research or titillation or maybe both. A considerably more important find was a lightweight, sterling silver belcher chain with a heart-shaped drop engraved with the initials 'YK' found in the bedroom. The report was typed but Phil had added a scrawled pencil comment saying it was lucky Yvonne Kitson didn't have a middle name starting with 'K' or they may have overlooked the chain mistaking the 'YKK' for the logo of the zip company.

However, most significant of all, in Graeme's workshop at the bottom of a waste bin, they found an empty display box. Fitted inside the box was an insert to securely hold two knives of the type used for the killing. The knives themselves were missing but the lining had the printed name 'Top Hat Suppliers.' Alex was gleeful at the discovery of this new and vital piece of evidence. The joy was only marginally tempered when he read the result of dusting for prints revealed nothing as the box had apparently been wiped clean before being discarded.

There was a distinct spring in their steps when he and Sanjay marched into the interview room to speak to Kitson and her lawyer.

Following the formalities, Alex wasted no time in mounting his challenge. "We've come a long way since we last spoke. We now have irrefutable evidence implicating you and Graeme Armstrong."

Kitson's face paled and she clasped her hands tightly together to stop them from trembling. "I told you before we didn't do it."

Alex led the questioning, following the same route he had with Armstrong. Not unexpectedly, he made little progress on what he'd already learned, with the lawyer parrying any time he considered his client in danger of incriminating herself.

"Graeme claims he was unaware that you were in the school on Monday," he stated, hoping the implication of him turning against her may be enough to drive a wedge splitting their mutual support."

"I hadn't told him in advance I was going. I didn't make up my mind to do it until Monday morning. I told you before that I'd called in sick to the Academy because of the audition. It was only as an afterthought that I decided to go to Eastfarm."

Alex brow wrinkled assessing her answer. She corroborated Armstrong's statement and potentially implicated herself in the process. Was she being honest, naïve, or was it some sort of smart double bluff?

"And you didn't see him once you'd arrived?" he pursued.

"I looked about for him but didn't see him anywhere. I'm guessing he was working backstage at the time. I spoke to Sheila and a few of the others, but I couldn't ask for him as Graeme didn't want anyone to know about our relationship, not yet."

Alex nodded in acknowledgement. "Now, I understand you are heavily involved with South Caledonian Players?"

"I've told you all about that already." Kitson's voice was testy. "It's how Graeme and I first came together."

"Is this really necessary?" her lawyer interceded.

"Yes, it certainly is," Alex asserted. "I'm not asking about you and Graeme. I'm enquiring about your level of responsibility."

"I was one of the regulars, still am actually, but I'm not on the committee or anything."

"No, but I understand you have access to the costumes and the props store," Alex continued.

"I don't have the keys or anything, but I am allowed in to look for anything I need for a performance or to check what's available."

"Yes, so we've been led to believe. Are you aware there had been a set of knives kept in the store which matched the set used to kill Sheila?"

Kitson's jaw dropped and her lawyer grasped her wrist as a warning to stay silent.

"I can also inform you that these knives are no longer in the store and they can't be accounted for in the Club's records."

"I didn't know," Kitson responded.

"The box containing them had gone missing. However, I can tell you it's now been found. I learned about this only this morning, in fact. The fascinating thing is where it was found. It was hidden in a bin in Graeme's workroom; furthermore, there were no knives in the box."

"It can't be," Kitson replied. "Either you're lying or someone is trying to set him up."

"Not just him," Alex continued. "You too had access to his workroom, didn't you?"

"What are you talking about? I've never been there; Graeme's not taken me back to his house."

"So you're telling me it must have been Graeme?" Alex tried.

"No, no, I didn't say that," Kitson cried.

"Come now, Chief Inspector, don't put words into her mouth," the lawyer admonished.

Alex eyes stayed fixed on Kitson, completely ignoring the solicitor.

"If you're telling me you've never been to the house, then how can you explain us finding this?" Alex held up an evidence bag containing the bracelet.

Kitson gasped, her hand automatically reaching forward. "Where did you find that? I lost it ages ago."

"We'll ask the questions," Alex stated, withdrawing the bag quickly.

"I haven't seen the bracelet for months. I'd no idea what had happened to it. It's not worth a lot of money, but it has great sentimental value. My parents gave me it for my sixteenth birthday."

"Why should we trust anything you tell us? A moment ago, you stated you'd never been to the Armstrong house but that's where we found your bracelet."

"I didn't lie," Kitson protested. "I told you Graeme never took me to the house and he didn't. It was Sheila who invited me over for coffee and to discuss a play. I've already told you that I knew her before I got together with Graeme. It must have been near enough a year ago."

"Just for coffee?" Alex quizzed.

"What do you mean? I said it was to discuss a play."

"We found your bracelet in the bedroom," Alex asserted.

Kitson looked puzzled. "I don't know what you're suggesting but you're wrong. I've only been to the house once and it was to see Sheila. I'd remarked that it looked a beautiful home because I appreciated the artwork she had and she showed me round. She gave me a tour."

"And this included the bedroom?"

"She walked me through each of the bedrooms. Maybe it fell off when I was there," Kitson replied tartly, not rising to the bait.

"And Graeme's workroom?" Alex continued.

"We didn't go in, but Sheila pointed it out to me. She opened the door to show me it but said Graeme didn't like his stuff being disturbed, so we never went inside."

"And you maintain the bracelet must have fallen off. You didn't remove it. There was no struggle, no impassioned embrace. You were there in the bedroom and it just fell off."

"I've no idea how it got there," Kitson pleaded.

"Very convenient," Alex commented.

"My client has given you a full and credible explanation, Inspector. Besides, don't you think it a bit odd if her bracelet fell off in the bedroom for it not to have been found and still be there a year later? Someone has obviously set her up," the solicitor stated.

"Precisely my thinking. Not the setting up, but the whole story she's given us – very odd and hardly credible. We only have her word for any of it and it doesn't ring true."

Before Alex had a chance to continue with his interrogation, there was a loud knock on the door, which then opened a fraction and Phil poked his head through.

"What is it? Can't you see I'm in the middle of an interview? This better be important."

"It is important, Sir. I'm sorry to interrupt. Could I have a word?" Phil meekly asked.

"Interview suspended," Alex announced to the recording device. "Deal with the formalities, I'll be back in a minute," he directed Sanjay. "Now, what's the emergency?" he asked Phil while hastily rising and leaving the room.

"It's Sandra, Sir, she needs you."

Chapter 21

Sandra had left the flat at the same time as Alex, meeting with Peter at their office. She had a clear idea in her mind what she hoped to achieve. Her first priority was going to be Kevin Speirs and she arranged for him to be lifted. From what she already knew, his father was likely to be a problem. Consequently, she wanted to ensure everything would be done by the book and he had the opportunity of representation before she spoke to him. Realising this could take some time, she decided she and Peter would fill this hiatus by visiting Campbell.

She first had Peter confirm Campbell's mobile was still active and in the Greenock area and then they set off along the M8 to find him. The route took them past the Erskine Bridge. Although it was the other side of the river, Sandra was aware they were passing only a short distance from where Patrick Carson's body was discovered the previous morning. She rarely travelled this way and found the coincidence unsettling, doing it twice on successive days for different reasons but potentially related to the same case.

They found his address, it looked dilapidated, and was a flat with a main door entrance in a traditional red sandstone tenement located within throwing distance from the river.

Tam Campbell opened the door after the first knock. He was small and wiry with pinched, rat-like features. He'd obviously been expecting someone but was surprised to find Sandra and Peter at his door, becoming rather nervous after they showed their warrant cards. He looked past them, cautiously checking for onlookers up and down the street, then, apparently satisfied, he showed them through to his front room. It was a smoke-filled, cluttered, combined kitchen and sitting area, which nevertheless boasted a fifty-inch widescreen television currently tuned to a twenty-four hour poker channel.

"We need you to tell us everything you know about a Mr Devosky," Sandra started.

"Devosky? I don't think I've ever heard that name before," Campbell answered, but he was clearly lying. His brow shone from perspiration and his hand shook.

"We understand you are the owner of a mobile with phone number…" Peter recited the number.

"So?" Campbell challenged.

"This number was used to call and receive calls from a Mr Gilchrist within the last couple of weeks."

"The only Gilchrist I can think of is my optician and I haven't seen him for months. I don't know anyone else called Gilchrist," he stated. "Whoever it is must have been mistaken if he's told you I spoke to him. Maybe he got the number wrong."

"There is no mistake, Mr Campbell. We have his telephone records from Vodaphone, and just to be certain, we've also checked yours from Tesco Mobile."

"How can you do that?"

"It's not important. What is important is that we are one hundred percent certain calls were made from your phone to him."

Campbell looked deflated but continued his denial. "It wasn't me. I've no idea who he is."

"Who else has been using your phone?"

"I can't tell you," Campbell replied.

"That's not good enough," Sandra demanded. "We're investigating some very serious crimes, and unless you can tell us who's been using your phone, then you're the one in the frame."

"And if I do tell you, then you'll have some even more serious crimes to investigate and I'll be the victim," Campbell answered.

"You shouldn't be more afraid of him than you are of us," Peter added, attempting his most threatening tone.

Campbell only raised his eyebrows in response.

"Listen, we have enough to put this man away. But we need your help to confirm we have the right man," Sandra tried.

"If you already have enough, then you don't need me."

"We need your information too," Sandra admitted. "What does he have on you?"

"He owns me, that's all. I was really stupid and built up a gambling debt. I'm sure I was cheated but it doesn't matter now. He bought over my debt and now he owns me."

"Who was the debt to, to start with?" Sandra asked.

"I'm not saying."

"Okay, how about you say nothing and we'll tell you who we think it is. All you have to do is nod if we're right." Sandra thought she'd try the same technique which she'd been successful with the day before.

Campbell nodded cautiously.

"A man used your phone and made you take calls for him."

Campbell nodded.

"The man's name's Devosky."

Campbell's gesture indicated the name wasn't familiar.

"You're not familiar with his name?" Sandra asked.

Campbell shook his head.

"But he's East European, Ukrainian or Russian most like?" Sandra tried.

An affirmative nod.

"Six feet in height, broad shoulders, brown eyes, dark hair and clean shaven with a scar above his lip on the left running across to his ear." Sandra asked.

Campbell nodded firmly but increasing terror showed in his face as Sandra ran through the description.

"And he lives around here?"

Campbell firmly shook his head.

"But he runs this area?"

Nod.

"Have you seen him in the last few days?" she continued.

Another negative.

"We heard he might have moved away," she prompted.

Campbell's face brightened but neither agreed nor disagreed.

"And have you heard where he might have gone?" Sandra asked.

Campbell's shrug wouldn't have looked out of place on a Frenchman. One simple gesture indicated - don't know, don't care and most importantly, don't want to know. Sandra suppressed a smile, Campbell's action reminding her she'd only been home from France for a few days and causing her to muse for a moment why she hadn't stayed there.

"Fine, that will be all for now, but don't go too far. We might need to talk to you again," Sandra stated while moving towards the door and stepping back outside.

"I've said nothing and I'll say nothing so don't waste your time," Campbell announced loudly, presumably for the benefit of any eavesdroppers outside.

"It was the best we could hope for under the circumstances," Peter said to Sandra once back in their car.

A short while later, they arrived back at their office. Sandra was stopped by a young constable she hadn't met before. "Excuse me, Mam, we've picked up Speirs as instructed. He's in interview room two and his lawyer's with him, a first-class pain in the ass he is too."

"Speirs or the lawyer?" Sandra asked.

"Both," the constable replied. "The whole way in, Speirs was complaining and making threats. Wait for this; he was claiming his father paid our wages so we'd better do what he wanted. At first I thought he was talking about bribes and asked him to explain. What he meant was his dad was so rich and paid so much in taxes that he was paying for us. When I didn't show what he thought was appropriate respect, or maybe it was fear he was looking for, he said he wanted our badge numbers and would be making an official complaint. I gave him our numbers and told him to go for it. He's not really that influential, is he?" A tinge of worry appearing in his voice.

"Don't lose sleep over it, Constable," Sandra reassured. "What's the problem with the lawyer?"

"Nothing out of the ordinary. A bit marbles in the mouth and seems to know what he's on about so best to treat him with care."

"Okay, thanks for the warning."

When Sandra and Peter entered the interview room, Speirs and his lawyer were standing chatting near a window against the far wall.

Having taken on board what she'd been informed on her way in, Sandra decide to start in an aggressive fashion. "So nice to meet you at last, Mr Speirs. We haven't met before, but I've heard so much about you in the last few days, I feel I've known you for years. Now, before you start with any threats, your daddy's money isn't going to do you any good here. He can't buy your way out of this one."

Sandra's intention had been to rile Speirs and put him off his guard. His reaction was far more extreme than she's anticipated. He ran and threw himself at her at the same time shouting, "Fucking bitch!" Sandra didn't see it coming. Peter reacted quickly but not fast enough to stop Speirs catching her in something close to a rugby tackle, thudding her sideways against a table and ricocheting onwards into a wall. Within moments, Peter had grabbed him and pulled him back, restraining Speirs flaying arms before they reached their intended target. The lawyer hadn't moved; he was still standing against the far wall, shocked, with his hand covering his mouth. Sandra lay whimpering on the floor.

Peter yelled for assistance and hit a panic button. Within seconds, two burly officers charged in and cuffed Speirs before dragging him screaming from the room.

Peter turned his attention back to Sandra. She remained lying on the floor having hardly moved. Her complexion was a ghastly grey colour, other than a large, blue bruise on her cheek where she'd collided with the wall, she was holding her side, in obvious pain.

He cautiously raised her blouse free of her skirt to examine the wound and could see some surface skin was torn and bloody, but more concerning there was a growing black patch below.

"We need to get you to the hospital straight away to check for internal bleeding and get you an X-ray. I'm worried that you may have broken a rib or two."

"No, no X-ray, absolutely not," her voice rasped.

"Why, what's wrong?" Peter asked.

"I'm pregnant. Get me to hospital quick. I've got pains. I don't want to lose my baby."

* * *

By the time Alex arrived at A&E, Sandra was being attended by a doctor. He reluctantly obeyed the instruction to remain in the waiting area, but unable to settle, he anxiously paced the floor, his face grave and his eyes watery. Peter too was in the hospital reception, sitting with his elbows on his knees his head clasped in both hands.

Spotting him, Alex marched across and placed his hand firmly on Peter's shoulder.

Peter looked up surprised. "I'm sorry, Sir. I was too slow to stop it happening. I tried to help, but…"

"It wasn't your fault," Alex reassured. "From what I heard, you did everything you could. I just hope it's been enough."

Nothing further was said; both stared glumly at the floor awaiting news.

After what felt like an eternity, but was in truth less than fifteen minutes, Alex was permitted through to see Sandra.

Pausing outside her cubicle, he could see she was half-lying, half-sitting on a hospital bed with its upper section raised to a forty-five-degree angle. A cotton sheet draped over her legs up to her waist, she was wearing a loose, apron-like, disposable nightshirt on top. Her bruised face and side were evident.

The tears Alex had until then supressed flowed freely down his cheeks. He pawed at them for a second and then ran forward and grabbed her hand, holding it in both of his. "What have they said?" he asked nervously.

Sandra smiled weakly and whispered, "The doctor said I've been very stupid and I should take better care of myself."

"Do you mean...?" Alex couldn't finish the sentence.

"We'll need to wait and see," Sandra replied. "The bruise to my face is superficial, but being thrown into the corner of the table's broken two of my ribs and the bone's nicked the edge of my lung. Bloody painful but not too serious. I'll live," she smiled again. "But I've had a slight bleed. I'm still carrying our baby, but I'll need to take it very easy. They want to keep me in for a few days to keep a close eye on me."

"Thank God," Alex mouthed.

"So much for my first big case," Sandra said.

Gently, careful to not press against her wound, Alex held Sandra's face in both hands, kissed her brow and then cradled her head with his shoulder. "You already had it cracked. Don't worry, I'll make sure you get the credit, and anyway, that's the last thing you need to worry yourself with now."

Sandra closed her eyes for a second. "You're right, there's more important things than work, but it really pisses me off to have done all this work for nothing. Anyhow, I'll be happy in the knowledge Speirs is behind bars."

"He won't go behind bars if I get to him first. I'll kill the evil wee bastard."

Sandra pulled back from the caress and looked Alex firmly in the eye. "No you mustn't go near him. We can't give him any cause for complaint. You need to step back. I don't think you should be involved in handling his case, neither should Peter for that matter, nothing that could possibly give his lawyer room to claim he'd been unfairly treated after his attack on me. I don't want there to be any risk of him getting off on a technicality."

"I suppose you have a point but he's likely to need a new lawyer in any event. I've been told the one who witnessed your attack had near apoplexy. He probably can't be forced to give evidence against his own client, but if it wouldn't have given him professional ethics problems, then he might have wanted to. I've a funny feeling he won't be representing him for very long. But we've no room for complacency. I'm sure Daddy Moneybags will have a replacement arranged before we can blink."

Before Sandra could comment, a nurse re-entered the booth. "That's us ready to move you. A bed has been allocated on the ward. I'm afraid I'll need to ask you to leave, Sir. We need to get Miss McKinnon prepared. There's no point you waiting either because she's going to need rest. You ought to be able to get in to see her for evening visiting. It's at 7.00pm, but phone in first to make sure it will be okay."

"Thank you, nurse. Be sure to take good care of her, she's very precious," Alex requested.

"I only work in A&E, but don't you worry. I know the girls on the ward and she'll get the best treatment available."

"What're you going to do?" Sandra asked. "Please don't do anything stupid."

"I try not to make a habit of it. There's no doubt I'd like to strangle the little swine with my bare hands. You needn't concern yourself though, I'll stand well back and not have any direct contact. However, you can rest assured I'll keep a close eye on developments to make absolutely certain he gets what he deserves. I wouldn't mind going after the father as well. After all he's the Dr Frankenstein who's responsible for making young Kevin the monster that he's become. I suspect he'll have plenty of skeletons in his closet and I'm sure it won't be too difficult to release a few.

However, before all of that, I need to find out how Sanjay's got on. When I had to leave, I sent Mary in to join him to finish off Kitson's interview."

"Please be careful," Sandra said. Touching her abdomen, she continued, "I'm holding onto this baby full term and I want his father to be fit and well for his arrival."

Alex squeezed her hand and kissed her brow again. "I'll be careful and I'll be back this evening."

Alex found Peter sitting exactly where he'd left him. He filled him in on Sandra's condition and advised him to stay clear of Speirs for the reasons he and Sandra had discussed, adding he'd clear it with his superiors. They both left to return to work, although Alex sat outside for a long time before he felt ready to go back.

Entering the office, he was besieged by colleagues enquiring about Sandra's welfare and only after they were satisfied by his answers did they deluge him with congratulations about her pregnancy, the news having already spread through the inter-office grapevine.

"Would you like to buy a second-hand pram?" Sanjay offered, grinning. "As new condition, one careful driver, only three previous passengers."

"I'd better not," Alex replied. "You'll probably need it yourself for number four."

"I certainly hope not. I don't think I could cope with any more. Maybe I should get the snip just in case."

"It makes my eyes water just thinking about it," Alex chuckled. "Let's go back to your desk and you can bring me up to date on the interviews. No, better still, my office."

Sanjay collected his papers and disks on the way and sat down facing Alex, a broad smile covering his face. "I'm sure you'll be happy with this, Boss. Would you like to hear the recordings now?"

"I'll get to them, but first give me a run down. Did you get a confession? You certainly seem happy enough."

"Not quite, but it's close to the next best thing. The last you heard, we considered both Armstrong and Kitson as suspects. We'd spoken to both. They both denied any involvement and they both claimed the other was innocent too."

"Yeah, so where are we now."

"They're both still protesting innocence but neither one is quite as supportive of the other."

"Tell me more," Alex pushed.

"It started with Kitson. We challenged her about her lying. The old ground, lying to the education authority, not telling Graeme she'd be at the school. Claiming she hadn't been to the house before. We emphasised she'd been caught out and we couldn't trust a word she said. We knew she'd been to the house, we had the bracelet as evidence. We knew she wanted Graeme for herself but he would never have left Sheila. The only way she thought she'd get Graeme would be to get rid of Sheila. We knew she had access to the murder weapon through the drama group and she was at the murder scene to carry out the switch. Added to which, she'd left the school before the police arrived and she hadn't been forthcoming with any information. She broke down, protested she didn't do it. She more or less admitted all we'd said was true. Well, she could hardly deny it. She admitted she'd had conversations with Graeme about leaving Sheila and she realised he'd never do it. They'd also discussed how good it would be if Sheila wasn't about, but claimed they'd never discussed doing anything to get rid of her. I talked to her about the bracelet. I said if it was true she'd lost it months ago, then it couldn't possibly have lain there undiscovered all this time. The only explanation would be if someone had deliberately left it for us to find and the only candidate for doing that would be Graeme, to set her up and cover for himself. I added comments suggesting maybe he wanted his freedom from Sheila but not because he wanted to be with her. I reinforced it by saying he'd refused to talk to her since the killing and was using her as the scapegoat."

"What did she say?"

"Nothing at first, she sat for quite some time taking it in. I didn't break the silence, let her dwell on her predicament. Her eyes filled up but she didn't cry, I'll give her that. There were no hysterics. Then she whispered she couldn't believe it, she thought he loved her. How could he do it? She fell short of a downright accusation, but not by much."

"Well done, Sanjay. How did you get on with him?"

"A similar story. We ran through all the evidence, about everything he had to gain by Sheila's death, both financial and personal. He stayed resolute and supportive of Kitson until we asked why she wouldn't have told him she was going to the school. He was also unaware she'd been to his house. I laid it on thick about how she was looking to take Sheila's place. And he became a bit less certain. Even more so when I mentioned she'd spent time alone with Sheila at the house, that was after I confirmed Kitson's claim he'd never taken her there. I didn't say when it had been as we only had her word for it anyway. When I mentioned the bracelet was found in the bedroom, he became distinctly agitated. When I hinted that Kitson had thought he was capable of killing Sheila, he replied certainly no more than her. He inferred she had a cold calculating streak. Maybe not as much as Sheila, but she was capable and he didn't defend her when I suggested that she could have set up the whole thing. We're not there yet, but we're pretty damn close.

"What do you want us to do now?" Sanjay asked.

"They're both accomplished liars. Charge them both and keep them remanded in custody. It's not improbable they're both in it together, so let's not lose sight of the alternatives. We'll see who breaks first."

"There are a couple of other things, nothing startling but I'll fill you in for completeness.

"Your pal Brian Phelps called to say he hadn't managed to find out anything else yet but he'd keep trying. Then there was another call from someone who wouldn't give a proper name but said you'd understand what he meant if I said Shuggie called."

"Did he tell you anything or was I to get back to him?" Alex asked.

"Two things he said, firstly the man Richard you asked about had been doing some business with the east. I asked him to explain but that was all he'd say about it, to me at least. It sounded like some sort of code. He could have been talking about Edinburgh or China for all I could tell.

"Then he said something about there being another guy you'd 'not' spoken about, that's how he worded it and I didn't know what he meant."

"I've a fair idea what he was on about. What about him?" Alex remembered Shuggie refused to recognise Devosky by name.

"He said the word was he'd gone back to Moscow for keeps. Does that make any sense?"

"It does. It was someone Sandra was looking for. I'd rather we'd got hold of him but it's the next best thing. I can get back to Shuggie later to see if he's got any more details. Anything else?"

"We've checked all the phone records. Not surprisingly, there's a lot between Kitson and Armstrong, and in particular, there was a forty-five-minute call on Sunday evening at about five. At that time, she either hadn't decided to go to Eastfarm in the morning or else she wasn't telling him."

"Or else they're both lying," Alex added.

"Yeah, that's possible. Maybe they're working on the basis that if we can't ascertain which one did it, then we can't go after either," Sanjay responded. "There hasn't been any completed calls between them since Sunday. Kitson's dialled several times but it never connected. Which supports what she's claimed. Then looking at older records, there'd been calls back and forward between Sheila Armstrong and Kitson, but nothing in the last three months. Well, almost nothing. Sheila phoned her last Thursday but the call only lasted about twenty seconds."

"What did Kitson say about it?" Alex asked.

"She didn't. She had no recollection of it whatsoever. Didn't budge even when I told her we could prove the call."

"Strange, might it have been Graeme calling and using Sheila's phone?" Alex asked.

"I hadn't considered that. Do you think he could have been trying implicate her with all these little clues? The phone calls and the bracelet, realising she'd have no reasonable answer. It would have been incredibly devious, but we've know from the start whoever was responsible went in for intricate planning and was a bit theatrical. It fits with Armstrong being a stage manager."

"Check when the call was made and where they each claimed to be at the time," Alex instructed.

"One of the other numbers which was on Sheila's list was a young lad, a pupil at Eastfarm, goes by the name of Kevin Speirs. I've no idea what the connection might be, but I heard you mention the name recently and thought you'd want to be told."

"Thanks, Sanjay, good work. Speirs was the little thug who put Sandra in hospital. He was her prime suspect for killing Carson."

"Damn, I should have found out more. I was so immersed in this case. I heard what had happened to Sandra, but didn't know who'd done it so I didn't make the connection. What on earth can he have to do with Sheila Armstrong?"

"That's what I aim to find out. Sandra told me he was at Eastfarm and that he was interested in writing. That may have led to his path crossing with Sheila and the writing group, but at the moment I don't know any more.

"You press ahead with your enquiries. I'm going to have a word with the Super to see what's happening with Sandra's cases while she's laid up."

Sanjay left and Alex was informed Inspector Cairns, newly returned having recovered sufficiently from his alleged back injury, had been assigned Sandra's caseload. Knowing Cairns reputation for laziness and sloppy work, it was with some trepidation he called to ask what was happening.

True to form, Cairns was preparing to rely on the work Sandra had already completed and claim the credit for closing down the cases with the minimum of effort. He was ready to level charges on the McGuire brothers for the assault on Hardy, but was prepared to go easy on them if they would stand as witnesses against Speirs for his murder of Carson. He had arrested and charged Speirs for injuring Sandra, and based on this detention, he felt certain the McGuires would cooperate.

"What about Devosky and Zennick?" Alex asked.

"Who?" Cairns replied.

"Have you bothered to read the file or speak to Peter Lister?" Alex challenged.

"I only took over this morning, I've not had a chance to catch up properly yet. Now, with respect, I reckon I've done bloody well so far. Why, what is it to you? It's not your case, so it's a courtesy I'm even discussing it with you, Sir." The last word was laboured and reluctant and the 'with respect' had been said purposefully, clearly being ironic.

If Alex had the ability to reach through the phone line, he'd have throttled Cairns on the spot. Instead, he swallowed the profusion of curses on the tip of his tongue and spoke slowly and firmly using his most intimidating techniques normally reserved for dangerous suspects.

"Now, Mr Cairns, these may not be my cases, but it appears I know considerably more about them than you do and you're supposed to be in charge. Unless you want to make an enemy of me, you will do exactly as I say; and I warn you, I'm the last person you want to make an enemy of. Check my record if you don't believe me. I can assure you the problems you've been having with your back will pale into insignificance by comparison to the trouble you'd be inviting. Now, don't interrupt and listen carefully because I will say this only once. And don't smirk, this isn't 'Allo, Allo.' There is nothing I'm going to say that you'll find remotely amusing. When we finish this call, you will read all the files thoroughly and you'll call in Peter Lister to help you have a full understanding of the cases you've been allocated. Once you are properly in the picture, you will do everything in your power to hunt down Devosky and establish whatever links you can to Zennick. I also want you to see what involvement either of them have had with Richard Speirs, he's young Kevin's father. Once you've done all of that, you can assess who can be charged and what with. In your reports, you will give full credit for the sterling work done by DI McKinnon and DC Lister. Is that understood?"

"Y-y-yes, Sir," Cairns stammered.

"And one more thing. I want you to find out from Speirs what connection he had with my murder victim, Sheila Armstrong. Speirs goes to Eastfarm School, the one where Armstrong died. We have evidence they spoke on the phone last week and I want to know what it was about. Speirs has an interest in writing, so it could be quite innocent, but it seems too much of a coincidence to me and I want to know for sure, and quickly. Have you got that?"

Alex didn't wait for the answer; the affirmation was hardly out of Cairns mouth by the time the phone slammed back on its cradle. He sat breathing heavily for several seconds allowing his temper and his blood pressure to resume normal levels.

Chapter 22

Never comfortable speaking to a psychologist, Alex sat on the edge of his chair. Although he knew he was being ridiculous, he always felt he was the one being psychoanalysed. He sat wondering if it stemmed from some deep-seated insecurity dating back to his childhood, then chided himself for reading too much Freud and trying to self-diagnose. Better to leave it to the professionals, he concluded.

Alex spent some considerable time describing the case then sat back hoping for an educated assessment.

The clinician asked further probing questions and then surmised either Kitson or Armstrong could be responsible for organising Sheila's death. Either ones' profile could be made to fit and he couldn't give Alex an answer based on a desktop analysis. Besides anything else, Alex's views and interpretations could skew the evidence to suit his own prejudices. On a more positive note, he thought it most unlikely for them to have been working in concert for such a contrived crime and he did offer to come and speak to both suspects in order to give a better-informed opinion.

His assessment of Sheila's condition was hardly more helpful. He cited cases where brain damage or injury had been shown to coincide with changes in a person's temperament or moral code but gave examples where an apparent descent had occurred without cause and, of course, there were countless occurrences of people incurring such damage with no character changes being noted.

In the end, Alex left the consultation hardly any better informed than when he started.

Checking his watch, he realised it was rapidly approaching visiting time at the Southern General Infirmary and called ahead to check on Sandra's condition. He was informed she'd been taken to the maternity unit and he was put through to the ward. They, in turn, confirmed they were pleased with her progress but she still required a lot of rest. He would be permitted to visit, but only for ten minutes.

When Alex stopped to refuel his car, he picked up a bunch of flowers and a box of chocolates then raced onwards to the hospital. After a short while, he found a space to illegally abandon his vehicle showing a police on duty sign.

Approaching her bedside, he winced seeing her blackened face. Otherwise, she appeared well and looked rested.

"Hello, Love. Are they taking good care of you?" he asked, depositing his gifts, caressing her undamaged cheek and holding her hand.

"The staff are marvellous. They won't let me do a thing. I've been told I need to do nothing for a while so I'll get stronger for junior's sake, but I feel such a fake lying here doing nothing. What's been happening in my absence?"

Alex updated Sandra on progress. He explained about his frustrations, first with Cairns and then with the psychologist.

"It's bloody infuriating, being stuck in here when I should be wrapping up the cases. I'll be out in a few days. Why did it have to be reassigned?"

"You know how it works. At least Devosky seems to be out of the way. Cairns won't have the opportunity to screw anything up and, if he knows what's good for him, your name will be on the charge sheet and arrest warrant as chief investigating officer for the boys, so you can't be denied the credit."

"Yeah, I suppose. What about your case. Who do you think killed Sheila?" Sandra asked.

"I'm truly not certain. I know Sanjay's money is now on the husband, but I'm really not certain. I have this niggling doubt that there's something important we've missed."

"You seem to have covered everything, but I'm sure if there is something it will come to you before long. Are you working tomorrow or will you be seeing the boys?"

"I'd originally thought of going in for the morning and taking them to the footie in the afternoon, but I've changed my mind. Sanjay has everything under control and, other than keeping a watchful eye on Cairns, I can afford to take the day off. I'll call the kids, see if they fancy a swim in the morning and that will leave me free to come see you for afternoon visiting."

"It's okay, Alex. You don't need to come here at every opportunity, I'll be fine. You take the boys out for the day. Mum and Dad are coming to see me tomorrow afternoon. I phoned them earlier to tell them everything was alright. I couldn't risk them hearing about what had happened on the evening news; it could have given Mum a heart attack."

"I should have thought to deal with that myself. I'm sorry, Love. Irrespective, I'll be here to see you."

* * *

The car door was half-open, Alex stepping in when his mobile rang. Alex recognised the Superintendent's number.

"Hi, Charlie. You're working a bit late, aren't you? Or is it a social call? If you're checking to hear how Sandra is, the news is good so far."

"I'm pleased to hear it, but I'm sorry, it's no social call. I'm calling with some information, well, advice actually."

"Okay, go on," Alex said while manoeuvring his way to a comfortable seating position and closing the door with his free hand.

"You've been making enquiries about Richard Speirs. I'm on to tell you to back off."

"I can't do that," Alex fired back angrily. "I've heard he's wealthy and influential but his boy's a nightmare. He's the little bastard who put Sandra in hospital. The kid thinks he can get away with anything and the father will cover up. I'm guessing Daddy's not squeaky clean and I need to get at him. He does have some clout, or someone's in his pocket for you to be making this call."

"For the sake of friendship, I'll pretend I didn't hear that. I can understand you being upset with Sandra being hurt and the baby and all, but it doesn't alter the facts. I've had word from on high, Dick Speirs can't be touched. It doesn't stop us throwing the book at young Kevin. If it makes you feel any better, Speirs won't be interfering in his son's prosecution."

"What's this all about? Where's this coming from?"

"I can't give you details but you've been around long enough to guess for yourself. Speirs has his uses. This is on the QT but we'd never have broken Zennick's network without him."

"What about Devosky?" Alex asked.

"He wasn't important, only one of Zennick's minions, but with aspirations to climb higher. Zennick gave him a couple of simple tasks to carry out and he failed. When the boys screwed up, he was history.

He's scurried back where he came from and I doubt we'll ever hear from him again."

"If we knew all of this, then why wasn't Sandra properly briefed?" Alex asked.

"Come now, Alex, don't be naïve. The crimes Sandra was given to investigate were standard local work. Don't get me wrong, she stepped in at the last minute and she handled everything brilliantly. Too brilliantly, because she got a bit too close to some other rather sensitive work, but no harm done. Cairns was given the tidying up to do and that'll put an end to it."

"For Christ's sake, Harry, I can't let it go. Besides, I've already bullied Cairns to do some more probing," Alex argued.

"You can and you will. This isn't a request, Alex, it's an order. Leave Cairns for me to sort out. Now go home, have a dram and put your feet up. You and Sandra have both had a very successful week and you've earned it. Send her my best when you see her." The line clicked dead.

Once home, Alex felt restless. He was dog tired after the busy week with rare and unsettled sleep and he was worried about Sandra. The flat felt cold and lonely without her there, but the last thing he wanted was anyone else's company. Anger at Harry's instructions and with thoughts of all the investigations milling around in his head, he had no wish for a diversion of film or television. He took time to tidy up, clean the flat and hang away clothes and oddments which had been lying about since their holiday. Once done, he wanted to relax. He turned on his stereo and dropped a Metallica CD in the slot. It was their live S&M recording, one of his favourites. Although mentally resistant to Harry's instructions, he lifted a bottle of whisky and poured a generous measure. It was a fifteen-year-old Benlochy single malt, a souvenir he'd been gifted after a previous enquiry. Reclining in his chair, slowly the strong spirit and the familiar music had their effect. He felt hazy and closed his eyes.

Alex had no recollection of switching off the music, disrobing and going to bed but he knew it must have happened because the next thing he remembered was reaching out from under his duvet to answer the phone.

"Hello, Boss. Sorry to disturb your weekend, are you awake?" Sanjay asked.

"I am now. What time is it?"

"It's 8.40am. Are you free to come in?" Sanjay asked.

"I can if it's important. What's the problem?"

"No problem, Boss. But I just took a call from a lawyer by the name of Fairgrieve. He said he has received an important message from Sheila Armstrong and he needs to let us know about it."

"Is he a lawyer or a bloody clairvoyant?" Alex asked, gradually coming to his senses.

"I'm sorry? Oh yes, I see what you mean. No, he explained he'd been away on business all week and only checked his mail this morning. He's Sheila's solicitor and handles her business affairs. He received a package from her in the mail with a message to be opened in the event of her death. He said he thought we needed to see it as soon as possible."

"I'm on my way, Sanjay. When do you expect him?"

"He said he'd be in at about ten-thirty."

"Is that 'as soon as possible' in lawyer speak?" Alex asked.

"I guess. He said he had a few other matters to catch up on and then he'd come in. I'm sorry for calling so early but I wanted to catch you before you committed to anything else."

"You did the right thing, Sanjay, thanks." Alex rose, had a leisurely shower, dressed and breakfasted, then phoned his sons to reschedule seeing them in the late afternoon, after hospital visiting.

* * *

Archibald Fairgrieve was a man in his sixties, short but very dapper and wearing a starched shirt and a finely pressed, black, three-piece suit even though it was a Saturday morning.

Sanjay and Alex introduced themselves and showed him into one of the larger and more comfortable interview rooms.

He sat down, opened a briefcase and lifted out a DVD and a portable player. "I didn't know what facilities you would have so I brought this."

"If we can first go through the formalities," Sanjay asked. "We need to take your details and then find out what you've come to tell us."

Fairgrieve complied with the request and went on to give his explanation. "I've been Sheila Armstrong's solicitor for almost twenty years. I've negotiated her business contracts and property purchases and, of course, I prepared her will. Now, before you try to stop me, I've not come to see you about any mundane executory issue. As I told you on the phone, I discovered a package this morning which was posted by Sheila last week. It contains a letter stating I was to open the package in the event of her death but added I should not make it public for at least one month. As you can see, I am in breach of the instruction and I'm not even certain how I stand with regards to professional ethics because of it. However, after I realised the contents, I couldn't stand back and allow there to be a miscarriage of justice."

"This is very intriguing," Alex commented.

"Rather than give you any further commentary, I think you'd be best to see the film." Fairgrieve started the machine, inserted the disk and pressed play.

The screen illuminated with a picture showing Sheila Armstrong sitting on the couch in her lounge, a broad smile on her face, and dressed in the same outfit she'd worn on stage when they'd examined her body. Alex felt a chill run down his spine.

"This DVD will be my first and only film performance, I hope you enjoy it.

"By the time you're watching it, I must presume that I'll be dead and buried and my plans will have been successful.

"This isn't as I would have wished – it all had to be rushed at the last minute – but under the circumstances, it was the best I could have hoped for.

"Looking back, everything had been going well until I was diagnosed with this damned tumour. Graeme and I had a good life. My books were published and bringing in a comfortable royalty. There was even talk of some screenwriting work, and then this happened. It's been well over two years since it was first identified and I decided not to tell anyone. I wanted to spend my last days exactly as I chose and without anyone pitying me. I swore the doctors to secrecy and I've been a very bad girl knowing I'd never have to face the consequences, not in this world at least.

"But you don't need to hear about any of that. What you do need to know is that I was very disappointed with both Graeme and Yvonne. I loved them both, but they let me down and I wanted them to suffer. Because of my condition, I know they'll both survive me so I wanted to add a little bit of devilment to their relationship and make sure they never forget me or what brought them together, if they manage to stay together when all this is done.

"As I said, this had to be rushed at the end. I had hoped to have more time. I planned my finale to go out in a blaze of glory, on a proper stage, at the annual national writers' conference, in front of a large and prestigious audience. Instead, it has to be in a provincial school watched by a few of the local writing group and God knows who else might be milling about. But it was an opportunity not to be missed. I'd planned everything in such minute detail. I'd written the play, arranged the casting all to make the most impressive spectacle, but when the Doc told me the end may only be days away, I pulled forward the plans to make do as best I could. I've no doubt it will have been a memorable performance."

Sheila held up a box. "You'll have worked out all this already by now, but I borrowed these knives from South Caledonian Players so I could use the real one to do the switch with the dummy from the stage props. My only hope is that Bert will keep a firm grip and the end can be quick and painless. I've left enough clues here and there to convince the police that it was all carried out by Graeme and Yvonne. They should have suffered enough by now, so I'm happy they can be released, and you can all see just how effective my scripting was.

"My one regret is not seeing the look on his stupid, bloody, brother's face when Graeme is arrested.

"When you get round to reading my will, you'll see I've left my fortune and my royalties as a legacy to create a foundation for acting and writing. This house is in joint names and Graeme will be able to keep any money in our joint accounts, but otherwise he'll have to fend for himself.

"I'm feeling rather tired now and there are many small details I need to conclude. So, for now I will bid you all a fond adieu."

* * *

Sitting at Sandra's bedside, holding her hand, Alex hadn't yet got over his shock from the morning's revelations. Her parents had arrived early for visiting but left ten minutes before the end to allow the couple some privacy.

On hearing Alex's account of Sheila's video, Sandra was pragmatic. "You were always convinced there'd been more to it and you were right."

"I suppose, but it was the last thing I would have expected," Alex replied.

"What sort of bitter and twisted person would go to such lengths? Do you think her mind was affected by her condition or was the madness there all the time?" Sandra asked.

"In our job, we expect to deal with every sort of crazed lunatic but this was a whole new ballgame."

"Speaking of ballgames, weren't you wanting to take the boys to the football?" Sandra asked.

"We had a change of plans and I'm seeing them when I leave."

"Better get going then, the bell's already gone and you don't want to upset the staff," Sandra added.

Turning to leave, Alex spotted a large colourful bouquet of flowers in the corner. "They're beautiful, did your folks bring them? Shall I ask the nurse to find a vase?" Alex asked.

"They're not from my parents. I didn't get a chance to tell you. Before visiting started, I had a visit from Helen and she brought them. She said she was on her way somewhere else and couldn't be here at the standard visiting time. Truthfully, I think she didn't want to bump into you. She said you'd called for the boys this morning and told them what had happened. She felt sorry for what I was going through and hoped I'd be okay. She seemed very sincere. She said we all had a part to play in Craig and Andrew's lives and it would be easier if we could all be friends. She actually said she wanted to be friends."

The astonishment on Alex's face was no less than after he'd watched Sheila's DVD.

"You must have taken too many painkillers," he laughed. "I think you're hallucinating."

Dear reader,

We hope you enjoyed reading *Written To Death*. Please take a moment to leave a review, even if it's a short one. Your opinion is important to us.

Discover more books by Zach Abrams at https://www.nextchapter.pub/authors/zach-abrams-scottish-mystery-crime-author-glasgow

Want to know when one of our books is free or discounted? Join the newsletter at http://eepurl.com/bqqB3H.

Best regards,
Zach Abrams and the Next Chapter Team

The story continues in:

Offender of the Faith

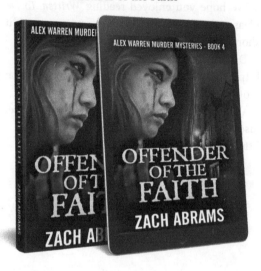

To read the first chapter for free, please head to:
https://www.nextchapter.pub/books/offender-of-
the-faith

About the Author

Having the background of a successful career in commerce and finance, Zach Abrams has spent many years writing reports, letters and presentations and it's only fairly recently he started writing novels. "It's a more honourable type of fiction," he declares.

His first novel *Ring Fenced* was published in November 2011. This is a crime story with a difference, following one man's obsession with power and control.

After this he collaborated with Elly Grant to produce *Twists and Turns* a book of short stories.

Zach's next novel, *Made a Killing*, is the first book in the Alex Warren series. It follows the investigation after the killing of a much hated criminal where an elephant tusk was used as the murder weapon was. This has been followed by *A Measure of Trouble* where Alex's team are seeking the murderer of a CEO killed within the cask room of his whisky distillery. The third, *Written to Death*, deals with a mysterious death during a writers' group meeting. These are fast-moving, gripping novels set in the tough crime-ridden streets of Glasgow.

Zach's quirky thriller, *Source; A Fast-Paced Financial Crime Thriller* has three investigative journalists travelling across the UK, Spain and France as they research corruption and sabotage in the banking sector while trying to cope with their own fraught personal lives.

Alike his central character in *Ring Fenced*, (Benjamin Short), Zach Abrams completed his education in Scotland and went on to a career in accountancy, business and finance. He is married with two children. He plays no instruments but has an eclectic taste in music, although not as obsessive as Benjamin. Unlike Benjamin, he does not maintain mistresses, write pornography and (sadly) he does not have ownership of such a company. He is not a sociopath (at least by his own reckoning) and all versions of his life are aware of and freely communicate with each other.

More in keeping with 'Alex Warren,' Zach was raised in Glasgow and has spent many years working in Central Scotland.

Written To Death
ISBN: 978-4-86747-756-4 (Mass Market)

Published by
Next Chapter
1-60-20 Minami-Otsuka
170-0005 Toshima-Ku, Tokyo
+818035793528
26th May 2021

Lightning Source UK Ltd.
Milton Keynes UK
UKHW041432110621
385334UK00001BC/67

9 784867 477564